THOSE OPULENT DAYS

THOSE A MYSTERY
OPULENT
DAYS

JACQUIE PHAM

Atlantic Monthly Press
New York

FIRST EDITION

Published simultaneously in Canada
Printed in the United States of America

This book was set in 12.5-point Baskerville
by Alpha Design & Composition of Pittsfield, NH.

First Grove Atlantic hardcover edition: November 2024

Library of Congress Cataloguing-in-Publication data is available for this title.

ISBN 978-0-8021-6380-6
eISBN 978-0-8021-6381-3

Atlantic Monthly Press
an imprint of Grove Atlantic
154 West 14th Street
New York, NY 10011

Distributed by Publishers Group West

groveatlantic.com

24 25 26 27   10 9 8 7 6 5 4 3 2 1

AUTHOR'S NOTES

Those Opulent Days is a work of fiction, and while the city names and historical events have been described as close to reality as possible, the characters are not, including the two emperors whose names are mentioned briefly: Bảo Khánh and Bảo Nam.

Bảo Khánh's character draws inspiration from Emperor Khải Định, who ascended the throne in 1916. He was the first Vietnamese monarch to travel to France, his reign heavily influenced by European culture and architecture, which he later incorporated into the construction of his lavish tomb.

Similarly, Bảo Nam, the son of Bảo Khánh in *Those Opulent Days*, draws inspiration from Bảo Đại, who was Emperor Khải Định's son and successor. He ascended the throne following his father's death in 1925, effectively becoming the last Emperor of Việt Nam.

For A Bob

THOSE
OPULENT
DAYS

PROLOGUE

"He's gone," came a weak voice from Cao Hải Duy's left. Soft, almost a whisper that struggled to carry with it the weight of two deafening syllables.

"He's gone," Duy repeated, the same way a child copied whatever adults said, without understanding the meaning. His head was spinning still, yet to wake from the euphoric opium high. A part of Duy hoped he never would, a stubborn refusal to accept his reality.

His friend was dead, just like the fortune teller had predicted thirteen years ago. A haunting memory Duy couldn't rid of. He needn't close his eyes, the scenery unfolding with ease, the details sharp.

That night when they were eleven, the moon was a cold and distant crescent on the boundless navy sky.

All the streetlights had just flickered off, following the governor's curfew, and the alleyway where Duy stood fell immediately into an oppressive shade of black. He squinted, trying to adjust to his surroundings—he couldn't see much. His hands had already lost their shape within the infinite darkness. The only thing relatively visible was the outline of Phong's well-worn notebook, tucked under Duy's arm. A treasure in disguise. Beneath its crude brown cover, the pages contained all the answers to the history exam that Duy and his friends would take tomorrow.

Duy hadn't studied, of course. What was the point? The year was 1917, and his nation—the fierce, brave Việt Nam—had fought the war and lost. More than thirty years prior, the French had come and freely split the land in three; they named the north Tonkin, the south Cochinchina, and the central lands Annam. They glorified their actions through propaganda—they hadn't just invaded Việt Nam, civilising a poor and underdeveloped colony. They had wiped entire cities off the map, bestowing them Westernised identities. The ground Duy currently stood on had once belonged to the Nguyễn lords and was known as Gia Định—but now, the French called it Sài Gòn. Even at eleven years old, Duy knew the obliteration of his entire country's origin would never be mentioned in history books penned by the French. Why should Duy bother memorising the tales the foreigners told about his own nation?

Besides, Duy and his friends had a different plan tonight.

A few days before, Duy had been visiting home from boarding school. Bored, he had snuck into his parents' bedroom, where he sometimes found interesting and exclusive items—Mother's lustrous strands of pearls, Father's intricate wooden tobacco pipe. That morning, her jewellery was nowhere in sight, undoubtedly stored in hidden cabinets only Mother knew how to operate. But she had left a piece of paper, lying crumpled on her rosewood dresser. Intrigued, Duy reached for it.

18 Norodom Boulevard—Master Cần

The delight in his eyes vanished, his childish giggle dimming. Duy knew what he was looking at: the address to the most famous fortune teller in town. His mother worshipped Master Cần, treated the old woman like a god. *You're too young to participate. Stop with the questions!* Mother would snap when Duy expressed his scepticism. *And don't you dare touch the offerings.*

Every lunar month, on the first day and the fifteenth, Mother would wake before the servants, preparing the freshest fruits, the fattest chickens, the most fragrant sticky rice. She would carefully place them atop gleaming silver trays, forming mountains of gifts. Dressed in her most humble outfit—a plain mustard-coloured linen tunic and pants, a string of solid wooden beads around her neck—Mother would leave for Master Cần's property, always warning the old butler: *The young master Duy needs to stay home today.* It seemed she could never risk his following her. Was she ashamed of him? Was she worried that Duy might offend her gods, tarnishing the holy connection she had been building?

Duy ought to discover what Mother was hiding. The piece of paper containing Master Cần's address felt like an invitation from the divine, an opportunity he couldn't bypass.

The plan formed quickly: come midnight on Monday, Duy and his friends would sneak out of the dormitory to pay the fortune teller a visit.

When he first broached the subject, Edmond had shrugged noncommittally.

We can leave one at a time. Duy suggested. *You know, to avoid detection.*

Sure. You can go first, since you have the address. Edmond waved a hand, seemingly indifferent—he didn't typically enjoy activities that weren't his idea.

Normally, Duy didn't mind such callousness, but now, as strange, frightening noises echoed from the darkness, he thought Edmond could have been more considerate. Shifting from one foot to the other—a kid in detention—Duy hated himself for not asking his friends to be punctual.

Thankfully, finally, a hushed unison of three voices came, Duy's blurry friends arriving in the shadows.

Sorry we're late.

Why are you all here at the same time? Duy asked, annoyed. He had been waiting in solitude for nothing.

It was me. Phong spoke over Edmond and Minh, his voice apologetic. Duy couldn't see Phong's expression, but he knew his friend was lowering his head, his body shrinking into itself. The rabbit of the group, as Edmond often teased. *I didn't want to go by myself.*

Duy softened—it was difficult to stay mad at Phong. His friend's timid words were like delicate feathers, dusting his irritation clean. He pointed to the end of the cramped alleyway instead.

Let's go.

They had barely moved down the dark, eerie street when a muffled woman's voice demanded.

Who's there?

The boys hesitated, then traced the sound to an ordinary crimson wooden door, dirt and gravel crunching under their steps. Like a reflex, they turned to Edmond, awaiting his direction.

Why are you all looking at me? Edmond's teeth chattered as he hissed the question. It was unnaturally cold for a summer night— the wind howled violently, whipping through tree branches. *Wasn't this your idea, Duy? Go on. Talk to her.*

Duy sighed but didn't argue. Edmond was right: it was Duy who convinced them to come here, Duy who had gathered the parcel of delectable treats Mother brought back from China—a gift his friends would never reject. Like Phong, Duy didn't want to come alone; he needed the company, his support system.

4

With a grunt, he announced himself.

My name is Cao Hải Duy.

Ah, I see. A strange, disembodied laugh streamed through the open window on the side of the house. *Madame Mai's darling son, the infamous young heir. Come.*

Another wind rose, lashing against the shaky panel, pushing the door open. A sharp chill raked down Duy's neck, like a warning. He ignored it, stepping inside, trying to stand tall, hiding his clammy hands in his trouser pockets—partly because he was cold, partly because he didn't want anyone else to see his trembling fingers. Behind him, the boys paused, exchanging wary glances.

What is that smell? Minh groaned, the instant he crossed the threshold.

It was a combination of dust, mould, and rotten food, Duy deduced. The space was dingy and reeked of neglect—it wasn't the establishment he had pictured. No place for Mother's gods.

He noticed a wooden door at the end of a corridor, its frame illuminated by two flickering candles afront. Their silhouettes danced on the wall opposite, unearthly. Duy swallowed the tension in the back of his throat.

Be brave, child, Master Cần urged. *Enter.*

The room was smaller than he expected, lit by hazy orange flame, an altar cabinet in the middle. There weren't any portraits or drawings of Master Cần's ancestors, only a brass statue of a smiling Buddha, surrounded by more candles, red wax dripping lazily down the ligneous surface.

Master Cần was kneeling on the glossy black-and-white tiles, her back facing the boys. She wore a dark brown tunic and a thin pair of trousers in a similar shade, a thick black skullcap on her head. Around her neck hung a string of beads, longer and larger than those Mother preferred. She was reciting incoherent phrases from a battered notebook; her head was low, in deference to some powerful but invisible force.

Why is he here? she asked, not turning around.

My mother always comes, and—

That's not my question. Why is he here? The French one.

She was talking about Edmond.

He is my friend.

Though her face was obscured, half consumed by murky shadow, Duy could imagine the curve of the fortune teller's lip, could discern the tinge of disdain on the tip of her tongue as she purred the words.

The French are not our friends. Now kneel, with your forehead on the ground.

Somehow, the old woman reminded Duy of Mother—the stern, clipped orders he always received. He listened, bowing with utmost respect for Buddha, a god he didn't believe in. Warm bodies enveloped him: his friends, following.

What is it you seek from me?

Master Cần was old, Duy realised. Ancient. She carried with her a puzzling kind of vitality; it seemed almost impossible to determine her age. There were countless lines drawn across her forehead—some short, some long, all deepened, all pronounced. Her eyebrows were thick, like dense white bushes. Her lips were dry, and whilst they weren't painted the bright red he had imagined, the crack on the bottom left corner was bleeding.

My mother comes here often. What does she want? What do you tell her? Duy sat with his hands placed neatly atop his knees, his gaze steady, trained on Master Cần.

The fortune teller tilted her head, laughing, like Duy had just told her the most amusing story.

Your mother wants to atone for the sins you committed in your past life, lessening your inevitable karma. It is no use, and I've told her so. You reap what you sow. Destiny is immutable.

And what is mine?

Master Cần took her time replying. She ran her fingers along the line of wooden beads, looking intently from Duy to Minh, Phong, and finally, Edmond. She shook her head.

Such a shame.

What is?

Master Cần tapped her forehead four times, her voice distorted.

The four of you. One will lose his mind. One will pay. One will agonize.

The silence expanded as the boys digested the fortune teller's prophecy, until Edmond broke out in a coarse, fake laugh.

We shouldn't have come here, Duy. The woman is clearly crazy. He raked his slender fingers through his curly, charming blonde hair. *Let's go. If we hurry, we could still play a few games of cards before the teachers wake up.*

Duy's eyes darted between Edmond and Master Cần, who had stopped speaking. The old woman remained completely still, like she had been frozen in time.

Master Cần? Duy prompted, but no answers came. Reluctantly, he gave a slight nod of acceptance and hoisted himself off the cold ground. One after the other, the boys exited the room, confused from the strange encounter—Edmond impatiently strode ahead, Minh following closely, leaving Phong and Duy behind.

Don't worry, Duy, Phong begun, patting Duy's back. *There has never been any scientific proof that fortune telling is real.*

Phong, ever the calm and rational scholar, Duy teased, trying to shield his disquiet with a weak smile.

Are you coming?

Yes. Go ahead. I'll just be one second.

Crossing his arms in front of his chest, Duy watched his friends' shadows grow smaller at the end of the long hall—he remained at the door to the altar room. There was something holding him back, some nameless thing gnawing at his gut.

It was Master Cần.

She had glided alongside Duy and was now staring directly at him. Her eyes gleamed as though they were freshly carved from precious obsidian—a smirk grazed her lips as she mouthed the loudest words Duy had ever heard.

The four of you. One will die.

A wave of dread coursed through Duy. Instinctively, he bolted, ignoring the burn in his lungs—he needed to escape this place. When his friends asked what took him so long, why he was panting, Duy lied, said he'd needed to tie his shoe. He decided to never repeat Master Cần's final prophecy, convincing himself he had imagined it. Together the boys rushed back to school, climbing into their beds, waking as though nothing had changed.

A harrowing wail pulled Duy away from the recollection, forcing him back to the present, where he now stood over his friend's corpse.

Die, one of them did.

A death by poison.

In the years that followed, Duy couldn't explain what he did next. How he reached that conclusion. He was so confident in what he'd seen—the white saliva foaming in the corners of his friend's mouth, the puddles of blood amongst the pool of purge. This was not ordinary alcohol or opium poisoning. The realisation shocked Duy, prompting him to immediately stumble out of the room, searching for the field telephone in the dining room next door—he called the governor. The alcohol and the drugs had rendered him naive, trusting that a corrupted French politician could be their saviour.

He couldn't have been more wrong.

SIX DAYS PRIOR

Phong

The grandfather clock in the corner of Phong's room struck midnight, its sound a deafening announcement. The day he'd always dreaded had arrived.

Phong thought he was alone and was startled by the sudden movement from the corner of his eye. The maid who had been fanning him. He had forgotten she was there.

She was either young or simply looked it—Phong couldn't tell. Her features were unremarkable: ordinary eyes, ordinary nose, and ordinary cheekbones that felt as though they could belong to just about anyone. They were alike, he found, the servants. The children of less fortunate parents who resorted to selling their sons and daughters in order to survive another day.

She lowered her head under his gaze, frightened she had done something to offend her master. Despite the aching emptiness under his chest, Phong laughed.

"I won't bite."

"I beg your pardon, Monsieur?" The maid was confused. Those three words may have been the most Phong had uttered in her presence. He was known as the quiet heir.

"Are you hungry?" he asked, another smile on his lips. A clumsy attempt to keep the maid's worry at bay.

"No, Monsieur, I am not." She shook her head the way she was taught.

"Of course you are. Servants aren't particularly well-fed," Phong said, pointing at his dinner tray. On top was a bowl of soup—what kind, he wasn't sure—and a piece of bread. "Take them to the kitchen to eat. Though I suppose they are a bit cold now."

"Tell the others it was an order," Phong urged when the maid remained in her spot, silent and scared whilst her stomach grumbled at the promise of good food.

"Yes, Monsieur," she bowed and stepped out, her grips firm around the tray, her pace quickened, like she was worried Phong might change his mind.

He hoped he had made her night somewhat better than his.

The wooden door creaked, and Phong was by himself, the way he was meant to be. His room was drenched in a heavy silence; the air smelled as dry as it was stale. The window to the left of his bed was sealed shut, denying the silver moonlight an entrance. Phong needed complete darkness to fully conceal the mass of his loneliness.

His breath was so soft, it felt like it did not exist. He could hear the faint shushing outside his bedroom as more servants walked past. Their discreet warning: their master should not be disturbed, today of all days—his birthday, the same day his mother passed away. Phong never celebrated it; he kept getting older, whilst his mother stayed forever young.

Turning onto his side, Phong blinked at the stack of paperwork, roughly a few years old. His plan to study abroad. In school, Phong was known as the smartest student. He could solve difficult mathematical equations within minutes, and his test scores were unbeatable. His teachers and his fellow students all spoke highly of him, believing he would excel in any field he chose to follow.

So, it came as a shock, naturally, when Phong turned eighteen and refused a once-in-a-lifetime opportunity to pursue his doctorate. People speculated and gossiped, searching for a reason that didn't really concern them, before forgetting and moving on to a fresher piece of news.

But Phong couldn't forget.

He kept the papers close, next to his pillow. A reminder of what he had given up. Physical evidence of a time when he wasn't such a failure.

Slowly, as though he had been approaching a timid animal, Phong reached for the pile of broken dreams and closed his eyes. Inhaling, Phong filled his nostrils with the maudlin scent of old, dusty papers. He saved the real reason behind his decision to skip school just for himself. Whenever Phong wanted pain—like he did today—he would uncover that secret, pulling it to the surface so he could wallow in it.

Phong had tried and tried to please his father, a scholar who valued education above all else. He brought home good grades and outstanding results, even securing that scholarship to Paris despite their family's wealth. In the end, it didn't matter; Phong's father glanced at the letter with the fancy stamp from that prestigious university with hateful contempt, his words cruel. *Is that really the best you can do?*

It was then that Phong finally understood: in his father's eyes, Phong would never be worthy. He was merely a living vessel

13

that connected his dead mother to this reality. His father kept Phong alive and gave him the Lê last name, simply because Phong was the only one left to walk the earth whose veins contained his mother's blood.

After that day, Phong gave up, ignoring his desperation to understand the meaning of his existence. Today, he turned twenty-four, with no job or higher education. He frequented Duy's opium club more than he did his own home. *My love can only love me there,* Phong had crooned drunkenly to Duy a few years prior.

Somewhere outside Phong's bedroom, the servants already started burning incense. The woody scent found the gap under Phong's door, invading his space with its thin grey smoke, making his eyes burn. Every year, just one second after the clock struck midnight, his father would head towards their altar room, where he would sit, keeping Phong's late mother company until the day turned dark—Phong's birthday an insignificant and unfortunate event his father didn't want to acknowledge.

This year wasn't any different. Phong knew he wouldn't be able to sleep, not with his father's heavy footsteps on the floor above. He slipped out of bed, turning on the light to gather his smoking equipment. This was a ritual he had been performing and perfecting for the past six years. First, Phong sat on the ground with his legs crossed, the metal tray turning yellow under warm golden light. With his back slightly hunched, Phong closed his eyes and remembered his fifth birthday.

His skin hadn't always been so pale; it was tan when Phong was younger. He did not know substances then, of course, only the innocent and childish marble games that he often played in the mansion's backyard. That day, Phong had sat under the toasty sunlight, enjoying the colourful orbs he managed to collect, when his father walked by, looming over Phong. He was wearing a black shirt and black linen trousers, his week-old stubble shading the lower half of his face. Tapping on Phong's shoulder, he signalled for Phong to follow him to the study room. The two of them sat in an uncomfortable silence, his father avoiding his eyes, Phong's eyes watching his father's expression—dark and tiring. The hardwood chair numbed his bottom, and Phong noticed the difference on his father's normally cold face, crueller somehow. When his father finally spoke, Phong's cheeks burned as though he had been slapped, the words bitter and hateful inside his ears. *We could have had ten or ten thousand of you. There was only one of your mother, in this entire world.*

His father leaned back into his chair, his hands clasped in front of his belly, Phong's juvenile cheerfulness wiped clean.

Now, he looked to the drawing of his mother that his father made mandatory in every single room of their mansion. The portrait in Phong's room was hung on the wall opposite his bed, a constant reminder of the person he accidentally killed. The woman within the golden frame was in her twenties, young and carefree. Her hair was black, gathered in a low bun behind her head. Her neck was long and slender, donned with a classy pearl necklace. She had an upturned nose, which she also gave her son, and her eyes were curved in the shape of teardrops.

Like on most days, Phong traced the outline of his mother's face whilst his resentment flared and bubbled into a small flame in his stomach. He could feel its fire, blue and seething with anguish. He hated his mother for abandoning him. She showed Phong the path to this world, pushing him over the edge that separated life and death. Without ever introducing him to the warmth of her touch, she left him there, something she clumsily dropped and forgot about.

The thought of her cold love made Phong anxious, the second stage of his ritual fulfilled.

Phong reached for the spirit lamp, a delicate thing with a brass base topped with a transparent, funnel-shaped chimney. He fixed a firm gaze on the malicious orange flame, his pulse thrumming with anticipation. His fingers palpitated, hastily rolling the gooey mass of opium into a round dough before pushing it inside the bowl of his golden smoking pipe. One deep pull and his surroundings blurred—his mother's death and his father's bitterness lost their shapes within his ecstasy.

And then Phong was floating. Levitating in a new dimension, where no sorrow could reach. He felt free, released from the anchor of suffering. His body turned inconsequential, his existence a portrait hung on someone else's wall.

Minh

A few hours later, in a grand mansion a few streets over from Phong's estate, Minh's thick eyelashes fluttered as he woke from the burning humiliation his dream had just brought. His hands twitched violently, itching for something to hurl across the room.

He despised it, the dream that wasn't really a dream but rather a memory that haunted his nights: the moment Edmond entered his life. How small, how insignificant he felt all those years ago. He felt this again when the images returned; their melody, the humming of a familiar song, stuck in the back of his head.

That early morning—4:00 a.m. on the dot, if he were to have glanced at the table clock on his nightstand—Minh lay with his back flat on the mattress, refusing to move, hoping he might fall asleep again. He needed the escape, detaching him from his current reality. When sunrise came, Edmond would be back in Cochinchina, polluting the air Minh breathed with his presence. Such a prospect made Minh anxious; he wasn't really himself whenever Edmond was around.

Minh had known this since that very first day, the day he could not stop dreaming about.

He could still see it, clearly, vividly—the start of their second year at boarding school. The classroom looked the same after summer break, the stale smell, the surface of the dark brown wooden tables and benches thicker with a layer of dust. The students, all slightly taller. Minh had walked through the iron gate with three servants trailing his steps, lugging his multiple suitcases in their frail arms. His face beamed with pride as he strode ahead, the kids at school worshipping the ground beneath his feet. His father was Khải Siêu, making him the richest heir to the biggest rubber plantation in Cochinchina, richer than Duy and his family's opium business, and certainly richer than Phong and his chemist father.

Minh squinted his eyes when he entered the dormitory, looking for Duy and Phong, his first and best friends. An inevitable connection, Minh's mother, Madame Nhu, had often said. They were the only three amongst a handful of Annamite students who were as wealthy as the French children. *Birds of a feather flock together,* she would later explain.

Edmond had arrived during recess, just as Minh was ordering the two biggest kids to form a makeshift palanquin with their arms—right hand holding onto the crook of their left arm, left hand holding onto the right of the person opposite. A traditional game, he had taken his time explaining. But Minh banned everyone else from participating, even Duy and Phong. They remained a step or two behind Minh's back, the two generals dutifully guarding Minh's kingdom.

Minh had barely managed to settle himself in the middle of the hollow square that the boys' limbs had created. He couldn't see where to put his feet, his hand shielding his eyes from blaring sunlight, when a voice came from behind.

This looks fun. May I play?

Minh turned his head, greeted with his first glimpse of the golden bloodline—the posture, the poise, the way that boy carried himself. The boy standing in front of Minh had fair skin, curly light blonde hair that grew to a rather feminine length, just touching his fragile shoulders, his eyes a beautiful shade of green. He smiled at Minh, his demeanour clearly relaxed, his hands sheltered inside his linen uniform pocket in the most natural way. The same uniform that Minh had been wearing, not in soiled brown like the rest of his class. A crisp white.

Ordering the kids to put him down, Minh faced the boy at last, noting the height difference between the both of them. The other boy, so much taller.

Who are you? he asked, his question coloured with a shade of annoyance.

My name is Edmond Moutet. Today is my first day.

Confidently, the boy grinned again, his right hand outstretched.

Minh ignored those five slender fingers, trying his best to summon his coldest voice.

This is a three-person game.

Oh, that's okay. Edmond had shrugged, paying Minh's hostility no attention. His face had brightened as he suggested another game. *This way, we can all play.*

The rest was a blur. Minh's shame was far too hot, burning the memories to ash in the process as the years went by.

He couldn't tell how or when it happened: one day he woke up in the dormitory and the boys no longer listened to his commands. Edmond's damnable smile and his artificial charm had captured their hearts. Blindly, they followed him, the way moths threw themselves at warm yellow light.

Back then, Minh did not know where to direct his rage, and it didn't help when Duy dismissed his complaints, pointing out how friendly Edmond really was, how they should all learn to get along. Suddenly, he was isolated; Phong remained quiet, always living within that sombre bubble, and now Duy. Angry and alone, Minh found himself sneaking into the school's kitchen and laying traps to catch mice. For an entire month, the teachers were terrified to find the pitiful animals with their bodies mangled, hidden in plain sight.

Now, trapped in his bed, Minh stared unblinkingly at the ceiling, his heart thumping. The bloody, filthy scenes that Minh had created with his bare hands both frightened and excited him, dimming the past echoes. Peeling the thin white blanket off his body, Minh breathed out a curse and sat up with his back against the headboard. He accepted that sleep would not return tonight. He lit the candle on his nightstand and watched as his room came to life under the bright orange hue.

Minh looked down at his brawny hands, wondering if he could ever release the grudge he had been holding all these years. Minh had naively believed that time would mellow his thoughts, that Edmond was his friend, not a physical reminder of his shortcomings. Yet as he sat with no companions but his old stories, he couldn't keep the jealousy from resurfacing.

A few years back, for Minh's birthday, they all agreed to go to Sài Gòn Municipal Opera House, a theatre built in the centre of the Clock Square. It was one of the few occasions that Minh truly looked forward to, an occasion arranged by him and not Edmond, involving cải lương—a blend of southern folk songs and classical music. His favourite form of opera. That winter was cold, and the day was gloomy and grey. Under the puffy clouds, four shiny cars came to a halt at the same time outside of the theatre, its façade ornate with inscription and reliefs, its roof an austere grey, the rest of the exterior painted in pale pink—a smaller and more humble reconstruction of the Petit Palais in Paris. Minh could still picture the four of them, getting out of their cars, an ensemble of wealth all dressed in navy wool and knee-length coats, wearing nearly identical black fedora hats. Minh still often laughed about this—how special they really were, walking out of their separate mansions in matching outfits, like a set of quadruplets.

Let's race to Duy's mansion in Đà Lạt. I want to ride horses today, Edmond had declared the minute his feet touched the grey cement, gesturing for his driver to hand him the car key, without waiting to hear his friends' opinions.

But we've agreed on the opera, Minh protested, before falling into a vast silence; his pride didn't grant him the energy to plead.

We can go after, Edmond. It's Minh's birthday. Duy tried to reason on Minh's behalf, and for this Minh was grateful.

Next to Edmond, Phong stood with his hands hidden inside the pockets of his coat, avoiding Minh's gaze and saying nothing, as Minh had expected. Minh hadn't known, still didn't know, what it really was—Phong's placid nature or his inability to refuse anything Edmond asked for. Later, Minh realised he had been bothered by this, too—how Phong consistently chose Edmond over him. When Edmond came down with the flu, Phong refused to leave his side, sulking next to his bed. Yet when Minh broke his arm from falling down the stairs, Phong only sent a bottle of wine. Edmond's favourite liquor. Minh knew Phong had done so without thinking, but it hurt all the same.

In the end, they all relented to Edmond's request, even though the trip from Sài Gòn to Đà Lạt would take them at least six hours, if not more, since the day already moved towards noon. Minh recalled the sharp slash of wind across his face as the four young men swerved their cars around the mountain pass, his mind trying desperately to understand why they couldn't seem to deny Edmond anything. Whatever Edmond wanted, Edmond received. Somewhere deep down, did they all feel inferior? Minh didn't know. He didn't hate Edmond, or at least he didn't think so. Perhaps it was what Edmond represented—someone better than him, someone easier to love, someone he could never be.

Despite Duy's efforts at filling the gaps, anchoring him to the group over the years, Minh still never felt like he truly belonged. He yearned for the bond between Edmond and Phong—the closeness and understanding that sometimes seemed even more profound than friendship. It was strange, he sometimes thought, how within their group of four there had always been two smaller groups— Edmond and Phong, an unbreakable pair, then Minh and Duy, the leftovers, forced to lean on each other.

For so long, Minh had been afraid that this would be his life, that he would have to walk the earth by himself, his soul a complex mathematical problem none could solve.

And then he noticed a housemaid he had never seen before.

He finally met Hai.

The thought of Hai eased the agitation panging inside his chest. Soon, it was replaced by a burning desire for her delicate touch. Quickly, Minh got off his bed, reaching for the tan trench coat hanging on a golden wall hook in the shape of a lion head. He draped it over his body and headed out the door.

Tattler

Crouching to the left of the Khải' mansion was a small, two-story flat where the Khải' servants spent the night. Its façade faced the east, absorbing most of the heat during scorching summers, making its rooms stiflingly hot, its residents miserable with sleep deprivation.

In her shared space on the top floor, Tattler sat sullen on the ground, letting out a frustrated sigh. Her hair clung to the side of her greasy neck, refusing to let go. Her scrawny fingers were numb from holding the battered bamboo fan all night, trying to keep cool. Had it been two hours? Three? Had she even slept at all?

She hated summer, hated the stickiness, hated the humidity, hated the fact that it would be easier to lose a limb than to get a decent night of rest because she didn't have a fancy ceiling fan like the one in her masters' bedrooms, with three wings and a whimsical black string in the middle that looked fun to pull at. Most of all, she hated not being able to complain. As soon as she opened her mouth, she would be deemed ungrateful; she would be beaten and reminded that her masters were more than gracious, more than generous, that she was a lowborn servant whose opinions did not matter.

They called her Tattler, though that wasn't her real name. Sen, it was. A lifetime ago, it meant lotus flower, the kind that rose from mud without stains. Resilience. Purity. When she first uttered it here, however, the people simply laughed, condescending. The common Annamites couldn't speak French, and they butchered the word *jeune servante*—which meant handmaid—with their clumsy pronunciation: *sen.* In this other life, Sen no longer meant a delicate flower, but a worthless servant. The identity her mother gifted her, forever distorted.

Change it, the other maids urged, *release yourself from the chains of fate*, and reluctantly, Tattler agreed. She now responded to the name of a stranger, allowing other servants to forget who she really was—that she was once someone's child, that she also once had parents.

The life she used to live, with her parents and an infant sister, had been purchased at such a meagre price. Still, she was taught to be thankful. As the years went by, perhaps she had forgotten it herself: the day her family sold her to the Khảis in exchange for a humiliatingly paltry sum to cover their seemingly never-ending debts sometimes felt like an ill-defined shard from a fractured memory she no longer wanted to possess.

She was blessed, she told herself, with the ability to quietly observe. She never missed a thing within the four walls of this mansion. From the stale and dull everyday occurrences—the glances between the young valets and the housemaids, the number of coins that the butler stashed in his trouser pockets at any given time—to the more fascinating indiscretions involving the masters of the house. Her mind held infinite knowledge, always ready to be utilised, helping her infiltrate a world that wasn't really hers.

She supposed that was how she got the name Tattler: the same way a person looked at a piece of furniture and called it a chair. The act of labelling objects according to their purposes. She was no longer a daughter, instead a servant who lurked in the corners, hearing others' well-kept whispers.

A muffled sound from the front yard caught her attention, and Tattler hoisted herself off the ground. She winced as she stood up, a dull pain gnawing at her shoulders; her body always hated the harsh, unforgiving ground.

Quietly, Tattler made her way over to the dinky window, ignoring the stifled groan from another restless maid, also struggling to sleep.

She was surprised. She did not anticipate this scene.

It wasn't one of the servants, their stomachs rumbling violently, their feet sneaking towards the main kitchen to steal a banana or two before the masters woke up. No, it was Monsieur Khải Minh. Madame Như's son. Tattler wondered why he was awake, and what he was doing in the servants' quarter at such an early, sinful hour. But the reason was walking clearly by his side.

Hai, his personal maid.

Hai, the rural girl from a village somewhere up North, with a heavy dialect that most of the servants couldn't understand. She wasn't wearing her usual shabby servants' attire, and her skin wasn't smeared with mud. Her petite frame looked as fragile and slender as a crane, her limbs delicate under an elegant silk dress, the kind Tattler had only ever seen Madame Như wear at extravagant dinner parties. Tattler squinted her eyes; Hai didn't seem uncomfortable or scared standing in front of Monsieur Minh. Across her lips, a genuine, warm smile. She looked . . . happy.

When had Tattler last felt that way? She couldn't remember, couldn't even imagine that same tenderness alighting her face. She watched as Monsieur Minh gently tucked a lock of hair behind Hai's left ear—her own ears suddenly grew hot with anger, thinking of the brutal beatings the young master had bestowed upon her whenever she accidentally did something he considered distasteful. He acted like a true gentleman now, holding the car door open for Hai, closing it dutifully after she had settled inside. It seemed that Monsieur Minh was well capable of kindness; he simply chose violence when dealing with Tattler.

25

Somewhere on her back, a half-healed scar throbbed its irritation. Tattler would see to it that Madame Như knew of this shameful and scandalous courtship.

When Minh and Hai finally drove off, Tattler smirked. The fools, she scoffed, as she returned to her place on the ground, her legs and arms splayed atop the blue-and-white ceramic tiles, stained slightly yellow. Her head ached from resting on the hard surface, but her muscles slowly relaxed; the knots of agitation cut loose when she envisioned herself kneeling on Madame Như's glossy floor, informing the mistress of her dear son's secret. Tattler smiled, her mind drifting away for a quick nap before the duties of her day began.

Soon, the sun would rise.

Hai

A soft breeze caressed Hai's sunken cheeks as the car lurched forward, passing the quiet neighbourhood, embraced by the gloomy grey blanket of early morning. Outside the car window, the trees remained tall, their branches fixed, their leaves still.

Inside, Hai tried to breathe slowly, to draw as little attention to herself as possible; her slim shoulders wavered lightly with each inhale. The weather wasn't as hot as she initially expected, yet between them the air was burning with the deafening silence of unspoken questions. She pressed her back against the leather seat, wishing the cushion would absorb all her worries. This wasn't her first time alone with Monsieur Minh, but it was one of the few occurrences where she started questioning her foolish heart— where the more she pondered it, the more she found their courtship fatuous, their future together bleak and dire.

She hadn't always been so glum.

Often, Hai recalled the day she met Monsieur Minh, *really* met him, the man she would soon love, the master who hadn't a reason to look her way yet did.

That morning, Hai had been on her knees, trying to save Tattler from another beating.

Tattler had been with the Khảis the longest, since she was a young girl, and so had declared herself the housekeeper, head of the housemaids, who was responsible for most kitchen chores. She loved delegating the tasks to newer, more gullible servants like Hai, who didn't complain. Hai never did, lowering her head and rinsing all the dirty plates and bowls Tattler pushed her way. Anything to make life less miserable. Soon, they found a rhythm, becoming two well-oiled cogs of a machine, doing their best to please the difficult masters.

Until Madame Như found residual soap bubbles on her favourite pair of chopsticks, the expensive ones with white mother-of-pearl inlaid at the tips. She had shrieked Tattler's name, a piercing sound that Hai could hear even from the corner of the kitchen, a world away from Madame Như's lavish dining room. She heard also the sound of Tattler's knees hitting the floor, her desperate pleas as she begged for pardon.

Hai's conscience didn't allow her to turn a blind eye. Cunning as she might be, Tattler shouldn't be punished for a mistake Hai'd made. She didn't hesitate, running to where Tattler was, confessing to Madame Như it had been her fault.

And there he sat, Monsieur Minh, on the other side of the table, his eyes curious, amused, boring into her. He had insisted no beating was necessary, that Hai only needed to become his personal maid. The mansion had gone silent at the suggestion; everyone knew what Monsieur Minh's intention was. His temper infamously cruel.

Yet to Hai, he had been anything but.

Monsieur Minh often laughed in her presence, his head tilted back, his eyes squinting. A sight Hai never believed exist. He was funny and he was smart. Charming. And despite what most servants thought, he was kind.

No warnings, no way to stop, Hai had fallen for him.

A dangerous game they had been playing when Monsieur Minh admitted he loved her too. Hai knew but relished in the safeness of his presence all the same, the assurance no one could hurt her as long as she was with him, the man who had never raised a finger at her, who reminded Hai she was a human instead of a nameless, soulless object known as a servant.

28

Two months later, he introduced Hai to his childhood friends.

At first, she was terrified at the prospect of appearing by Monsieur Minh's side, no longer as his faceless shadow, but as the woman he chose. She had never minded invisibility, not one bit; Hai only wanted the same thing Monsieur Minh had always longed for: profound, earnest understanding.

Later, though, when the three men nodded in her direction and smiled cordially, like she was one of their own, the chaos inside Hai's mind faded to a paler colour. She sat with her fingers relaxed around a cup of warm tea, and whilst such a beverage seemed odd and out of place inside a lively, modern dance club, no one ridiculed her. She shook her head to the invitation to dance, comfortably enjoying her own company.

Around her, the music dimmed to a slower tune, and the dance floor filled with young couples. They embraced their partners, swaying to the romantic melody. Hai grinned when she caught Monsieur Minh's eyes from across the room, her cheeks blushing as he discreetly blew a kiss in her direction. The feeling overwhelmed Hai, and she was embarrassed. Flustered, she looked away.

Her gaze landed, inadvertently, on Monsieur Phong.

He was lost in conversation, his eyes dreamy, fixing on the person opposite.

A quick glance. A brief touch. A knowing nod.

Hai recognised what she just witnessed almost instantly. This was exactly how she and Monsieur Minh communicated when there were other people around. This look stemmed from a particular kind of love—secretive and sinful.

When they finally left the dance club that day, Hai was quiet. She felt a strange sense of loyalty to protect Monsieur Phong's private affair, which she knew no one else had noticed. She couldn't explain why; perhaps she had pitied him.

What Hai didn't anticipate, though, was how her concern grew, how the knots of uncertainty tightened around her throat. She looked back now, and it seemed as though the thought had followed her from the dance club; its existence trailed her steps the same way a shadow would. Day by day, it consumed her love; she could no longer look at Monsieur Minh or feel his affection without feeling her worries, too. If Monsieur Phong could not afford to display his relationship publicly, then what was she doing? These powerful men could only love in darkness, it seemed.

Sometimes, Hai yearned for a piece of motherly advice. Cruelly, she indulged herself, imagining what her mother would say if she learned of Hai's taboo union. Maybe her mother would point out that Hai was being stupid. She would click her tongue, her tone dismissive as she described the men's arid effort. Hai could still hear it from time to time, her mother's perpetually scratchy voice. *Think of it this way*, the phantom inside Hai's mind would scoff. *Those men with their thin lips and their docile smiles. The promises they have given you, see them for what they really are—vain and fragile bubbles. Delicate prison walls.*

Or maybe she would be supportive. *It is rare, what the two of you share*, that same husky voice would say. *Those mundane things we worry about—a roof over our heads, or a bowl of rice inside our stomachs, they are not the reasons we exist. I've known of menial survival my whole life. I don't want the same for you.*

Now, sitting next to Monsieur Minh, no matter how hard she tried, Hai couldn't seem to summon either illusion. She no longer knew which path to follow.

Absentmindedly, her fingers brushed the cool, luxurious fabric of the dress she was wearing. Despite the comfort it was supposed to bring, she only felt suffocated. She couldn't appreciate the smooth, satin texture rubbing her supple skin, could only see her true, rustic and graceless self hiding beneath an outfit meant for someone else. A version of her that only existed because Monsieur Minh wanted it to; her body was a prisoner to what her lover had chosen and deemed appropriate.

She thought then of the different gifts he had given her, over the short period of time they had been together—a shiny, golden tube with a mild floral scent that Monsieur Minh called lipstick, a small and seemingly modest object that somehow still required extensive explanation. A pair of round sunglasses, which he instructed her to wear when they went to the golf course on sunny summer days. These were material things Hai never needed, the physical evidence that she was living a life that wasn't meant to be hers. They were symbols of Monsieur Minh's wishful thinking.

They were not Hai.

Hai was born the daughter of two farmers in the depths of poverty. Monsieur Minh was born the heir to the most powerful rubber empire in the colony.

Hai was named in correspondence to the order of her siblings' births, and even then, the irony was undeniable. She was the oldest, yet she was named number two because number one was inaccessible, strictly reserved out of respect for the royalty. Monsieur Minh's name, however, referred to a brilliant source of light, glowing as fiercely as the golden sun. Hai's name was an afterthought, something her parents decided upon as they held her slippery body, whilst Monsieur Minh's had been carefully thought of before he was conceived. He was entrusted with vast ambitions and greatness, whilst she was denied something as inferior and meaningless as the number one.

How could she ever love him with all her heart when they came from such different places?

As though he could hear her reservations, Monsieur Minh interrupted Hai's train of thought.

"Stop fidgeting."

Hai turned her head in his direction. Was it a suggestion or an order?

Monsieur Minh already stopped paying attention; his gaze was fixed on the world outside, unremarkable houses leaning against one another, their roofs a tedious terracotta. She always got nervous this way—she remembered his comment and his dismissive wave when she first expressed her wariness. He said her stress was unnecessary, that no one would even think to follow them out. Reluctantly, Hai often dipped her head and pretended to be fine, encasing her warm fingers in his.

"Monsieur." This time, against her best judgement, she summoned the courage to articulate her worry. Her breath felt urgent.

"I told you to drop those stupid formalities when we are alone."

There was a hint of annoyance lacing Monsieur Minh's words, prompting Hai to press her lips shut, sealing the escape route of a hasty retort. She wanted to exclaim her frustration that they were not equal, that they did not come from the same upbringing, that they had been playing a dangerous game, that neither of them would escape unscathed. Instead, Hai swallowed the argument, nodding the way she always did.

"Yes, of course."

Gone was the honorific. Still, the obedience stayed.

In that moment, Hai pictured herself inhabiting the body of a water buffalo, common and replaceable, its coarse grey back growing heavier and heavier, carrying each passing moment of silence.

At last, the car came to a stop in front of Monsieur Minh's house, the one he bought shortly after they started seeing one another. Hai stepped from the vehicle and stood in front of its black wrought iron gate, mesmerised by the solemn beauty of the property—its sharp rectangle shape, its brown timber windows with plantation shutters, its fading white paint and its creaking wooden floors. She could hear the reverberation of the doors' moans, protesting when they were pushed with force. Whilst these features agitated Monsieur Minh, Hai found their peculiarities endearing. It wasn't Madame Nhu's perfect, impeccable mansion, with treasures overflowing from one room to the next, and it did not belong to Hai. But it was a safe place where she could seek solace. Here, she promised, she would not stray back to the dusty road of her past, nor the ambiguous and uncertain future ahead. Her shoulders relaxed, her affection guarded by this one sturdy present, however fleeting.

Drawing a breath, Hai moved inside, escaping the water buffalo's hefty frame. Grudgingly, the animal retreated to a dark corner, waiting.

Edmond

"Welcome back, Monsieur."

The old driver hastily bowed his head to his young master, his gaze glued to the grey cement ground, awaiting permission to look up. Edmond could tell that he was trying to keep still, but the man's age betrayed his good manners, his back groaning with a faint crack. On his weathered face was a visible discomfort. He decided to not comment on it.

"Did you bring the other car? I didn't see it," Edmond asked instead, narrowing his eyes, trying to search for the extra vehicle he had requested for his luggage. "Here, take this."

Without waiting for the driver's response, Edmond withdrew his fingers from the tan leather briefcase's handle, letting its heavy body thump onto the ground. The old servant gasped helplessly as the bottom of the expensive bag touched the road.

"Oh, don't be so dramatic." Edmond grinned teasingly; he was in an unusually good mood. "This old thing I couldn't care less about. Now, where is the second car?"

The driver wasted no time, undoubtedly trying to preserve Edmond's breezy manner, standing up straight with a muffled whimpering sound. Gesturing to his left, the old man dipped his head slightly.

"This way, Monsieur."

Edmond nodded, and together, they started walking in silence.

The sky above their heads was a bright turquoise, free from even a dash of white cloud, which normally helped ease some of the harsh sunlight. Beside the valet, Edmond grimaced. After the month-long vacation with his mother in France, he found this return to Sài Gòn disturbingly repulsive. When he first stepped off the train, Edmond almost fainted; the heat was overwhelming. It felt as though the temperature had turned into a blade, searing his pale skin. His wavy locks of light blonde hair stuck to the nape of his slender neck. The white silk handkerchief, with the tiny flower that Marianne, his old nanny, had carefully embroidered on a corner, already became overly damp, and couldn't keep the trickles of sweat from running down his forehead. Reaching for the pair of round sunglasses in the inner pocket of his pinstripe suit jacket, Edmond mumbled, more to himself than to the driver.

"I could never understand why Father insists on running the business here, in this wretched heat."

Around them, a few naked kids hovered behind a line of parked rickshaws, their heads full of lice. Their scrawny bodies appeared to vibrate with savage anticipation; even from a distance, Edmond could see their desperation to steal a loaf of bread from the vendor at the corner. The woven basket was perched on the edge of the pavement, its belly filled with hot, steamy baguettes. The youngest, Edmond assumed, for he also looked smallest, with most of his ribs showing, followed the owner's movements carefully, the same way a hawk watched its prey.

Edmond's steps faltered; he wanted to observe what happened next. Like witnessing a wild animal in its natural habitat, hunting for lunch after a long period of hopeless starvation. The child stood half naked, a pair of faded brown shorts covering his lower body. An animal without most of its fur, its pink skin showing.

"I'm itchy," the kid told the rest of his group, his small fingers scratching his bare feet violently.

"Shut up," the tallest and fattest replied, threatening. "Focus. Or else."

Edmond blinked, wondering how many loaves of bread that arrogant leader had inhaled, leaving behind only crumbs for the younger to eat. A nameless sensation announced its presence at the back of his throat, and he didn't like it. Still, Edmond pointed at the child and turned to his driver.

"Go get him something to eat." His voice was hushed, trying to conceal the pity. Edmond never wanted to care, never wanted to sympathise. Yet there he stood, helping anyway.

A gust of scorching wind rose, making Edmond uncomfortable, prompting him to take his suit jacket off and roll up the sleeves of his white shirt. He was thirsty; he normally didn't drink when he travelled. He missed it, the warmth in his stomach as the liquid settled inside. He swallowed his saliva, the thought of smooth, silky wine making him even more eager to leave. Draping the jacket over his forearm, he searched the crowd for his driver's balding head.

"Let's go," he ordered when the old man returned, his pace quickening. He didn't bother turning his head to marvel at the kid's bewilderment; he knew that the happiness he just created was only temporary. As soon as the bread was consumed, the small child's hunger would no longer be ignored as easily. The boy had been introduced to satisfaction.

It was lunchtime, the sun now higher in the sky, a round and fierce dot of bright orange. The street was bustling with people buying and selling meat, fish, and vegetables. The road was tight and soon, Edmond no longer had the space to just himself, sticky bodies constantly pressing against his skin. His cheeks grew pink, his face flustered as he clumsily kicked a pannier full of oranges, their peels a deep emerald green, a world of difference from the bright, cheerful colour of the oranges in France. He mumbled an apology, shocking himself, the old driver, and the vendor in the process.

Just ahead, Edmond could see slabs of red beef and pink pork laid on a flimsy wooden plank. An old woman settled herself behind the counter, her face drooped like a hound. Her left hand was waving a palm-leaf conical hat, a fruitless attempt at cooling the searing weather, her right hand swinging a stick back and forth over the animal flesh to keep the flies away. Next to her stall, nestling in the corner of the busy street, was an elderly man's stand. His hair was completely white, bunched together into a lock secured by a black rubber band. He dressed in all black, and wore an unusual hat, hollowed in the middle. The Annamite's traditional costume, Edmond knew. The man sat himself atop a pale beige bamboo mat with a pathetically worn red trim, his legs crossed and his back stretched over a thin scroll, his fingers firm around a dark brown calligraphy brush. Edmond could not understand the words he wrote, but he watched the man in awe nonetheless. His green eyes darted between the elder man and the child, who had been waiting patiently at the man's side, her small hand slowly grinding the ink against the hard stone slab.

Edmond was not used to crowds like this, buyers and sellers from the other side of the world whose gazes discreet yet prying, curious on his skin. The reason he disliked leaving the comfort of his home in the middle of the day. The street was quickly filling up with more haggling and yelling; the seemingly infinite outdoor space somehow turned claustral, forcing Edmond to peel his heavy feet from the ground.

The driver had parked the black Cadillac under the shade of a young banyan tree, its roots still small compared to the others Edmond had seen, though he was certain that as time passed, they would also grow so stout that the ground would crack, yielding to their strength.

"Would you like to drive back alone in this car, Monsieur?" the driver asked quietly, carefully.

"What? No." He breathed out, exhausted from both the walk and the weather. "I need the extra car for my luggage. Did no one inform you properly?" He cocked his head towards the direction they had just come from, pointing at the two other servants he had travelled with, who were now standing in the middle of the station exit, guarding seven bulky trunks.

"My mistake. I'm terribly sorry, Monsieur. Let me start loading them in the car at once."

"Be careful. They are extremely fragile," Edmond commanded before climbing into the back seat, settling his bottom on its plush cushion, his long legs comfortably stretched out. "I do not want to look at broken bottles of wine."

"Of course, Monsieur," the driver replied before turning to his left, motioning for the other men to come and take the key for the second car. He started whistling as he filled the boot with Edmond's luggage, and somehow, hearing this, Edmond smiled.

For the first time in a very long time, Edmond wasn't even drunk.

* *

The drive from Sài Gòn railway station to 1 Charner Road—where the Moutets' mansion stood—wasn't long, but Edmond had grown restless. The humming of the car's engine felt endless. He called to the front.

"Go to Bonard Road, where the car dealer is."

"At once, Monsieur."

From the entrance, Edmond could already see the salesman, his eyes sparkling with hunger. The man was dressed in Western attire—a black, polished three-piece suit, with his hair in a sleek coif. He greeted Edmond with a smile so wide, Edmond felt sorry for the salesman's cheek muscles, how they must have hurt. Ignoring the man's many questions, Edmond wandered the shop floor, which was really a glamourised garage, with only two cars in the middle, begging to be purchased.

Edmond's eyes landed on a black car, which he instantly recognised as the famous 1928 Peugeot 201. Famous because there had only ever been one, in the entire colony, which belonged to Bảo Nam, the emperor of Annam.

Until now.

Edmond smiled as his slender index finger traced the silver bumper and the round headlights above. The car wasn't necessarily his preference, but because the so-called king owned it, Edmond decided that he must have it, too. This piece of land belonged to *his* people, anyway—he would not give anything up to a monarch who couldn't manage to keep his own country.

"I'll take this," Edmond called to the salesman, who had been clearly holding his breath.

"My valet will hand you the cash. An extra five hundred piastre for you," Edmond continued, his generosity now an order. "Go get your family a hearty meal."

Even later, Edmond didn't understand why he had given the man the extra cash; he only knew that he felt sorry. Perhaps it was because he bought a car out of childish rivalry, over a man he had never once met. Meanwhile, the fate of another human being, his hunger, his children's hunger, rested entirely in Edmond's hands.

After they left the shop, Edmond sent the valet home with the old car whilst he headed for Duy's opium club in his brand-new Peugeot. The drive was smooth. Yet somehow, the hum in his ears grew louder.

Duy

Duy had first toured his family's opium factory on his fifteenth birthday.

When they entered on that overcast morning, Duy was overwhelmed. The interior, a dingy and smelly space.

That day, there must have been over one hundred people working; the vast land was divided into multiple sections. To his left, there were wobbly wooden tables topped with raw opium atop, waiting to be rounded into fist-sized balls before being wrapped inside glossy green banana leaves. One by one, they would be transferred to the section on his right, where a group of young men waited, their limbs as frail as twigs, their upper bodies naked, linen trousers covering their lower halves. Their shoulders and chests were thick with black dirt and glistening sweat. They would grunt, the sound haunting Duy's juvenile ears, as they swung the iron hammers down, scraping the impurities off the blocks of opium.

Duy and Father observed from the corner of the factory. His gaze innocent, curious, Father's watchful.

Duy noticed many Chinese boys. He knew they were Chinese because of their signature hairstyle—the back was grown long and braided, whilst the front portion was shaved clean—something he remembered from the lessons Mother had taught. An attempt to connect him to her ancestry. A queue, he believed that was what the hairstyle was called. The boys were sitting in a separate section with massive copper basins crowding their sides, their hands swiftly washing the blocks of freshly processed opium.

Come.

Father called for his attention, and he followed. He couldn't help but wonder: Who did these boys blame for the fact that

Duy stood tall, whilst they crouched low? These boys were Duy's age, but their fates placed them somewhere below him. In another universe, they would have gone to the same school, would have attended the same class, would have been friends. In this life, this reality, however, they remained Duy's workers. Duy's property.

Soon enough, the question slipped into the black hole in his mind, where no light could reach; Duy had forgotten his pity towards those boys and their ashen faces, smeared with toxic chemicals from the addictive substance. His attention was now captured by a much quieter area, the only room with three locks on the outside door.

Without any instructions from Father, he stepped in, captivated by the unusual cleanliness of the space.

This is where we keep our inventory, Father explained, his words slower than usual, as though he had been allowing Duy the time to absorb the significance of his existence to their family's empire. *Once a month we come here to count the physical product, to ensure nothing has gone missing.*

Duy swallowed his saliva reflexively; the endless rows of carefully stacked golden boxes made him anxious, like he was in the presence of some dark force, as alluring as it was deadly. His index finger had traced the top of them absentmindedly; the brass lids were carved with either the letter B or Y, indicating the opium's origin. He attempted to recall what Father had said the day before, how B meant Benares, that the substance was imported from India, and how Y meant that the drug came from China. He nodded solemnly, noting the different numbers on the bottom right corner of each lid—5, 10, 20, 40, and 100, specifying how heavy that particular block of opium was in grams.

You.

41

Father called out to an older man, who Duy assumed to be the manager because he was fully clothed, his hands obnoxiously clean.

Why is this row missing two boxes?

The man stammered as Father narrowed his eyes, the quiet room going completely still. Duy could almost hear the poor man's heart, shambling in his chest.

Kneel, Father ordered plainly, his fingers tightening around the icy, hard metal whip he had taken off the rusty hook hanging by the door. Duy stiffened upon seeing the weapon; its body was hefty with multiple slender rods, connected to one another by silver rings. It must have been twice the length of his arm. He had seen Mother use the same kind to discipline the foolish servants who dared to steal. *Bian,* she called it.

An instinct, how Duy took a step back, fearing for the old man's fate—he had positioned himself at Father's feet, obedient like a house pet.

Duy, this way.

Father waved him over, and despite the thumping trepidation rippling through his body, he listened. As his skin registered the cold, unforgiving feeling of the weapon, Duy finally understood the reason for his factory visit that day. He was there to learn a lesson, imparted by Father.

His first kill.

He was unable to utter a single word; his expression was the one form of communication he managed to control. Pleading. *Father, I'm too young for this*, he wanted to cry, even as he knew Father would never accept such meekness.

In the years that followed, Duy continually failed to see where the strength had come from that day. He only remembered that his cheeks felt hot, as though they had been stung, that the veins across his forearm bulged, their bodies a faint jade green, like worms wiggling, infecting his blood. He attempted to ignore the sound, refusing to register the man's wail—a sound so desperate that Duy pretended to hear a wolf's howl instead. He stopped after the first two strikes, panting. But Father was not happy. His gaze, like steel, poking Duy's flesh. He ceded, resuming the brutal beating. It ended when the man slumped at Duy's feet. The flesh on his back was torn open, the skin flaking off, red blood and yellow fat oozing out. The crisscross pattern of his wound looked like a seal—over the man's short fate, over Duy's new identity.

Now, nine years later, Duy opened his eyes, gasping.

Duy realised—after a minute of disorientation—that he had fallen asleep whilst reviewing the tedious monthly report that preceded his upcoming factory check. Once a month, precisely one day before the walk-through, that same dream returned to haunt his sleep. A loud echo from a past Duy could never escape.

You will never forget it. Your first kill, Father had commented, a hint of pride nestling under his assurance.

"Monsieur, Madame Mai has requested your presence at the shop. At once."

Duy was sitting in his favourite armchair, his legs resting atop its supple hand rest, when the middle-aged valet entered. He didn't answer, rolling his eyes whilst suppressing a loud sigh. Judging by the anxious look on the servant's face, Duy could tell what had prompted Mother's summons.

Edmond's return.

He must have made his appearance at the club already, an entrance so unexpectedly grand that Mother had urgently sent for him.

Despite the brilliant orange sunset outside his window, Duy drowned the rest of his bitter black coffee in one gulp; the liquid smoothed his throat and mind. Letting out a hiss of satisfaction, he stood up and gestured for the housemaid to help him get dressed. For a moment, Duy stood hesitating in front of his wardrobe, unsure what to wear. He disliked formal suits and dress shirts, but he hated the idea of looking sloppy in front of Edmond's effortless charm and poise even more. Duy hated that this made him uncomfortable; after all, they had seen one another half naked, with their legs scraped and their skin smeared with mud in the school yard, all those years back. Why must he now bother with the vanity of material things? It was because of his family, Duy supposed. The way Father's eyes softened whenever he talked to that fat French governor, the way Mother fussed over high-born French opium addicts.

In the end, Duy opted for a navy suit jacket. Before draping it over his broad shoulder, Duy signalled for another servant to polish his Western-style shoes whilst he adjusted the chain of his silver pocket watch; its body glimmered across his navy vest, its buttons a straight and impeccable line. Duy winced, the stiff collar of his white shirt kept pressing against the skin of his neck. His discomfort was unbearable: his hair was pushed back into a coif, the stubborn strands weighed down with a generous amount of expensive hair gel. His skull felt heavy from carrying the unnecessary product, his best features subsequently restrained, for they looked best with his naturally flowing hair.

"All done, Monsieur," the servant announced at his feet, his hands, quick and knowing, gathering the brittle brush and the box of shoe polish.

"Thanks."

Like a reflex, Duy expressed his gratitude. His servants adored it, the way Duy pretended they had a choice. He traced his reflection in the mirror, remembering his mother's comment every time she saw him wearing navy blue. *Childish*, she would say, worrying that the business partners might not think him capable. Smiling now, Duy glanced at the bruises on his knuckles: some were new and raw with an aching purple, some had already turned a faint moss green. He could no longer recall the reason for his injury, only the fear on his competitors' faces. Navy blue dominated his wardrobe all the same.

"One more thing, Monsieur." The valet took a piece of neatly folded paper from his front pocket. Another request from Madame Mai. "Madame asked that you handle this before seeing Monsieur Edmond."

Duy nodded at the driver as he headed towards the car. "Go to the common club first."

"At once, Monsieur."

Duy leaned back in his seat, searching for the squashy head-rest to soothe the pulsing exhaustion in his mind. Most days, time unfolded this exact way, a tedious routine—there would always be a disturbance, a commotion, a business meeting that required his attention. He was sick of it. He never asked for this; he had never wanted this life.

Like Phong, Duy had previously planned to study abroad. Though unlike Phong, Duy wasn't a bright student. He simply hoped to utilise the distance to delay his inevitable inheritance. But he couldn't have seen it coming—the week before Duy was supposed to leave, Mother had fallen sick. To this day, Duy didn't know whether her illness was real, but he had stayed regardless. At first, he sent the university a long and sincere letter explaining his situation, delaying his enrolment. By the time Mother was healthy again, however, they had withdrawn their offer. *You are meant to stay here, by my side.* Mother had squeezed his shoulders, trying to comfort him. Quickly, one year had folded into the next, and before he knew it, Duy had been running the empire for almost six years. The days he spent doing what he wanted—frequenting jazz clubs downtown, trying to figure out who he was outside his family's identity—reduced to a smudge.

Now, as he sat in the back of the car, Duy wondered when he had started to change. His dream somehow became the exact thing Father had predicted—not a warning, not guilt or remorse, but simply the permanence of that memory. His first kill. Duy had ended more lives than he could save, and he was just as corrupt as the politicians he used to hate. Was it still a crime if Duy didn't feel good committing it? Or, like his cruel father, was Duy too far gone?

Outside his car window, vendors scattered around the entrance of Cho Lon. Duy sighed, his breath dense, fogging the clear glass.

His stomach rumbled, announcing its hunger as the car lurched past a brown wooden hawker cart, a dried squid hanging at the top, an assortment of fruit resting on a makeshift table below. Duy estimated the owner of the stall to be in his thirties, from the moustache on his top lip—still black and shiny. He was pushing his cart in the opposite direction, and Duy eyed the four tiny wheels rolling beneath. They made a spine-chilling squeak against the cement pavement.

Duy's car never made any sound.

"We are here, Monsieur."

From the front seat, the driver was speaking. Duy nodded, noting the battered wooden door from the corner of his eyes. This was a common den. A neglected, nameless two-story building, which his family utilised as a front for their other, less savoury activities. It sat at the very end of Cho Lon, an area the locals had always referred to as Chinatown.

Duy had been here countless times over the years, but the scene had never changed. The road was average, not too small but not too big, enough for two cars to move side by side without colliding. The pavement, though, was crowded with food stalls and their seating arrangements; the short, flimsy wooden settings blocked most of the walkway. The other buildings in this area were also two-story structures, all rented by local businesses. The ground floor was the place for food, the Chinese national dishes Duy's mother loved, which he had only tried once or twice. Above, on the second floors, there were spaces reserved for passersby who needed a place to rest overnight. In front of the restaurant or balcony were signs and banners that overwhelmed Duy. Their bodies were bright and loud with big foreign hanzi characters he didn't understand. He could barely hear any Vietnamese or French. The chatter was all in Chinese. Stepping from the car, Duy ignored the cautious eyes from the crowds of men and women, gathered around his flashy vehicle, watching him. His expensive suit did not belong here.

Duy inhaled, his lungs filled with the comforting scent of bone broth. The smell soothed his tired muscles. He missed Mother's cooking; it had been so long since Duy last attended a family dinner.

Exhaling, he tried to prepare for the scene that awaited him inside the den. Duy loathed handling the daily commotions caused by these peasants—the raunchy Frenchmen and their mindless arguments over their favourite bar girls, the addicts who had sold most of their earthly possessions, who could no longer afford another puff, their desperate pleas for generosity.

Duy could hear the fight amidst the bustling noise on the street, the sound of bodies being pushed against the thin wall. He didn't hesitate, drawing the shotgun from the inner pocket of his

47

jacket and fired it into the air. The veins around his wrist tensed with his grip, and the club fell silent for just a second before one of the French tirailleurs started cursing.

"What the fuck was that?"

"What happened here?" Duy smirked as he let the door swing shut behind him, speaking directly to the tirailleur in French.

It wasn't the first time Duy visited the common club, but still, the mangy space surprised him. The room was small and square, every vacant space utilised for a worn bamboo mat or a splintered panel bed. The only source of light came from the smoking lamps; their flickering flames cast a ghastly glow on everything they touched, further highlighting the patrons' frail rib cages. One body settled against the next, all mingling sweat. At least no one seemed to mind, Duy shrugged. The high was too exquisite.

He couldn't move, couldn't bear the thought of walking further inside. He tried his best to not look at the walls, but his peripheral vision betrayed his determination. The half-hearted attempt his family had made to renovate this place before its opening was showing at last—the paint had started to peel off, revealing black and green mould underneath. The black metal hooks for customers' coats and hats were now a brassy orange. He shuddered.

The portly tirailleur standing in the centre of the room was momentarily stunned. He panted, eyeing Duy. His breath was short, not from fright or terror but from exhaustion. It appeared he had just beaten a man to death.

"Who are you to cause a disturbance? The fine for such offence is five hundred piastre. Pay up, or I will send you to the station."

Duy said nothing, noting the wet, fresh streaks of blood on the tirailleur's knuckles before turning his gaze to the corner of the room, where a crumpled body lay.

48

"Hey!" the tirailleur called. "Are you deaf?"

"Did you kill that man?" Duy asked, his face an eerie shade of calm, a waveless sea moments before a violent storm.

"What man?" The tirailleur laughed, tilting his blonde head of hair back as though Duy had told him a funny joke. "That isn't a man. That is an Annamite. An animal. A rodent."

Duy sighed. He had hoped it wouldn't come to this.

"So you don't regret your actions?" He kept his eyes fixed on the tirailleur's forgettable face, imagining what it would look like thirty seconds in the future, after he drew his gun.

"Why should I?" the tirailleur challenged, his fat finger now pointed at Duy's face. "Do you regret when you kill an insect? I should hope not. I'm cleaning the street, you see. This land is already crowded as it is."

Duy shook his head, scoffing. He could never fathom it, these foreigners' audacity and entitlement. They trampled over his country's sacred ground, where soldiers had sacrificed their blood, declaring it theirs. They breathed under his country's sky, filling their alien lungs with his people's air, and still, they belittled everything. Even that title, tirailleur. They originally invented the term for the Annamite infantrymen who had given up fighting for their own nation, aiding the French in their maintenance of the colony. Yet soon enough, it'd become a slur, a tasteless private joke amongst French soldiers that referred to the cursed souls who were assigned to lead a herd of uncivilised sheep that were Duy's people.

In his eyes, they were also the devil who had forced his family's hands. They created miseries that the addicts sought to escape with deadly substance, parading the business in front of Father as the quickest way to generate wealth and preserve power. It wasn't Mother's sudden illness or Duy's guilt that halted his abroad education, he realised. It was them, these fair-skinned and strange-eyed

49

foreigners with their arrogance, their cruelty. They were the reason Duy could never discover who he would be beyond the drunk opium smoke, the reason he wandered through life without any ambition. They had chained Duy to this colony just as they did his father. They moulded him into a greedy young heir whose top priority was money, for profiting from others' misfortunes was the only way that allowed Duy to protect those he loved.

The thought made Duy's index finger twitch around the chilly trigger, and the tirailleur noticed the gun in Duy's right hand a second too late. A deafening sound. His bright blue eyes dimmed.

After, Duy stared at the tirailleur's body, blood hot around his ears and neck. The role could have easily been reversed. If you stripped off the flashy money and the self-proclaimed titles, Duy knew that an Annamite like himself was nothing compared to a nameless French infantryman.

"Get this piece of shit out of my sight."

He left just as one of the workers stepped forward, struggling to hoist the dead weight of the tirailleur over his scrawny shoulders.

Duy jogged towards his car, his face still flushed with anger. His back no longer carried its fearless composure; his soul felt deprived of energy. His throat yearned for the warmth of the imported whiskey from the silver flask he kept in his jacket, right next to his gun.

"Dare I ask . . ." The driver hesitated to say more once they settled inside. "Are you alright, Monsieur?"

It took him longer than usual to respond, his stare empty at the world through the car window.

"It could have been either of us, you know? Me or the *Annamite* that tirailleur killed. That's the power of having power, old man."

He needn't say the rest out loud. This had been the reality of their country, the country they had lost, the country whose victories only existed in long-forgotten history. He wasn't a patriot, Duy knew that. Quite the opposite, if anything. Like most Annamite children who were *privileged* enough to attend French boarding schools, French was more his mother tongue than Vietnamese had ever been. His family had even assisted in the French administration and exploitation of Vietnam—the hefty monthly payments to French political parties, the constant acquisition of land, forcing the poor onto the streets. Still, in the presence of the arrogant colonisers, Duy longed for his country's liberation, his streets' freedom from these foreigners. The only thing he didn't know for certain was this: If his wish came true, would he want Edmond gone too?

THAT NIGHT

"So, what happened here?"

Pierre's chest fell and rose laboriously; he had just finished inhaling a heavy dinner before coming here. The corner of his unkempt moustache was still wet with residual fat, the gaps of his teeth green with hastily consumed water spinach. A bamboo toothpick rested in his jaw, bouncing each time he breathed. He smacked his lips, the taste of boiled chicken rising from his stomach; he had left his meal in a hurry. His sage green uniform seemed rather old, its colour now faded, its back a shade darker, dampened with sweat.

Pierre had driven in a haste, following the governor's order, the superior whose words meant more to Pierre than the Bible's teachings. He believed in his governor, enough to always do what he was asked, enough to accept the demotion to a tirailleur without protests, a title often bestowed upon the *local* infantry soldiers and the unlucky Frenchmen who managed them. Before the occupation, Pierre had been the artillery unit's finest member, one who fired cannons with absolute accuracy. He had been praised, respected, even, until the last battle that marked the end of Pierre's glorious active duty days. He emerged a broken man, two of his fingers blown off by the same heavy weapon that helped propel his career in the first place. Now, he was the leader of a common troop that roamed the streets each nightfall, maintaining security order. The infantrymen of infantrymen.

Unlike the friendships he'd made back at the artillery unit, Pierre didn't trust his current subordinates. How could he? A lifetime ago, he was trained to kill people who resembled them on the battlefield. Anyway, he suspected the feeling was mutual. They were told to beware of white-skinned, light-haired men. Pierre hated it, the tension, the qualms. A smart move by the governor to appease the colony though, grouping Pierre and these *locals* together. Or at least, that was what Pierre told himself. He needed a good reason to tolerate his comrades' tease, the way they hollered that he was a tirailleur as though he had been born a citizen of this poor, forsaken city, just as he needed a good reason to continue being the patriot he was raised to be, to serve his country no matter its leader's agenda.

To run the governor's *errands* at a moment's notice.

The piece of paper with the house's address sat burrowed at the bottom of Pierre's trouser pocket, heavy like a cannonball he used to fire—a private property on top of a secluded hill, deep within the pine forest of Đà Lạt. He was ordered to arrive as fast as he could, and no other information followed. Why the secrecy? He was baffled, but as usual, he needed no explanations. The words *yes, Monsieur* flowed easily off his tongue, the obedience as natural as a reflex. Subservience was the first thing they taught him.

The small house where Pierre had received the call was already in the past, its owner's name already forgotten. Though he would remember the food they had provided him, the same way they offered sacrifices for their gods, to have their sins pardoned.

When his black patrol car first approached the opened front gate, its headlights flickering, the building was shrouded in the velvety carpet of night, its blinding white façade obscured—he could only see light coming from the living room window, a grand rectangle with intricate oriental ornaments atop a transparent glass panel. The amber cast fondled a few tall, carefully trimmed bushes at the front, preventing him from gauging just how wealthy these people really were. Now, Pierre took his time, his light brown eyes alert, his gaze settled briefly on the three young men, who remained silent in absolute bewilderment, or perhaps it was fright. He wasn't good at understanding people's facial expressions, but this was not a problem. In his line of work, it didn't matter which investigation style he adopted. It only mattered how many criminals he managed to detain. The promises he had made to his superior—the oath to uphold and maintain justice—were a comical joke, a façade to further the French propaganda. They knew better than anyone that the foundation of this colony was built on repression.

Pierre's question echoed, his words bouncing off the walls of the massive living room. He lifted his left eyebrow, noting the exorbitant agarwood furniture.

There was a corpse lying in the middle of the room with a thin blanket covering the head—but this did not repulse him. If anything, Pierre was glad. The bigger the crime, the heftier the sum he ought to receive; it was far more vital to determine the resources these people possessed, rather than to uncover the redundant truth. After all, truth was malleable. The most generous always won.

The tirailleur nodded in approval when his eyes caught the sturdy mahogany settee in one corner of the room, where a gold-inlaid grandfather clock also stood. Real gold, he was certain. His fat fingers clenched, an attempt to shield his blatant excitement when he saw the grand copper chandelier. He tilted his head back then, admiring the ceiling above—a magnificent mural painted in a warm yellow hue; the elegant cranes, with their slender legs and their graceful bodies, effortlessly strode towards the feathery stroke of rice paddies. There were four majestic white columns, with brass carvings hugging their crowns, and light bulbs in the shape of candle flames glinting along their sides.

Pierre was in awe, captivated by the extravagance he didn't think could exist. He forced himself out of the trance, remembering there were protocols he must follow. Protocols that dictated how he should act, what he should say.

First, he reached for the baton, tapping its tip against the expensive tiles. Each touch was curt. A dare, provocative.

The rubber weapon was slender, deceptively harmless. Pierre doubted the young men knew the things his companion had seen, the bodies it had beaten. He had no intentions of using it now, of course. Power was all the baton was meant to convey.

Second . . .

Pierre didn't have the chance to get to the second step.

He caught the pinch between one of the young men's eyebrows, much like the annoyance Pierre sometimes spotted on the governor's face. There was no jagging breathing, no reluctance to hold his gaze.

No fear.

The pieces finally seemed to fit—the discreet and urgent order from the governor, the secluded property, and now the opulent interior design. They could only mean one thing.

He was inside the vacation house of Cao Hải Hà, the most powerful opium lord across the colony.

His grip loosened and the baton fell to the ground. The payment Pierre dreamed of receiving promptly evaporated as the realisation sank under Pierre's veins; he wished he hadn't been so callous, asking a foolish, unauthorised question amidst his childish excitement. Pierre was preparing an apology for his bad manners, his arrogance—there existed another comprehensive set of rules when it came to dealing with the rich Annamites—when one of the men rose from his seat. He picked up the baton without flinching, like to him, it was an everyday object, insignificant, incapable of causing him harm.

Like he was invincible.

The man gave Pierre the weapon, clearing his throat and offering a hand.

"My name is Cao Hải Duy. I'm the owner of this house."

Before he could utter a proper response, Duy corrected.

"It's my father's. But well . . ."

His voice trailed off. Everyone knew his father's name.

"Monsieur." Pierre spoke carefully, chewing over what to say next. He could feel his pale face growing a shade whiter. The healthy flush dimmed under his skin, his expression ghastly. Pierre's weathered eyes seemed to blur, dazed; he failed to notice Duy's battered suit and beaten posture. Anxious, as though he were in the presence of the opium lord himself, Pierre pretended to cough, a brief chance to arrange the words under his pink tongue before trying again. "Monsieur, please, call me Pierre."

His head dipped low, humble, almost pitiful, just the way the governor wanted. Pierre stared at the glossy marble floor, the reflection of his own troubled expression gazing back.

He knew of these young men. He had never met them, but everyone knew their names. They were half Pierre's age—a bunch of twenty-somethings—yet their prestigious families had bequeathed them unimaginable power whose radiance drastically outshone the soft halo of their youth. They stood so high on the peak of an exclusive mountain, its location was elusive to a lowborn like Pierre; it was a place where even the strictest laws couldn't reach, where for every fractured shard of glass their reputation couldn't repair, their money could fill in the cracks.

He wondered why he hadn't seen their faces before, though he supposed their families could only do that much—protecting their features from the front pages of newspapers whilst talks of what they did, where they went, and who they loved, freely roamed the colony. Within this affluent society, rumours travelled faster than rain touching dry grass, whispers spreading quicker than infectious diseases.

There were four of them, Pierre knew. Khải Minh, the only son of the late Khải Siêu, sole heir to the most successful rubber plantation of Cochinchina. His face might have been hidden from the public's prying eyes, but his family's resources and their control over the vast forests in Biên Hòa were in plain view for all to see. The city housed thousands of refugees who abandoned their lives and fled from the war, only to surrender as servants to the greedy and cruel rubber trees. The boy had been sent to a boarding school, Pierre was certain of it, that private French school on the outskirts of the city, its black iron gate always opened for fair, blonde, French children. And occasionally, the wealthy Annamites whose families the French reluctantly relied on. The French ruled the colony, but they didn't understand its people—they needed locals, rich enough, corrupt and ambitious enough, to supply them with insight and cash.

It was during their first school year that the boys had met—Duy, Minh, and Phong. Pierre was embarrassed that he actually remembered all the gossip his wife had told him. The third boy, Lê Hữu Phong, son of the most renowned chemist in the colony, Lê Văn, was said to be the quietest. He was smart, too. All quiet people were. The boys had walked into each other's lives as desk mates, and as the school year stretched by, they grew close.

57

The story of the boys would have been ordinary, a group of rich heirs—boring and predictable—had it not been for the unexpected arrival of Monsieur Leon Moutet, the smart and capable diplomat who saw Annam for what it really was: a fertile land with riches he could easily exploit. His family had come during the boys' second year at school, and it didn't take long for Edmond Moutet, Leon's only son, to assume control over the group, his hair so blonde and shiny.

It was as funny as it was strange—Pierre remembered his wife's exclamation as she told him the story—and he agreed. No one understood why Edmond lowered himself to associate with the other boys. They might have been equally wealthy, but still. The other three were *just* Annamites. Against all odds and speculation, though, one season had shaded into the next, and on and on the boys grew up together, an ordinary tale turned mythical as their group became an inseparable unit. They walked with confidence, the ground beneath their heels polished just for them.

But now.

Pierre gasped helplessly, as though a hand had risen from his gut to squeeze the back of his throat. His eyes widened at the realisation: it was one of these four young men, the body lying motionless on the floor.

"Why don't we take this inside for a drink?"

Duy was speaking now. His left arm was stretched outwards in the direction of the formal dining room, his broad shoulders and startling height blocking Pierre's view; on his lips was a diplomatic smile that didn't reach his black eyes.

Of course, a drink. The most logical course of action upon witnessing the death of a close friend. Pierre nodded and followed Duy, like a puppy with its tail between its hindlimbs, his shadow a sad, impotent shade of grey trailing from behind. At the very least, he was thankful he wasn't offered an opium nugget, despite the knowledge that it would immediately ease the ache throbbing in his temples. The pulse felt like a warning, reminding Pierre to be careful.

It was going to be a long night.

* *

Pierre's father was a war hero.

Or so he was told.

His father died on the battlefield in 1861—the battle that marked the French victorious establishment of its newest colony, Cochinchina—not long after Pierre's mother, alone in a cold, dingy rented room back home, learned she was pregnant with their only child.

It was believed his father had used himself as a human shield, protecting his comrades against the enemy's attack. Everything Pierre's mother did in the years that followed was to honour that sacrifice. The sacrifice for the greater good, she called it.

She raised Pierre to have faith in their country the way others believed in God, to follow the government no matter the demands. Pierre obeyed. Even at a young age, he understood the implication—his mother needed such belief to make sense of her husband's death, and she needed Pierre as an ally.

Otherwise, what was it all for?

Pierre buried the question at the pit of his mind, a question too frightening to ever confront. To even think it was to betray the mother Pierre loved and the father Pierre hadn't met yet admired all the same.

These thoughts played in Pierre's head in a loop as he found himself stuck in the Caos' dining room, as he fought against the untrained reflex to make a snide comment at the rich but coloured man before him. Pierre sometimes wished he could do as he pleased—to make his unsolicited remarks without repercussions, perhaps, or to compliment aloud Cao Hải Hà's grand mansion, or to tut his disapproval at the young heir and his visibly excessive opium consumption. He wished he had the liberty to act like a real human, but he had been following the governor's protocols for long enough—what to say when he encountered the average Annamite men, what to do when he brought them into the station, how many slaps were one too many, how low he should dip his head in the presence of the more powerful, French and Annamite alike—Pierre could no longer tell what constituted as humanlike.

He shifted miserably on the hard mahogany bench—left then right, then left again—thankful there wasn't any protocol that banned him from at least trying to ease his discomfort. The wood was stiff under his plump bottom.

Pierre couldn't fathom how much money the Caos had wasted on this piece of furniture, but he was certain it was a huge squandering. It felt not unlike his own splintered dining chair, unwelcoming, poor quality. Surely the drug lord could spare some extra gold to acquire a snuggly, handcrafted, French leather sofa?

You idiot, a voice inside his head laughed mockingly, *what do you know about luxury anyway?*

His face went hot with shame, his hands now folded neatly in his lap. Pierre wondered if everyone felt this way, humiliated by the mere presence of these tycoons.

Across from him, Duy sat in silence, staring at the space behind Pierre's head, as though he had already forgotten asking the tirailleur here in the first place. That look unnerved Pierre; the suspense and the stillness had already grown restless. He wished to grab the young heir's face with his hefty palm, demanding an explanation. But he couldn't. *Do not speak unless spoken to*, another thing the governor had taught Pierre.

In front of him—where a few minutes ago, Duy had instructed his butler to leave a steaming cup of tea—was an ornate dining table. Its four legs were beautifully curved, shiny from timber polish. Pierre inhaled, the smell of expensive materials filling his nose. Back home, in the dingy room that Pierre rented, his cheap table was always wobbly, despite the many pieces of paper he had folded over the years for the shortest leg to stand on. *Fuck it*, he would curse, and his wife would shake her head, dissatisfied. They had never been able to maintain a pleasant dinner; the meal always ended with his wife's relentless complaints—how she shouldn't have left France, following him here, how his wage was a level too low, how their living condition was a mere footstep away from poverty. Her list went on and on, often met with Pierre's muted anger. He would tell her—ordering, almost begging—to forget it, that things were fine, that they were lucky to have a roof over their heads whilst people were dying left and right. Pierre couldn't afford having his own wife planting seeds of doubts in his heart. Whatever choice he made, he made it for his country, for the greater good, just like his mother had taught him so.

It wasn't easy, of course, not when Pierre was constantly surrounded by riches that sat right before his eyes, close enough to ache for, yet too far to reach. The riches he once imagined he would have possessed had he the courage and belief of his own to pursue another career—what, he didn't know, but Pierre liked to think he would have had a few options. The riches he could offer his wife, like that glass cabinet in the corner of the Caos' dining room, its shelves heavy with bottles of vintage wine and imported liquor. He stared at the fancy crystal decanters that glinted under beaming light from the grand chandelier, and swallowed his saliva.

61

He would sacrifice everything for just a taste of that warm amber liquid. The cheap, flabby wine his meagre wage allowed him to purchase was an insult to the beverage.

Just then, Duy seemed to wake from his daze, turning his stare back on Pierre's face. His eyes held a murky sheen, his voice thick, clouds around its edges.

"Why are you here?"

"We got an urgent telegraph to report to this address at once, Monsieur," Pierre replied, sitting straighter in his seat. His delivery, his posture, they were the textbook display of the protocols the governor had created.

Duy looked away now, avoiding eye contact. He was high, Pierre could tell.

After a while, Duy drew a breath, then pointed at the telephone field in the other corner of the dining room; the silver ring with a rectangle cut of deep ruby gemstone on his left thumb caught a glimmer of light, sparkling.

"I did not call you, hmm, did not ask for you. Who sent you here? Hmm?"

Duy struggled with his words, the question like a fish bone stuck in his throat.

In that moment, Pierre was terrified. When Duy first introduced himself, Pierre only knew that the young men in this house were powerful. What he hadn't realised, however, was just how powerful they really were. He glanced back to where Duy had pointed, a clot of tension blocking his mouth. The phone lay harmlessly on top of a timber stool, its appearance rusty and crude. But Pierre understood—such a phone was a tangible signal of the most powerful family in this colony. It was proof of immensely close ties to the military.

It was no longer wealth and opulence that Pierre was dealing with. It was wealth, opulence, *and* authority.

The daunting realisation made Pierre even more uneasy; he picked at his next words, hoping to say the right thing. In his years patrolling the streets, Pierre had come to learn that opium addicts were extremely paranoid, especially whilst the smoke constricted their minds.

"Monsieur, the governor has important matters to tend to tonight, so he ordered me to respond to the scene and report back."

When Duy started shaking his head frantically, Pierre's heart sank a level lower. He held his breath as Duy continued.

"This won't do. You must get the governor here at once."

"What happened, Monsieur?" Pierre pressed, desperate for information. He could not return to the station empty-handed, incompetent just like the time he had emerged from the battlefield with two less fingers.

"Perhaps I wasn't clear enough over the phone. Tell the governor that his presence is required by the Cao family. My butler will escort you out now."

Without another word, Duy stood up and walked towards one of the large rectangle windows, keeping his back turned against Pierre.

Duy was trying to hide beneath his sternness, Pierre knew. He was certain he saw a glistening tear rolling down the young heir's high cheekbone. In another universe, Pierre imagined he would have been able to give the young man a soft pat on the back, a clumsy display of sympathy. But in this lifetime, his actions were bound by the governor's expectations. In this lifetime, Pierre accepted the order and left the dining room, obedient as ever when he followed the old butler, brown spots dominating his paper-thin skin.

On his way out, Pierre noticed that the wooden door to the living room had been sealed shut. Despite Pierre's attempted eavesdropping, he couldn't make out the low mumbles coming from inside as he walked past. Before he could inch closer, his ears strained and his neck craned—a final attempt to please the governor—the butler prodded him forward.

"Exit is this way, Monsieur. Monsieur Duy would appreciate if you could follow his wishes."

Pierre considered the old man, who adapted a rather austere façade, his lips unsmiling. The respect for his young master was stronger than the sight of a Frenchman.

With a reluctant sigh, Pierre nodded; he was not in a position to create a commotion. But it was hard, leaving this mansion. His feet suddenly found the act of walking laborious. What had he managed to uncover? What could he possibly say when he informed the governor that he had no information? Duy had shed a tear for the friend he had lost, but who would cry for Pierre when his job was taken away for good, when the life he already struggled to lead crumbled to the ground? His shoulders sagged with the weight of these questions, his sympathy towards the tragedy fully depleted. How painless and simple dying was. The corner of his lips twitched in a scowl.

The night was dark and full of terrors—Pierre remembered the expression from the stories his grandmother used to tell when he was a child. He must have heard that phrase a million times over the years. But it wasn't until now that he truly understood its meaning. As he started his patrol car and began the winding drive, the road ahead looked like a direct path to hell, trees lying shallow under the blanket of eerie blackness, their low branches scratching at his murky windows, screeching for help.

FIVE DAYS PRIOR

Madame Nhu

The sun fell from the sky earlier than Madame Nhu had expected. It was the middle of summer—as she admired the stunning sunset from her window, she thought it should have remained bright a tad longer. On the horizon, a remnant of bold orange light divided the ether in half with one vivid streak, as though someone had been pulling invisible strings, rotating the radiant morning curtain to this inky evening.

Inside, the twilight already started casting its dark gloom down her beloved living room, yet Madame Nhu took her time strolling from one corner to the next. She was in no hurry to light a candle. She was busy humming a soft tune, which she no longer remembered the name of, as she strategically placed the lacquer cigarette holders on the tables near the entrance—she imagined most of her guests would stop here to smoke. Had anyone been watching from outside in that moment, they would certainly have failed to see the most powerful widow in the colony: instead, they would see a black shadow slowly swiping the white marble floor of the Khải' mansion with the tail of an extravagant velvet dress.

Madame Như made her way to the front yard, where she instructed the servants to gather the thick piles of money into the empty wicker baskets she had left outside.

"Bring them to the living room," she ordered. "If any notes go missing, so will your fingers."

Madame Như's threats had never been just threats. She was a woman of her word.

Back inside, Madame Như settled on her favourite inlaid chair, its back centred by a circular marble plaque, which was flanked by ruyi sceptres in black zitan wood—a symbol of good fortune used during the Qing dynasty. She had renovated the grand mansion a few years back, before her late husband's passing, with French architecture as its main aesthetic. She had been happy with the changes. Still, this chair and what it represented—the finer things, even during a more *uncivilised* time period, according to the French—were her pride and joy.

For a while, Madame Như sat in the dark, her breath soft and slow. She reached for a white handkerchief, dabbing at the nape of her neck where droplets of sweat had gathered. Her velvet burgundy gown was not summer attire, but she didn't care. It made her look younger, and it complimented her petite figure so well, it hardly mattered that the weather didn't agree. After all, the summer party was tomorrow night, and Madame Như needed the rehearsal.

Madame Như ran her fingers along the coffee table, hoping to find the box of matches she had previously prepared. When she couldn't, Madame Như mumbled a curse but refused to stand up and turn on the light. Madame Như was wealthy, her lifestyle lavish, her estate filled with expansive and precious collections of paintings, sculptures, and décor, yet the lights were only turned on when darkness had completed its descent. When the servants were feeling extraordinarily bold, they would call Madame Như stingy behind her back. Whilst of course she never learned of such audacity, she sometimes still defended her decisions, to herself more than to others. She wasn't ungenerous, heaven forbid. No, she simply wanted to do things her own way, with her own set of rules. She held a bright flame to what she wanted people to see, and she hid the rest inside darkness.

Madame Như was always in control.

Her willowy fingers found the matches at last. She picked at one randomly and struck, watching its flame, a hue darker than orange, brighten a corner of the living room. The pearl necklace hung loosely around her neck, its surface glimmering in the flickering candlelight each time Madame Như swayed.

She stared at the baskets the servants had just carried in. Each note of money was thin, nearly weightless on its own, yet together they turned heavy as stacks of bricks.

Perhaps this was the reason for Madame Như's monthly compulsion—pulling all of the Khải's money out of the family's vault, inspecting to see if it had grown any mould or mildew. Every month, she left them in the yard to dry under the sun, with at least six servants standing guard. A three-hectare piece of land covered in cash; its ashen ground turned light brown if seen from above.

Under the unsteady light of the lone candle on her coffee table, Madame Như might have imagined the smirk on the face of the man printed across the one hundred–piastre note. He was the governor-general of French India—she recalled her late husband's condescending explanation when she'd asked. Now, as she turned the cash to the other side, avoiding the man's prying gaze, Madame Như saw the gate to Thái Hòa Palace, a brass urn to its left. A half-hearted French attempt at honouring the monarch of her country by putting their imperial city on the same paper as a common man, a man without any royal blood inside his common veins.

She shook her head at the thought. So what if that was the case? *Swim with the flowing tide*, her father had always taught. It wasn't her place to worry about her king becoming a puppet to the French. They held all the true power.

Dropping the money back in the basket, Madame Như took a deep breath, her stomach half-contented, half-empty. In the lonely hour of the endless evening, she sometimes found herself yearning for her late husband. He was familiar. He was stable, her ally. But he was no longer here.

She needn't the sensual touch of another man, she was sure of it. She was too old and too proper to think of such things anyway. She needn't the money or the riches. What she needed, Madame Như thought, was protection for her family, for their reputation. She needed protection for her strong-willed, ill-tempered, and perhaps—if she dared to be honest with herself—*mildly* violent son. She needed to know that if Khải Minh were to involve himself with something unspeakable, he would be safely hidden.

Madame Như had known this since the day her husband died. She had been afraid, had always worried. It was a dangerous thing, to be a lonely woman.

She started looking a long time ago, preparing herself for a problem that had yet to exist. She considered the bachelors her age, but it was no use. Their affluence paled compared to her own family's, and they weren't even nice to look at. Madame Như didn't have a lot of options, she knew. In truth, there was only one family above her own station.

The Moutets.

Even the sheer mention of such name made Madame Như shudder; there was always something sinister in Leon Moutet's crooked grin. That charming smile he flashed—she could tell it was an act. A mask, concealing the real Leon Moutet from the public's knowing eyes.

Of course, Madame Như had heard the rumours—Leon's troubled marriage, his strange and wicked fondness for the exotic Annamite young women. She knew the association would bring her more harm than good, but what could she do? Leon Moutet was the only man in the colony who could help shield her son and every other thing that she held dear, should an unforgiving storm arrive. What of a little fear, then, when there was so much she couldn't afford to lose?

Madame Như gently rubbed her temples with her index fingers; if only her son could be slightly more manageable.

"Madame."

Outside the living room, Tattler bowed her head to announce her presence.

"How many times have I told you to not come here if I haven't asked for you?" Irritated, Madame Như snapped, the lines on her forehead intensifying.

"I'm terribly sorry, Madame."

As if she had rehearsed this performance a thousand times over, Tattler immediately dropped to her knees, rubbing her hands together to beg for forgiveness. "I beg your pardon, Madame. The cook is ready for you to come and taste the food for tomorrow's party. That is all, Madame."

"Oh, would you quit that!"

Madame Như couldn't keep a disgusted sigh from escaping, her glare a sharp blade nicking Tattler's skin. She loathed seeing the servants crying, their heads pressed to the ground, their backs arched like frail bridges, welcoming the masters' stomping foot-steps. Were they aware of their own pitiful reflexes?

"Oh, and . . ."

Tattler hesitated, glancing up at Madame Nhu's face, await-ing permission to speak.

"Spit it out." Madame Nhu narrowed her eyes in Tattler's direction; she hated the servants' reservation even more than she did their timidity.

"Yes, Madame. Well, the thing is . . ." Tattler stammered again, and already, Madame Nhu could guess where this was going. She might be the owner of the mansion, but she knew that in Tattler's eyes, her son was far more terrifying, with a temper that even she had never been able to restrain. She traced Tattler's gaze, which was now fixed on the baskets of money, smirking when the servant finally breathed out.

"This is about the young master, Madame."

"What of him?"

Madame Nhu raised her right eyebrow. One half of her face was hidden in ghastly grey shadow, the other half sceptic, warning Tattler to tread carefully.

"Yesterday, Madame, I, uhm . . ." Tattler took a deep breath and finished her report in one quick exhale. "I saw Monsieur Minh and Hai dressed up, getting into his car and driving out of the mansion in the early morning. Before you even woke up, Madame."

Tattler's left index finger paused on her right as she listed the oddities she had observed, her short nails thick and black with filth.

"Was that so?" Madame Nhu kept her tone flat, free from any dismay. "We have more to take care of before the party tomor-row, do we not?"

Madame Nhu stood up, acting as though she had not heard such diabolical news. Her hand found its way towards an imaginary fluff from the sleeves of her gown, and absentmindedly she brushed it off. Her feet briskly delivered her into the corridor leading to the main kitchen, leaving Tattler where she knelt on the floor, speechless, wondering when she would be rewarded with the few spare coins Madame Nhu had promised upon receiving *worthy* information.

It was officially nighttime. An abrupt gust of wind arrived and snuffed the candle flame.

Minh

Minh headed towards the plain writing desk in the left corner of the room, quiet enough not to wake Hai. The sun had set an hour ago, but she was still sleeping. This private estate was their haven; they needn't rouse when the outside world did. Society could not see them here.

Flipping through torn envelopes and crumpled receipts, Minh looked for the telegram he had received the other day. How many times he had held this piece of paper within his fingers, he could no longer count. The skin on his forehead bunched with worry; he had yet to land on a solution.

There had been rumours circulating for a while. Some of his workers were planning a strike. Let them, Minh had shrugged when he was first informed. Daring. It wasn't as though those people had anywhere else to go—the scraps Minh had granted them were more than generous. Why were they complaining?

Such audacity.

I could round them up and execute them all. Quick and efficient, Minh had said when he discussed his problem with Duy. *It's absurd, worrying about such ungrateful idiots.*

You can't do that. Duy had shaken his head, handing Minh a crystal glass full of wine. *This is just a rumour. We don't even know if it's going to happen. You would be killing innocent people. If it were me, I would investigate first. Find out who is leading the movement, and take it from there.*

Minh hadn't been pleased, hearing Duy's advice, but he hadn't let it show. Duy had always been soft. How his friend had managed to successfully rule the opium business, Minh could never fathom. He couldn't imagine wasting his energy and effort in the pursuit of justice; he wanted his problems to disappear as soon as possible.

Still, Minh supposed Duy had a point—there had been no commotion just yet. He would wait for the strike to happen without interfering. By then, it would no longer matter what he did next. Once the workers made their move, Minh could be as brutal as he pleased.

He walked back to his nightstand to get his favourite pen. He could send someone with instructions, Minh knew, but the act of writing his command on a piece of paper and sealing it inside an envelope made him feel like an emperor. Royal.

After he was done, Minh returned to bed, gently sitting down on the edge, turning to appreciate Hai's sleeping face. Softly, he brushed Hai's cheek; her silky skin soothed the dry patch on his fingertip. Oh, he loved her so.

He adored every fibre of her being—her long strands of black hair, which flowed through his fingers like silky water, the rosy blush on the tip of her small nose, which only appeared when she accidentally got sunburnt. Her round chin, its frame as earnest as a luminous full moon, a darling fullness that occurred merely once a month. He adored the way Hai hugged her chest when she slept, an instinctive self-preservation Hai never managed to shake, even when she was with him.

He adored her, every part of her. The first woman Minh had been with. His lover. The first to soften him after what happened with Phương Liên, his first heartbreak.

He hadn't thought about her in a long time. Minh wasn't surprised. Edmond's return brought with him the humiliation and hurt Minh had suffered as the result of his friend's existence.

Phương Liên wasn't a traditional beauty, one with silky black hair and round, innocent eyes. Over the years, her features had melted into something downright average, forgettable. It was her energy that stayed with Minh.

That random winter evening when they met, Minh couldn't recall what Phương Liên was wearing, who she was with, only the laugh she had. A laugh as bright and warm as a morning spring sun. Summoning all his courage, Minh had walked up to her with what he thought to be a charming story, expecting she would allow him the chance to dance with her along the slow tune that was playing in the background of the jazz club. Their conversation was easy, genuine. Phương Liên shielded her mouth with a glass of wine and laughed her wonderfully peculiar laugh, and Minh was pleased. Yet somehow, he could tell she wasn't interested, not in the way he had hoped she would be, anyhow. Her eyes kept flickering to the side, her breathing more rapid each time she did so. Minh knew what he would see once he turned his head, but for once, he prayed his instinct was wrong.

It wasn't.

There Edmond was, leaning over the counter, deep in conversation with Phong. He looked as though he had been carved from precious stone, his slender frame almost ethereal, the tips of his blonde hair playful above his shoulders.

A part of Minh knew his anger was unreasonable, pathetic even, that it had been a coincidence, how Phương Liên had spotted Edmond. Why wouldn't she? Edmond and the rest of Minh's friend group, Duy and Phong, were all there, drinking and smoking in the corner, boys pretending they were grown, hardened men.

The rest of Minh blamed Edmond all the same. It was just like Edmond to steal Minh's spotlight the way he did when they were children, when Edmond was enrolled in the boarding school. It was just like Edmond to win a fight that had yet to begin.

It was just like Edmond to—without so much as uttering a single word—steal the first woman Minh had fallen for.

Which was why Minh had brought Hai to that same jazz club they frequented. A childish challenge to see what Edmond would do.

He had introduced Hai to his friends before excusing himself, spending longer than needed at the bar counter, pretending he didn't know which drink to order. Soon, he realised it wasn't an act. Minh couldn't focus, almost breathless, his heart thumping inside his ears. He was playing a dangerous game.

He didn't know when the wine glass appeared, only that it was slippery in his grip, his palm sweaty. He was certain the barmaid had asked if he was alright, and stubbornly he nodded. He stared at her until she became frightened, squirming out of his gaze. Minh couldn't muster the strength to spin around and watch his scheme unfolding.

A roar of laughter forced him to.

Duy had made a joke; his friends were having fun without him, oblivious to his absence.

But Hai wasn't.

She remained where Minh had left her earlier, her hands wrapped around a small cup of tea. He cocked his head and narrowed his eyes. Minh saw a glimpse of himself in her. Her face was impassive, but the grim line of her lips told the truth that Hai was uncomfortable, a misplaced flower in the wrong vase. Much like how Minh had felt his entire life.

Hai didn't pay attention to what was said at the table, didn't look Edmond's way. She was watching Minh with the same intensity she always had, the intensity that made Minh believe he was the only one for her.

She needn't do a thing, softening Minh's frown with her sheer existence, and he strolled towards her, straight in a straight line.

Dance with me? he had asked, a touch of shyness behind the question. The moment was tender enough to warrant a request instead of the usual commands.

Hai nodded; her lips blossomed with a faint smile. Minh held her hand, guiding her to the dance floor. They swayed to the soulful music in the background; the knots in Minh's throat loosened. Little by little, they disappeared.

It was simple and easy, being with Hai. Her love pure and innocent. Steady.

Since that day, Minh had been confident in her heart. Assured she would always choose him. Two lost souls finding each other.

The only woman who could save Minh from himself.

Not long after, Minh bought this place. He first took Hai here on a damp, rainy morning. Holding Hai's hand in his, the same way he did that day at the jazz club, he showed her the many different rooms within the mansion. *This is where our kids will sleep*, Minh said as he led Hai to an empty space at the end of the corridor.

Are you happy, he asked, *knowing I will always take care of you?*

Later that night, Minh got drunk on wine and love. *You, my dear, are the queen of this house*, he exclaimed, laughing blissfully. *Inlaid furniture, gold decorations, you say the word and I will make it happen*, Minh had declared, snapping his fingers to demonstrate how quickly he could fulfil Hai's wishes.

Don't. Hai shook her head, avoiding his eyes. She told Minh that she was uncomfortable, her existence like a precious brooch atop the lapel of Minh's most expensive suit. *I never asked for such exhibition.*

Minh was angry. His ears turned the colour of a bottle of claret and his fists clenched tight. He couldn't grasp Hai's silly reasoning, couldn't accept the secrecy of their courtship. In truth,

Minh did not know if this was because Hai's fear was so exaggerated it seemed unbelievable, or if his tantrum was the direct result of her refusal.

In the end, Minh relented and agreed to Hai's request—no elaborate furniture, no fancy clothes. He nodded his head and stretched his lips into a thin, cold grin whilst his pulsing mind attempted to ease its agitation with images of animals dying. An impulse Minh always indulged in when he felt upset: remembering the rats he had killed when he was a young child. Somehow, those creatures had become a part of him, their bodies mangled and lifeless. Minh carried them wherever he went, their memories like a bucket of water poured over his raging frustration.

When the meagre fixtures arrived—a bed, two bedside tables, a desk, a chair, plain white curtains, plain white duvet and pillow covers—Minh once again found himself conjuring the relief he felt when he ended those rodents' lives. He wanted to scream at Hai, but couldn't, because like a gentle fairy, Hai strolled over and took his hands, whispering her gratitude for his generosity, his understanding. Before Minh knew it, his demons had vanished, leaving him breathless with the realisation that he needed Hai—that she was indeed the only person who could save him.

"Are you hungry?" Next to him, Hai stirred and opened her eyes. She asked the question automatically, already resuming her role as Minh's personal maid.

"Are you? I can order the cook to make something for us." Minh smiled again and tucked a strand of hair behind Hai's ear, an act he imagined she found endearing.

"No, no." Hai shook her head and quickly got up. "I'll cook for you."

It wasn't an offer of love—or perhaps a small part of it was. But Hai always insisted on cooking for Minh, on doing his laundry, polishing his shoes and sewing the loose buttons on his shirts. It hardly mattered, the nights they spent lying together, the air thick and dense with promises of a brighter future. Hai would forever think of Minh as her young master. Minh hated this.

"Don't be silly." Minh smirked and reached for Hai's slim wrist. "The servants in this house serve you the same way they serve me. Now, come here."

Before Hai could protest, he pulled her into his embrace. "I've got something for you."

"I told you. I don't need anything. People might think I'm using you." Hai sighed, repeating the same words she always said to him.

"People this, people that." Minh wasn't pleased with Hai's concern. He never was, but still, he plastered a neutral expression on his face to conceal the boiling annoyance in his gut. "You care too much what those fools think."

"You're right. I'm sorry." Hai reached for his hands, pacifying. "Forgive me. Yes?"

He supposed she noticed the flatness in his words, the tension between them loosening.

"Of course. How could I ever stay mad at you?"

Minh turned to open the top drawer of his bedside cupboard, the screeching sound making him grimace. He pulled out a jewellery box, square and covered in black velvet. His smile deepened as he revealed its contents to Hai: a stunning jade bracelet. Its radiance, an alluring green, brightened the dimly lit room.

"I want you to have this. I will ask Mother to marry you."

A statement, a firm decision, not a question that required Hai's answer, not a discussion that awaited her input. That had been the nature of their courtship—he led, and she followed.

After a silence that lasted a beat too long, Hai looked at Minh and nodded obediently, as Minh had expected her to. He was pleased, holding Hai tight against his broad chest. He finally understood what it meant, happiness. He would defend this feeling with his life.

Phong

Phong stood in a daze, his calves exposed, his lower body covered by only a thin pair of underpants. He refused to look at the young woman waiting near his feet, his dark brown eyes trained anywhere but her timid face.

The metal on the buckle of his belt made a clang as it landed on the hardwood floor.

The sound couldn't jolt Phong awake. He was occupied by the thoughts of his friends—this had been the longest Phong had gone without seeing either Minh or Duy. He often disappeared when Edmond was away, Duy had commented once, and Phong couldn't deny it. It was true, his dependency. Edmond was the only person who had ever showed Phong that he was good—that he was enough.

He remembered the day so clearly, all those years ago. When Edmond first walked into their lives. Minh was so eager to prove he was the leader. But Edmond only smiled through Minh's bravado, his face dimpled and handsome.

A few days after Edmond's arrival, the boys received their maths test results. Dropping his body down in the seat next to Phong, Minh nudged his elbow against Phong's ribs, annoyed.

How did you get a 10? I only got a 7. Did you not give me all the correct answers?

You always skip class. The teacher would have known you copied someone else's work.

Phong shrugged, thinking he had done Minh a solid favour.

But Minh wasn't happy. *And you call yourself the smartest*, Minh retorted mockingly. Whilst Phong knew that Minh didn't mean to be cruel, he still sensed chills pricking at the tail of his spine. Like déjà vu—how familiar that sentence sounded. How much like Phong's own father.

I've never called myself that.

Like a helping hand, scooping Phong up as he started to fall, Edmond had walked over, glancing at Phong's test and exclaiming in utter admiration and delight.

This is excellent! Can you tutor me?

Phong looked up, surprised at how genuine Edmond seemed, his gaze flying past the creases on Minh's forehead. It didn't take much convincing. Phong agreed almost immediately, and they quickly became inseparable. The rest, as the saying went, was history. It was as simple as that. Need, and respect: Edmond made Phong feel seen and heard.

"Monsieur . . ."

The young woman hesitated near his feet, and Phong knew why. His body remained cold, no matter how hard she tried. He finally looked at the escort, staring directly into her black, round eyes. Randomly, he thought of longan, and couldn't help but laugh. How appropriate of him, to think of a fruit during a supposedly sensual time.

"Do you want me to . . ."

"Leave."

Phong nodded, confirming the woman's unasked question.

Pulling his trousers up, Phong reached inside the pocket for a few spare coins and dropped them in her expectant palm.

"Thank you, Monsieur," the escort whispered softly before hurrying out.

Now, alone in the private room he had booked for the rest of the month, Phong didn't know what to do with himself. People rented this space to smoke opium, and he couldn't do so just yet; he was waiting for someone. Trying to distract his thoughts, Phong started examining his surroundings, as though he hadn't been sleeping here for the past few days.

He was at Duy's finest opium club, Lavie. At first, when the establishment was built, the Caos didn't put up a sign—the white building was intended to be an exclusive institution, only granting access to the elite. Slowly, the nouveau riche came and decided to call it what it really was—a reason to live.

Phong wasn't sure if he would call the substance his raison d'être, but he knew that it helped prolong his hopeless love. It didn't matter whether he wanted the bewitching smoke; Phong *needed it.*

My love could only love me here. Phong had said so himself.

Phong's space was called the Red Room, though in truth he no longer remembered why. The hue from the spirit lamp was always more orange than red, the blankets and bedsheets a shade of burgundy. The walls were covered with black-and-white scrolls, the door and the furniture a tedious dark brown. Perhaps it was a metaphor, Phong supposed. The more he smoked, the less human he became, and whilst he didn't bleed, he felt he could sometimes see his blood evaporating, condensing as opium smoke invaded his veins.

Abruptly, the door swung open, revealing a slender silhouette. He stared at the figure unblinkingly, half-startled, half-amused.

"You're early." Phong grinned in utter delight.

The dim room was now filled with a sweet and smoky scent of sandalwood, a scent that Phong had missed and yearned for all this time. He inhaled deeply, feeling his muscles relax.

"Wine?" Phong smiled, already pulling out two crystal glasses.

"Brought my own. Here."

They clinked their drinks, washing their throats with the smooth liquid, their eyes flickering with desire.

"Want a smoke?" A laugh, and Phong nodded.

Together, they smoked.

Duy

One will die.

They always came back, those three serrated words, isolating Duy. He had no one else to turn to.

Duy never thought one day he would return here—to the place he tried so hard to outrun. He leaned against the filthy brick wall, the same way he had a decade ago, debating whether this was the right decision. Years had passed, yet Duy was still haunted, imprisoned by fear—he knew what he had heard. Like a sharp blade, the way those words had grazed his skin.

Every year, as the anniversary of that fateful night approached, a recurring nightmare would return. He would struggle to fall asleep, only to be jolted awake a few hours later, accosted by the memory of Master Cần's wrinkly skin, shapeless identities crawling beneath. For the last decade, Duy had calmly dried his glistening forehead, flooding his thoughts with alcohol and opium. Obsessive as he was about Master Cần's prophecy, Duy never admitted his belief in it, not even to himself.

This time was different. Duy couldn't determine why—a change in the air, a change within him. The images were more vivid than ever: his friends and their deaths. Duy didn't, couldn't, confide in anyone; it was inexplicable, how certainly he knew. Something sinister was near.

The night was dark as it had been eleven years prior, yet nowhere as eerie. He wasn't exactly alone—mosquitoes buzzed around his ears, trying and failing to drown the monotonous tone coming from Master Cần's property. Someone was chanting along to the deep sound of a tocsin—a hollow, sphere-shaped instrument made from hardwood. Duy felt compelled to move closer. A desperation, almost, like a person stranded on a desert, sprinting towards a mirage, hoping for salvation.

He stopped at the familiar crimson door. It was wide open, a figure hunched on the steps at the entrance. Flimsy candlelight helped Duy discern: the figure was a man, his ears twitching faintly as he registered Duy's footsteps. He didn't acknowledge Duy's presence, only continued to mumble phrases Duy couldn't understand.

Duy didn't want to interrupt, standing awkwardly with his hands inside his trousers pockets. He observed the man—his black tunic and linen pants faded and slightly torn, his head shaved clean, round and shiny, reflecting chilling moonlight.

Impatient, Duy cleared his throat.

"I'm looking for Master Cần."

"You are Cao Hải Duy, aren't you?"

Duy should have been surprised; he had never seen this man before. But he remembered how quickly Master Cần determined Edmond was French, before she'd even seen him. Secrets didn't seem to exist under the old fortune teller's roof.

"I am," Duy confirmed.

"She always told me you would come."

The man chuckled, then stood, turning to greet Duy. He was young, perhaps the same age as Duy, his face juvenile, his eyes sombre.

"You just missed her. Master Cần passed away last night."

Duy stared at the man, unblinking. He almost wanted to laugh, mistaking the man's detached announcement a tasteless joke. But when the moment passed and no one smiled, Duy's stomach sank. Over the years, he had accumulated complicated feelings towards the old woman; still, the news of her death was not something he had prepared for.

"How did—" he stammered. "How did it happen?"

"It was a natural death. Old age."

"I see," Duy responded. He swallowed dryly, then continued. "She told you I would come. Did she mention anything else?"

"That's all," the man said, with an indifferent shrug.

Duy sighed; this wasn't what he expected. He felt increasingly dizzy, nauseous; he shouldn't be here.

"I, uhm. I should go." His voice was hoarse.

"You could stay. If you want to," the man offered. "I'm Master Cần's only student. Her protégé. I'm about to perform her funeral ceremony, to send her off. I'm sure she'd like to have you there, to help bid her farewell."

Duy hesitated; he wanted to leave, but he also needed an explanation. Maybe it was all in his imagination, but he wondered how he had sensed Master Cần's departure. Maybe now was the time for Duy to send her prediction off into another world, alongside her.

He nodded, then followed the man into the courtyard.

Five candles had been placed on the ground in one straight line, an ethereal orange hue glowing from their tips. Aside from their cylinder bodies and a thin cushion for Master Cần's student to kneel on, the land was empty. There was no coffin, no sign of the fortune teller's earthly body. Duy frowned—the simplicity of the ceremony baffled him.

Keeping his back to Duy, the young man started chanting a few more incoherent phrases—he was reading words aloud from a thin scroll. Then, without warning, he tore the paper to pieces, tossing them in the air.

A white rain, those falling shreds.

Some descended slowly to the ground; some plummeted towards the fire, turning to ash. A single shred landed on Duy's left shoulder. A touch so brief, he almost didn't notice. Its frail body felt significant between his fingers, its content—two messy, handwritten words—a jab in his eyes.

too late

Master Cần's final message.

Goosebumps dominated Duy's skin. His friends were all he had; their existence grounded him, bounding him to an aimless life he wouldn't know how to otherwise lead. Duy couldn't lose his anchor, selfish as it might sound. Still, the images returned, as he'd envisioned them all these years—Edmond trapped under a crushed car, Minh with his ribs broken and his face beaten in, Phong crumpled on the ground, blood running down his neck. They terrorised Duy, closing his throat. His surroundings went still—he looked up to discover that he was alone, that Master Cần's student had gone.

Duy didn't run. His feet were chained down by some invisible force. He remained standing, trembling with rage. He couldn't dismiss the prediction anymore. He believed it, wholly and fully— someone he loved was going to die, and like an inadequate fool, he couldn't do a thing to stop the wheel of fate. Duy carried no weapon, no trick under his sleeve, only the same question he had asked since he was a young boy. Which one of them would it be?

Edmond

Edmond stumbled towards the timber chest of drawers in the corner of the Red Room. His head was spinning, his mind hazy with opium smoke. His instinct was to climb off the bed, his nose scrunching in disgust at the flashbacks of his actions.

He tried to be as quiet as possible—he didn't want to wake Phong, who could only ever seek peace within the realm of sleep. That, and because Edmond couldn't bear hurting Phong in any way. He tried not to wonder how Phong would feel as he woke to find the room empty. Again.

Darkness compromised his vision: Edmond couldn't see much with the candles already snuffed. He let his fingers wander aimlessly atop the ligneous surface of the drawers. When they brushed against the fluffy towels, he sighed, relieved. The wet cloth was his saviour, cleansing his sticky, sinful limbs. His body shivered; the sharp iciness jolted the last drowsy cells awake.

Clothes were scattered across the polished wooden floor. Remnants of drunken desires. He picked up a shirt at random, breathing in the dry and earthy scent of vetiver—it belonged to Phong. Edmond didn't allow his brain the chance to hesitate; he draped the shirt over his body, the fabric caressing his skin as though he was enveloped in one of Phong's earnest hugs.

He straightened his back, resisting the urge to sprint out of the room with his leather shoes tucked under his arms. A condescending smirk tugged at the corner of his mouth; he wanted to say goodbye before leaving, but his cowardice only allowed him the strength to muster something wordless.

Phong was lying on his side, his face in the direction of the window, bathed in a sprinkle of greyish moonlight. His eyelashes fluttered like he was dreaming, his lips no longer the straight and grim line he always wore when he was awake. A loose strand of hair drooped down Phong's forehead, and very gently, Edmond reached out to brush it away. Such action didn't mean anything, he reminded himself.

That same sentence he had been reciting from the beginning.

It was six years ago, a balmy summer night much like the present one. The four of them—Edmond, Phong, Minh, and Duy—arrived at the Caos' mansion to celebrate Duy's decision to stay in Annam. In truth, it wasn't a joyous occasion; they all knew abandoning his study in Paris was not something Duy wanted. But denial was the sole emotion they all excelled in.

Time passed in a silent blur. Duy was always the sunshine of the group, and without his usual cheerfulness, Edmond, Phong, and Minh were lost. They couldn't do much to console their friend, other than ensuring that his glass was constantly filled to the brim with the finest wine. There were expensive cheese, breads, and fresh fruits on the glass table, untouched. They were eighteen-year-old adults, and adults didn't eat whilst they sulked, did they?

Back then, Edmond had yet to evolve into a heavy drinker; both he and Phong could drink their weight. When the clock struck twelve in the morning, Duy and Minh had fallen asleep, their bodies curled atop the uncomfortable mahogany benches, crumpled jackets turning makeshift blankets.

I'm heading out for some fresh air. Do you want to come? Edmond peeled himself off the plush velvet armchair, his cheeks rosy. Amidst his tipsiness, Edmond couldn't recall what his other friends were wearing, couldn't tell what colour his own trousers were, but he remembered very clearly Phong's beige shirt, the first three buttons undone, his smooth chest exposed. Phong had kicked off his shoes earlier; on his feet was a pair of ordinary black socks.

Sure, Phong agreed, and soon, they were sitting on the stone staircase, passing back and forth a new bottle of wine. Black silhouettes of tall pine trees dotted the horizon beyond.

Do you think Duy should have stayed? Phong asked, leaning back on his elbows, his face tilting towards the starry night sky. He had misplaced his glasses somewhere, his eyes squinting.

Edmond considered the question, his slender finger stroking the tip of his chin.

He did what he had to do, Edmond said. *There aren't a lot of choices for people in our position, you know?*

Yeah. Phong nodded. *Yeah, I do know.*

They looked at each other, the kind of look that spoke a thousand words. There was electricity in the air, and Edmond felt as though he was hypnotised. A soft night breeze arrived, ruffling Phong's hair. A subtle tease, inviting Edmond to run his hand through those dreamy black strands. Before Edmond could catch it, the delicate moment slipped away, flowing out of the gaps between his fingers. He averted his gaze, stifling a sigh. The wine was doing something to him, his heart hammering inside his chest.

Edmond shook his head and shifted to the left, expanding the space between him and Phong. His friend didn't seem to notice, oblivious to Edmond's confusion. They resumed drinking in silence, until their hands met as they both reached for the alcohol. The touch was brief, so imperceptible Edmond could argue he had imagined it.

But he hadn't, and neither had Phong.

The bottle made a clang as it rolled down the bottom of the staircase, the noise not loud enough to wake Edmond from his daze. He was spellbound, pulled in Phong's direction. They kissed, or perhaps Edmond initiated it; he couldn't tell. The whole world had stopped moving. He closed his eyes, the honesty far too overwhelming to be confronted. He saw no darkness but the pale pink bloom of tenderness, his hands instinctively cupping the sides of Phong's face. For the first time in a long time, the tight knots inside Edmond's stomach loosened, the walls he had built crumbling. He was home, a place he never knew existed, next to a person he didn't realise he had been searching for. The hesitation, the fear of rejection he had collected over the years, vanished. Was it love, Edmond wondered. Surely not, that seemed too small a word.

After an eternity, the kiss slowed, Edmond pressing his forehead against Phong's. His eyes were still closed; he let Phong see the world for them both—Phong wouldn't see what Edmond did, wouldn't feel embarrassed or guilty being with a French man.

Somewhere nearby, an animal ran deeper into the woods, startling the quiet night, and like a naughty child who got caught smoking, Edmond gasped, his right hand pushing Phong away.

I . . . I . . . he stammered, waking from a fever dream. *Please don't . . .*

I won't. Phong needed no explanation, shrugging the way he often did. *I won't tell anyone. Nothing happened, right?*

Right. Edmond lowered his head, his voice small. *I mean, I don't know.*

He said something else, he was sure of it, but he couldn't recall. He was confused, frightened—he was raised to be proud of his heritage, his people. It was one thing to be Phong's friend, another entirely to feel the flutter in his heart, the butterflies in his stomach whenever Phong was near. What did it say about him, the great Edmond Moutet, when the only person who knew him, who *really* knew him, was an Annamite man?

That night, Edmond failed to answer the question, and he continued avoiding it ever since. One lonely moment not long after that summer, he got himself drunk, the ground melting to liquid

91

under his feet. The interior of the Red Room was shifting left and right when Edmond entered, surprise written plainly across Phong's face. He marched to where Phong was standing, and without any hesitations, he pulled Phong into his embrace. The heat from Phong's body, and the dry scent of vetiver, became a soothing whisper in Edmond's ears.

You're home.

Afterwards, alcohol and opium turned necessities, something Edmond needed to consume prior to seeing Phong. He would nurse the crystal glass in his hand, his throat burning. A bottle quickly multiplied, the session ending when Edmond's mind was tamed to oblivion. His affection alone would have been enough to fuel his courage, he knew, but his shame, his struggle was far larger, heavier.

Self-destruction knew no bounds.

Now, he heard a body turning, bedsheet and blanket shuffling, and like a magic trick, the memories were interrupted, the images of the first time Edmond revealed his feelings evaporating. He blinked and saw that Phong now lay with his back against the window, his face obscured by the many pillows Edmond had arranged to be his replacement. He didn't know how much longer he could continue down this path, his heart pleading yes and his mind saying no. Somehow, he had become a soldier who fought a battle he couldn't seem to win.

The night was inky when Edmond stepped outside, his pair of shoes dangling on the tips of his fingers. A tear escaped the corner of his eye, warming the side of his sunken cheek as it rolled towards his angular jawline. Its body, glistening under the chilling moonlight, a precious gemstone. Behind him, the door to the Red Room closed, the sound jarring.

THAT NIGHT

"The tirailleur is gone, Monsieur." The old man bowed his head.

"Good," Duy said. "You may leave now, too."

"Monsieur."

The housekeeper retrieved his steps, chin tucked to his chest, his manner timid and cautious. It didn't matter that Duy was looking out the window, that he could not see the man's exit; the servants were required to express their reverence through even the most trivial acts. In truth, Duy never bothered himself with such silly etiquette, least of all in a moment like this.

He didn't remember much of the conversation with the fat French man from earlier, his frazzled mind protected by opium. But the substance had worn off now, leaving Duy sober. Painfully so. He watched the murk swallow Pierre's car, its taillights vanishing down the road. Duy found he still couldn't move from the window. It was a safe space, the world outside his family's mansion. Once he turned around, he would have to face his childhood friends, and Duy didn't think he could. His head was still spinning, his questions an entangled mess of cobwebs. He closed his eyes, defeated. He pictured Master Cần's smug face, aflame next to his bubbling resentment. Thirteen long years Duy had feared her prophecy, driving himself to the brink of madness, searching for a way to cheat this exact fate. Often, too often he stood in front of the mirror, staring at his pupils the way he would a crystal ball, running through different scenarios: accidents, natural disasters, even war. None of it had mattered. His efforts had been useless. The old woman's words had materialised anyway. It shocked Duy, of course, his friend's death, but the smallest part of him was also relieved. He no longer had to fight, resisting the inevitable. He could focus on more pressing matters now—he could figure out who had done this terrible thing. He must. Duy knew, with a painful conviction in his chest, that one of them was responsible.

One of them was a murderer.

He always thought he was used to seeing blood—the soulless corpses of servants, or his competitors. But now, as he stared at his trembling hand, Duy realised he wasn't nearly so hardened. Everything around him seemed foreign, his dining room a space from a parallel universe.

He winced. The cut on his left cheek, where he shaved early that morning, was throbbing. Duy wasn't trying to summon the horrid moment, but it came nonetheless.

Earlier tonight. They had all been drunk and high. In the kaleidoscopic limbo between reality and ecstasy, he could still see himself in the middle, with Minh to his left and Phong to his right. Edmond sat in his favourite leather armchair opposite the three of them, crooning drunkenly as he continually took big gulps of wine. It was almost midnight, the living room a quiet, foggy space from opium smoke. Duy couldn't see much. A gurgling sound started, and Duy's silent world was torn in half; he was petrified. Someone started vomiting, but he could not make out a face; everything was spinning. It took Duy a second too long to right himself, to clear the cloud around his head. When Duy finally noticed the stiffening body, he screamed.

Phong! Phong!

A reflex, how Duy had pleaded for Phong's help, relying on his friend for assurance, like he had done so his entire life.

No one answered, just Duy and his friend, who had transformed into a corpse lying on the cold floor, the sickly purple veins across his pale skin bulging like venomous snakes.

Now, Duy sighed, sitting down on the mahogany bench, pressing his hot forehead to his palm. His head was still aching. Duy was flushed, the excessive amount of alcohol he had consumed now catching up, burning his organs from within. Hastily, Duy started rolling his shirt sleeves, revealing the tan skin underneath. His heart fluttered, its rhythm frantic, at the sight of dry blood, from when he held his dying friend in an embrace. Duy flexed his fingers, ensuring the muscles were still alive after the numbness of the drugs. His hands were clean, or at least they *seemed* clean—he wasn't so high that he could forget committing something that atrocious, right?

Duy shook his head violently, ignoring the nagging ache. He wasn't a righteous person, he knew that, but Duy would never, *ever*, hurt his friends, no matter how tight the opium's grip.

Who could it be, then? Had there been anyone else in the room with them? Duy couldn't answer. There must have been someone else. There simply had to be—how could any one of them hurt each other? They were like brothers. They always had been.

And just like that, Duy was transported back in memory.

Hurry up! Duy heard his younger voice and saw his worried face, behind Phong's back.

This was his favourite story, one he recalled often. It was a chilly winter morning when they were fourteen. They were given an unexpected test, and Duy, Minh, and Edmond all groaned; they hadn't studied. In the end, they once again relied on Phong. Duy was the most impatient, his eyes darting back and forth between his empty sheet of paper and the clock hanging by the door. He had counted to twenty before tapping at Phong's back, nudging him to hurry. Behind him, Minh and Edmond were just as restless, their pencils scratching against the wooden table. When Phong finally dropped his paper to the ground, sliding them backwards in the direction of Duy's table, the three of them copied every equation, number by number, without any doubt. They all trusted Phong, in a deep and wordless way. They had grown up together like that, believing they would always be able to rely on one another—an undying, loyal brotherhood.

Duy didn't realise he had been crying—the fond anecdote no longer brought him happiness, only a sudden hollowness. Could he still trust the other two? Duy grimaced.

Bracing himself, Duy rubbed the heel of his palm against his eyes, ordering himself to stop crying. He needed to move, to solve this before the governor arrived, or all three of them would be in danger.

Duy stepped away from the bench, walking circles around the room, desperate for a solution. He compared each possibility, searching for the most plausible explanation. All the complaints Duy had helped ease, all the disputes he had helped solve—one by one, Duy scrutinised each scenario. In the end, one face brushed Duy's mind, leaving him breathless. One suspect.

No. He waved the image away. That couldn't be right.

FOUR DAYS PRIOR

Madame Nhu

Madame Nhu paced back and forth inside her bedroom as anger heated her flesh, quickening her bloodstream. Her son had just left, after babbling about marriage to that lowborn maid of his: a ridiculous notion. She gazed at the photo of her late husband, wondering in desperation. *Why did you leave me so soon?*

Above her mahogany nightstand, her husband, Monsieur Khải Siêu, trapped inside the black-and-white photo of his younger self, continued his silence. His watchful eyes followed Madame Nhu's anxious footsteps, demanding and scrupulous. She shuddered against her will, picturing him alive and well, sitting in the black leather armchair she still hadn't the heart to use since he passed, a cigar resting on his lower lip.

I was a fool, leaving this empire in the hands of a woman, he seemed to say. *Did you not see the Frenchmen lurking, preying upon your careless mistakes, trying to assume control over our plantation? What about my heir? You have always been too soft on him. He is blinded by lust, and it is all your fault.*

Madame Như blinked, attempting to interrupt her vivid imagination. She couldn't.

Monsieur Khải remained in front of her, wearing the same burgundy silk gown he had worn the day she found him on the floor of their bathroom. His frame looked sturdy, as though he had still been alive, his feet still tapping against the ground with that old, patronising pace. Madame Như was chilled. It was as though Monsieur Khải had never really left; his disapproval was a blunt carver, tearing Madame Như's flesh into pieces.

The thin skin on her face stung with humiliation, and Madame Như pressed her mouth shut, biting her plump lower lip to stop a scream from escaping. She wanted to ridicule her late husband—*Look at me*, she wanted to point and laugh, *I have outlived you.* It was no use, though. The illusion was the product of her own criticism.

Madame Như supposed she had harboured a fair amount of suspicion, even before Tattler confirmed it. She had simply hoped the atrocious relationship could not be real. Perhaps her late husband was right—she was weak, and her heart wasn't cold enough. *She would be strong and ruthless now*, Madame Như thought. There was too much on the line. She needed a solution before it was too late, before her family's reputation was ruined for all eternity.

You cannot stop me, Mother.

Her son had been determined when he informed her of his decision. He didn't ask for her permission, didn't even need her blessing.

Either you stand aside and allow our marriage, or you find yourself another heir.

Once more, Madame Như's face flushed red with embarrassment—how could she accept those disgraceful words from her own son's mouth? Minh had even threatened her! How absurd.

In truth, Madame Như had always been terrified of Minh's temper—she had tried her best to fan his violence elsewhere. She gave him space, time, and even power to do as he pleased. Not once had she ever questioned his actions, no matter how sadistic and ruthless they could sometimes be. Madame Như assumed Minh would eventually grow out of this violence, becoming more sensible. She never expected him to be so reckless, special as he was. How could he leave everything behind for a woman? Madame Như was baffled. Had Minh really no worries for his future, his responsibility?

Madame Như threw herself down on the leather armchair, glaring sharply at Monsieur Khải's photo. No, she most certainly had not failed. It must have been that inferior maid, filling her son's head with such audacity.

Oh, what could she do now?

As a reflex, Madame Như twisted the ring on her middle finger—a gold emerald in a square cut, adorned by sparkly diamonds on both sides. Her dowry from when she married Monsieur Khải. She rarely took the thing off, not even when she bathed. It was a reminder of Madame Như's happiest day, a representation of everything she needed to protect.

She still remembered the moment her father called her to his study room.

She was sixteen years old, a traditional beauty with pale skin and jet-black hair. Obediently, she stood in front of her father's writing desk with her head lowered, listening intently to his every word. He had always been her hero.

Our family's friend, her father began, *has a bachelor son around your age. I see that it's only appropriate for the two of you to join hands, strengthening our relationship with the Khảis.*

Madame Nhu had nodded dutifully, a butterfly eagerly flapping its wings inside her stomach. Her mother had been preparing her for this her entire life; Madame Nhu had been ready to serve the man she would later call husband.

When the good day came, Madame Nhu was taken to a mansion that wasn't her family's, and she sat on the edge of a strange new bed in a strange new room on the third floor, one with a grand balcony overlooking an immaculate garden, waiting for her strange new husband to enter. It was almost midnight, and she had grown slightly restless, but Madame Nhu wasn't unhappy; she had always known that weddings were extravagant events, that her future husband needed to drink to show his gratitude towards their guests. She held onto her patience, and when the clock struck two in the early morning, her husband appeared, stumbling towards the bed, lifting her veil.

That was the first time Madame Nhu and Monsieur Khải looked directly at each other. She married that young man without any hesitation, trusting her father's choice without any doubt, and even in all the years that followed, without a single regret. Their lives together unfolded predictably; their fates had already been determined. Madame Nhu gave Monsieur Khải an heir, and Monsieur Khải had spent the rest of his life teaching his son how to rule the empire.

This was the only love Madame Nhu had ever known. A wedding borne of their families' mutual benefits, instead of mutual affections. A marriage that lasted because of loyalty. No foolish courtship could achieve such a thing, Madame Nhu wanted to tell Minh—though in the end, she couldn't. She was afraid of what he might do should she misspeak, provoking him.

Now, Madame Nhu stood up and made her way to the balcony of her bedroom. Her feet were cold atop the black-and-white

100

shiny marble floor; the fishtail of her silk robe trailed silently behind. She rested her hands on the white rail, a soft smile brushing her lips as she marvelled at the beautiful malachite bannisters and the grand garden below, with its various flowers—dozens of different kinds of roses and orchids. She adored their delightful fragrances, adored her ability to create something so magnificent with *her* family's affluence. She watched from above as the servants busied themselves, knowing that whilst their heads were low, their stomachs were full and their pockets were heavy with the spare coins she sometimes gave them when she wanted to be generous. Perhaps their hands hadn't always been clean and their conscience hadn't always been clear, but Madame Nhu believed that her family was the reason these servants had a roof over their heads, that these men and women prayed not to a mythical god but to her ancestors. Her family, the gracious saviour in their unfortunate stories.

Madame Nhu shook her head, her index finger twitching in anger. Her heir might never understand the implications of his existence. She rubbed her temples, longing for those nights when she only bothered herself with simple things, like table arrangements, the menu, the most appropriate colour schemes for the beautiful dresses the tailor would sew. Madame Nhu missed presenting herself obediently next to her late husband, wearing a fake but dulcet smile, allowing the wives of her husband's subordinates to take her wrists in their hands, listening to their praises and childish giggling over her newest, exclusive piece of jewellery. Oh, how she loved to stand with her waist cinched by a Western-style gown, her neck warm against her favourite mink-fur cowl. She needn't any schemes then, as her only job was to ensure her mansion's impeccable appearance. The compliments filled Madame Nhu's existence with a sense of purpose, of pride. During each party, she would lead her guests down the hall, cosy with candlelight on both sides. At the end of the corridor, before they entered the banquet hall, Madame Nhu would position a magnificent pair of golden candelabras. The figurines underneath were carved from expensive, precious black marble, the women's sculpted faces graceful and lifelike, hypnotising every person who passed them by. The praise would erupt as she and her guests eased inside the banquet hall, where the walls were covered by French windows with tasteful arches and elegant beige curtains tied by thick, velvety golden ropes, whimsical tassels hanging playfully. The ceiling was supported by beautifully sculpted columns, each complex and intricate, with serpentine coils.

These days, the women no longer shrieked and squealed over what Madame Nhu wore to her parties. She found herself constantly on her feet, moving from one person to the next, expressing her gratitude for their appearances. She needed to maintain her connections after the unforeseen death of Monsieur Khải; the banquet hall her late husband used to open for such occasions was now closed to outsiders.

Suddenly, an idea sparked. Madame Nhu thought of the party later that night, and she chuckled. It seemed she had successfully sought a way out, after all. A coy smirk grazed the corner of Madame Nhu's lips—how simple but effective this elegant ploy would be. Once again, she was thankful for her brilliant mind. It had gotten her this far, after all.

"Tattler!" She rushed to the door, calling out the corridor. "Tell Madame Hai to come and see me. Make sure you use her title correctly."

Hai

Hai didn't want to come to Madame Như's bedroom, but an order was an order, and she never disobeyed.

"Madame, you asked for me."

Hai hesitated outside the dark wooden door. Her voice sounded weak, even to her own ears.

Madame Như didn't say much, only smiled, terrifying, as she appeared to greet Hai. She stepped aside, gesturing for Hai to enter.

Hai kept her head low, gazing at the floor under her bare feet; the interchanging slabs of black-and-white marble reminded her of the rare antique chessboard Monsieur Minh had struggled to find as a birthday present for Monsieur Duy. She wondered if Madame Như knew how to play chess, but she dared not ask.

In the few short hours since Hai had last seen her mistress, Madame Như already changed into yet another outfit, a habit she developed after the passing of Monsieur Khải. Madame Như was now wearing a black velvet dress with short sleeves and a cream lace shawl with fringe hanging over her slim shoulders. Her left wrist was decorated with two jade beaded bracelets, and each time she moved, they made a slight rattling sound. Hai's mistress was no longer barefoot, a pair of oxford shoes in shiny leather and low heels under her feet. Hai recently learned about oxford shoes because Monsieur Minh had suggested buying her a pair. Naturally, she declined, and he was unhappy. The whole incident was nerve-wracking, but now Hai was pleased with the small piece of knowledge she had gained.

She was told to sit in front of Madame Như's dresser. The furniture was made from inlaid wood with a shiny oval mirror in the middle and two black-and-gold ceramic table lamps on each

103

side. It was completely dark outside, and so the lamps were lit; Hai could feel her round cheeks warm by the hazy yellow light.

Despite Madame Nhu's direct, verbal order, Hai couldn't shake the uneasy feeling, sitting in this chair. The emerald brocade cushion with golden tassels in four corners atop Madame Nhu's dressing stool felt wrong under Hai's body; she wanted to stand up and remove the cushion, to place it where its beauty could be properly treasured.

She shifted slightly in her seat, praying the chair wouldn't make any noise, exhaling in utter gratitude when it didn't. Hai didn't know what else to do to ease her bulging nerves, and her scepticism that Madame Nhu had waited until Monsieur Minh was away from the estate to call her here only intensified Hai's worries. She tried to blink her doubts away. Monsieur Minh would never let anything happen to her. Time and time again, he promised her so.

Despite her self-assurance, Hai remained uncomfortable, her jaw clenched, a survival instinct. Her knuckles turned bone white around the edge of her frock—a shabby brown tunic with dark oil spots splattered across the front—so tightly, it was badly wrinkled when she finally loosened her grip. She could feel Madame Nhu's eyes on her fingers, and for a second, Hai didn't know what to do with her own limbs. They said nothing to each other—Madame Nhu was busy with her soft, gentle humming, and Hai was occupied with her anxiety. She pictured her reflection in the mirror, still too scared to look up, an invisible rope wrapping around the nape of her neck, like a python constricting its prey. It wasn't new, this feeling, this fear; she previously felt it when she sat next to Monsieur Minh in his car. Hai didn't know if this was a bad omen, her identical disquiet, parallel in the company of mother and son alike.

"Stay still," Madame Nhu ordered, dusting Hai's face with a floral scented powder. Though the smell was relaxing—it was similar to the roses Madame Nhu grew in her precious garden— Hai's heart was beating faster than ever. When Madame Nhu used the tip of her finger to brush the excess white off Hai's fluttering eyelashes, her stomach churned at the sensation. Hai had been taught to fear the master, to keep herself low, to know her place. She was new to this, didn't know how to react. She had shivered when Tattler called her *Madame*.

Keeping her eyes on the table, Hai blinked, taking in the sight of Madame Nhu's extravagant jewellery. The sparkly things did little to impress her—she could not appreciate what she did not understand—but she stared regardless. A way to distract her uneasiness.

Madame Nhu never allowed servants in here to clean, aside from Tattler. The diamonds, the precious gemstones—she feared the maids would steal from her. An irrational fear, really, because they were all terrified of Madame Nhu and would never dare touch her belongings. Tattler was proud when she was first assigned the task, Hai remembered, not realising that Madame Nhu chose her simply out of efficiency—should anything go missing, she would know immediately who the culprit was.

Hai settled her gaze on the intricate carvings along the table edges—the horns of mythical creatures, the detailed mimic of phoenixes' wings. She tried to guess how long it took for Tattler to dust and polish them—half a day, at least. Hai could picture Tattler's fingers, wrinkly and damp with a dirty rag in her palm, whilst the engravings shone brightly.

"Put this on."

Madame Nhu's voice rose from behind Hai's back.

Whilst Hai was daydreaming, Madame Nhu had gone to her wardrobe and pulled out a brand-new outfit. She now stood with her index finger outstretched, a white, five-piece aodai dangling on its tip.

"Madame."

Hai didn't dare argue. She dipped her head, accepting the dress with two grateful hands. She stood up, intending to move away from Madame Nhu's searing gaze to undress.

"Stop wasting time, my dear. You can change here." Her mistress raised a hand, blocking Hai's way.

Hai was stunned at the thought, embarrassed, her cheeks already flushing pink.

"Change," Madame Nhu repeated, ignoring Hai's hesitance. "This way, I can teach you about the meaning of the dress you are about to wear."

Hearing this, Hai's heart skipped a beat. She was a peasant, her knowledge of this fancy and sophisticated world so modest and raw. The aodai she was holding had multiple intricate flaps, sewn together, a symbolic creation she hadn't the mind to understand.

Reluctantly, she drew in a sharp breath, her fingers deliberate as they unbuttoned her worn brown tunic. Her naked skin burned under the light, the pink across her cheeks turning red. Quickly, Hai fumbled with the five buttons as Madame Nhu stepped forward.

"Here."

She offered her gracious, timely assistance, fastening the round, thick knots in place in a swift and knowing motion. Madame Nhu's hands followed the fabric of the two front pieces, then the two back ones, then the subtle line of threads and stitches connecting them.

"See here? These signify the four parents one ought to serve and obey. One's birth parents, of course, and one's parents-in-law."

"And here." Madame Nhu didn't wait for Hai's reply. "The small flap sewn to the inside of the front piece signifies the person who wears the dress. When one drapes this sacred outfit over their body, the four parents are always watching. The sins, the misdeeds they think of committing, should be forever banished, as long as they have this outfit on."

"Yes, Madame."

Hai replied promptly, though she didn't quite understand the implications of Madame Nhu's words. Was this really an innocent lesson to prepare Hai for the party, or was there some deeper meaning that Hai was too naive to see clearly?

"You look stunning."

Madame Nhu ignored the reservation on Hai's face, exclaiming the compliment in a genuine voice. Her smile didn't seem to reach her eyes, yet it appeared so kind, Hai suddenly hated herself for always being overly wary.

Madame Nhu turned Hai's shoulder back towards the mirror, signalling for her to look at herself. Hai obeyed, her eyes stopping briefly on Madame Nhu's reflection before falling down to the strange girl in the shiny mirror, with her black and lustrous hair braided into an elegant low bun, lips pink and ears heavy with a pair of clip-on pearl earrings.

"Now," Madame Nhu said, finishing her charity work, as she clasped a gold chain around Hai's long neck. "This will complete the outfit."

"Madame." Surprised at her master's benevolence, Hai stammered and turned around. "This is too much. Truly, I don't deserve such a beautiful thing."

"Hush." Madame Nhu chuckled. "Don't you want something to match your beautiful bracelet?"

Hai felt a dip in her stomach. Of course Madame Nhu knew of the bracelet that Monsieur Minh had given her. The comment stung, as though Hai had been slapped; the gold chain turned into a shackle, and the bracelet felt just as confining.

Her mind drifted back to the day before when she sat in front of Monsieur Minh in his private mansion. She could still see it, the jewellery box in black velvet, with its clasp undone, and its mouth hanging open, beckoning. She didn't know what she should say in response to Monsieur Minh's statement; she wasn't sure whether she could accept the gift at all. *It belonged to a* real *madame,* she thought to herself, *this exorbitant treasure.* She would only soil its surface, submerging it under filthy dishwashing water.

Somewhere in the shadowy corner, the water buffalo—the creature Hai often envisioned herself inhabiting—reappeared, uninvited. Its back was heavier once more with the doubts Hai never dared express, its four hefty legs thumping violently atop her chest. She couldn't breathe.

At last, she had looked directly at Monsieur Minh, plunging herself down the velvety brown orbs of his gaze, trying to search for the courage to defy everything she'd ever known. Yet, she had only found Monsieur Minh's oblivion, and his perpetual trust that the world was pliant to his wishes, that happy endings truly existed.

Hai couldn't bear disappointing him. She had said yes. Of course she had.

"So? Tell me." Madame Nhu interrupted the memory. "Do you love what you see?"

Hai was in awe; she couldn't believe her own eyes. Not even in her wildest dreams had Hai ever dared to imagine looking this way. The only two dresses she had ever accepted from Monsieur Minh were the white silk dress she always wore when they went to his private property, and a lilac chiffon ball gown with exquisite lace tracing its hem. Hai never knew how to style them, never had any jewellery to adorn the outfits. As such, she had always looked like a rural woman playing dress-up.

Today, however, Madame Nhu completely transformed her. Hai looked like a young lady from a noble family, born to marry Monsieur Minh. She absentmindedly touched the jewellery around her neck, ignoring the shame that prickled under her skin. After all, Hai had expected a brutal beating once Madame Nhu discovered her relationship with Monsieur Minh. This seemed a far less vicious punishment.

Hai supposed she was too umbrageous, too defensive. Had she been this way with Monsieur Minh, their love would never have had the chance to blossom. *Maybe*, Hai thought, *it wasn't a bad idea to let her guard down, to have a little faith in good intentions.* Madame Nhu might not be happy, but she wasn't attacking Hai's courtship, either. Maybe she needed to trust Madame Nhu, the same way she trusted Monsieur Minh. Maybe once they spent enough time together, Madame Nhu would continue to soften.

Hai decided, in that moment, that she was happy. She picked her words carefully, her eyes two wells of endless gratitude.

"Madame, you are so kind to me."

She searched her master's face for an expression of approval, eagerly drinking in every moment.

"Don't be silly." Madame Nhu patted the top of Hai's head, as though she had been chatting with her own child. "You must call me Auntie."

Tattler

Tattler pushed the door to her bedroom shut, trying to enjoy her precious and fleeting time alone. Somewhere in the main house, she could hear the housemaids, arguing over trivial matters—she had used the chaos to slip quietly away.

She started picking at the dry skin on her lips, something she did when she was trying to think. Tattler felt a sting but didn't wince, distracted by the fuming irritation under her chest.

Madame Nhu asked for you. She really wanted to stop there, standing in Hai's room. But she couldn't. If Madame Nhu found out, Tattler would have been beaten to a pulp. So she'd said the word, *Madame*, maintaining a neutral expression, her nails digging into her palms to stop the corner of her mouth from twitching. Almost immediately, soft pink flushed Hai's cheeks—oh, the pride in them. Tattler was enraged.

As she recalled the encounter, Tattler realised her anger hadn't disappeared. She yanked her hair with the force of her frustration, gathering the mass into a thick lock and securing it to the back of her head with a black rubber band. She placed her seething face inside her cold palms, attempting to calm her jealousy. It didn't help. Tattler couldn't stop picturing Hai with her clueless face, sitting in front of Madame Nhu's dresser, staring at the antique mirror Madame Nhu treasured more than any piece of jewellery. Looking up at the ceiling of her fan-less room, Tattler heard the question, loud in her ears. *Why not me?*

Tattler understood the reason for her envy. She had never really liked Monsieur Minh, so it wasn't because of love. She wanted what Hai was about to get—a powerful last name, a rich husband, absurd wealth. There was a time when Tattler thought she resented such opulence, when she was first brought here. Her fingers were always red and raw after an entire day of being submerged under water, cleaning the estate. It felt as though Tattler had sliced her own flesh, using her own blood to keep the grand staircase and obnoxious furniture shiny. Constantly, she wished for a hammer large enough to break the whole structure to pieces—she would close her eyes, dreaming of powdery mist twirling through the air as marble shattered to millions of ugly shards.

Later, however, Tattler realised she only loathed rich people because she wasn't one of them. Her hatred helped fuel the fierce ambition she didn't realise she had. It scared her, the similarities between resentment and hope.

After that, Tattler tried her best to please her masters, to look for any opportunity to escape the life she was forced to live. She had been traded for a few crumpled notes of money—but Tattler knew she deserved more.

So much more.

She deserved a room of her own, with a fancy ceiling fan above an expensive wooden bed. She deserved a deep sleep on plush pillows and a mattress. She deserved meals of foreign delicacies, the boiled spinach and cabbage reserved for the dogs and cats she would raise as pets. She deserved fine china, instead of the hideous earthenware pots in unglazed terra cotta.

She deserved a chance to make such a life happen.

And perhaps, tonight was Tattler's chance.

In preparation for the party, Madame Nhu had ordered freshly sewn attire for her servants—white shirts with black vests for the valets, light blue tunics for the housemaids. Running her index finger along the line of her top buttons, Tattler smiled. She didn't have to wear her usual faded brown uniform, and this relaxing colour made her slim face even prettier.

She would position herself in the corner, Tattler thought, a place she successfully scouted yesterday. The empty, forgotten space beneath the grand staircase. She would hide there, searching the crowd of guests for her own Monsieur Minh. They needn't be as rich—Tattler was impressed with her own generosity, her willingness to compromise. As long as she could live and breathe freely without worrying if she had offended her master, Tattler would be happy.

In that instant, as Tattler inhaled deeply, bracing herself for a long night ahead, she knew she would risk it all to escape this menial work, to search for the life she believed was rightfully hers. She couldn't lose to that foolish Hai.

"I'm coming," Tattler called out the door once she heard her name. Her voice no longer sounded irritated; instead it sounded cheerful. She whistled softly as she left the room. The last time she would ever see this place.

* *

Tattler was stunned and positively mesmerised when she reached the main house. The living room Madame Nhu normally kept dark was now bright with enchanting golden light. All three grand chandeliers were lit, their adorning crystal strands cascading like three shimmering waterfalls. This was certainly the biggest event Madame Nhu had organised in the last few years, and Tattler was even giddier at the realisation. The stars were aligned.

The whole property was drowned in a foreign melody, coming from the gramophone in the middle of the living room—the object was really more a decoration, a flaunt of wealth, than a practical device for playing music. Quickly, before anyone could notice her presence, Tattler retreated to her hiding spot, watching as the adoring guests made their way over to the gramophone's golden brass horn.

"Look at this clover engraving!" a thin, tall woman in a silk purple dress commented, her brown eyes bright with admiration. She nudged the shorter man standing on her left, pointing at the intricate, whimsical decorations, which Tattler had scrubbed clean just a few hours ago.

"Why, thank you."

Tattler heard Madame Nhu's phoney laugh at the compliment and watched her mistress's face swell with pride. Madame Nhu didn't know the song, but she pretended she did anyway, and Tattler smirked to herself when she noticed the guests' realisation. They played along, nodding their agreement, and Tattler was momentarily embarrassed on Madame Nhu's behalf. She imagined herself in Madame Nhu's position, how easy it would be for Tattler to navigate such a life. Her face would be innocent and clueless when she admitted she didn't know who the singer was, and the guests would have been thrilled, finally given a chance to prove their knowledge was superior.

"You, there." A plump man in a charcoal suit somehow spotted Tattler, calling for her. "Bring me some more wine."

Tattler only narrowed her eyes as she retreated further into the shadow of the grand staircase. It was comical—she had always hated this staircase, and now she was relying on it to execute her plan.

Just as Tattler suspected, the man was far too drunk to remember seeing her face. When she was certain she was safe, Tattler swept the room with her eyes one more time, determining who was sober and who was not. She frowned in distaste when her eyes caught the sight of a group of loud, entitled men. She could see, even from afar, how their scotch sloshed over the rims of their crystal glasses, how their minds were lost within the stories they were struggling to tell. Mundane, insignificant stories, yet on they spoke, and people listened.

A line of servants carrying silver trays blocked the group of men from Tattler's view, their steps urgent towards the hungry guests. Tattler looked at the trays on their hands, unblinking, feeling both admiration and eagerness. They had been polished so carefully their coats practically gleamed, their surfaces as shiny as Madame Nhu's precious mirror. Tattler took one step forward, craning her neck so she could see the rest more clearly. Her heart leapt as she studied the rims of the plates, which were decorated with elaborate and realistic birds, butterflies, flower wreaths, and enamel vines. Tattler knew without checking that the bottom of each fork and spoon carried a faint *P*— an indicator that all of them had been manufactured in Paris, then exported to Cochinchina. Whenever Tattler walked past the cupboard where these items were kept, she always stared. The letter *P*, ingrained deep in her memory, like a promise.

When Tattler finally peeled her eyes off the silverware, she swallowed hard, the corner of her mouth wet with saliva. She was hungry, and her stomach wasn't subtle. It growled at the sight of luscious green asparagus soup, fluffy white bread, and the assortment of cured meats, arranged into tasteful flowers on white ceramic plates. To the left was another long table, its expensive mahogany surface protected by a delicate linen runner with lace trim. Atop the surface was a line of fine bone china bowls, their bellies full of the party's special dessert—doubled-boiled bird's nest with ginkgo nuts soup. Such a delicacy: the pale white salangane nests costed a fortune, and Tattler knew this with certainty because she was the person unpacking and handling the deliveries. The chef, a short, heavyset woman in her mid-forties, had poached the nests one at a time to eliminate any impurities before stewing them in a simple sugar syrup for as long as possible. They could be served hot as a warming entrée during cold winter months, but because it was summer, Madame Nhu ordered the chef to serve them over ice. Once, when she was in a talkative mood, the chef described the texture to a curious Tattler: slightly chewy but not tough, soft yet not mushy, overall a delight on the tip of the tongue.

The dish sounded so incredible that Tattler was surprised, and even slightly offended, when she realised that none of the foreign guests touched them. They all walked past the dessert table with a certain disdain across their faces, their luxurious outfits suddenly appearing pretentious. They adored the opulence that came with wealth, but precisely the Western kind only.

Tattler bit back her annoyance; there simply wasn't enough space for the feeling. Her hunger already dominated her thoughts— she hadn't eaten since breakfast. The small piece of steamed sweet potato was long digested. She and the other servants wouldn't have their dinners until long after the party was over, and even then they would only consume the tasteless yellow Western potatoes mixed with half-cooked rice and paired with the saltiest dry shrimp. The leftovers from the party, according to Madame Nhu's instructions, were to be dumped into the waste bin. Madame didn't feel comfortable sharing the dishes with her servants, for she believed it was cruel to show them a glimpse of a life they could never lead.

The sudden commotion at the entrance brought Tattler out of her resentment and back to the task at hand. She wiped her mouth, her gaze following the sound to the front door, where the entire party was now gathering with their heads bowed respectfully. Somewhere in the background, someone adjusted the volume of the gramophone. The music dimmed to a faint tune, fading as the great Leon Moutet entered with his son, the young and handsome Edmond Moutet.

They looked nothing alike, Tattler thought. Monsieur Moutet, with his piercing blue eyes, Monsieur Edmond with his captivating green. Their hair was different, too. The older Mou-tet's hair was straight, clipped neatly, pushed back to reveal his pronounced cheekbones and square jaw. Monsieur Edmond's was curly, left to rain freely on his shoulders. Softer, more feminine. Kinder, somehow. He smiled brightly, greeting the crowd with a radiant confidence whilst his father appeared rather frantic, his head craned in search of something. Or someone.

As the sea of people hovering around the Moutet family quickly dissipated, Tattler saw Madame Nhu pushing forward, her face glowing under the light of the crystal chandeliers.

"Monsieur Moutet!" she called. "So glad you could be here. I wanted to introduce you to someone. This is my son's good friend."

Tattler watched as Monsieur Moutet stepped forward, kiss-ing the back of Madame Nhu's hand. He then turned in Hai's direction.

"Splendid," he exclaimed with excitement. "I have a fine bottle of wine in the back of my car. We must toast!"

He winked at Madame Nhu. It was quick, subtle, but Tattler never missed anything.

Within seconds, Monsieur Moutet returned with two full glasses of wine, presenting Hai with the glass on his left, keeping the other for himself. Tattler's eyes widened as Hai tilted her head and finished the drink. Madame Nhu—their master, for heaven's sake—remained empty-handed.

One by one, images of Hai as a shabby housemaid flooded Tattler's mind—Hai with her feet under sluggish puddles of mud, Hai with her clumsy fingers as she prepared the day's meals. They seemed like memories of a different person, not the woman Tattler was looking at. In front of her was a young, noble lady with clean skin and smooth hair, who wore an expensive outfit and a dainty gold chain around her slim neck. She looked as though she truly belonged to this world. Life wasn't fair, Tattler grimaced.

"Edmond, you should stop drinking."

Monsieur Minh's familiar voice rose from Tattler's left, and for a second her entire body jolted when she thought he had discovered her secret spot. No, he couldn't have seen her; she was already crouching, a sneaky rat. She took another step further into darkness, averting her gaze to observe Monsieur Minh and his group of childhood friends. Today, they all wore similar outfits—black suits, white shirts, and velvet black bow ties.

"Oh, shut up," Monsieur Edmond snapped, his fingers turning white as he tightened his grip around the neck of the wine bottle. "Why should I? Even when my mind is drenched in liquor, it's ten times smarter than that know-it-all brain of yours."

Tattler was shocked. Nobody spoke to Monsieur Minh that way—she was certain that her master would turn violent very soon.

To her surprise, Monsieur Minh simply shrugged, even as the tips of his ears flushed crimson. Was he scared of Monsieur Edmond?

"Oh, quit it, you two. Must you squabble every chance you get?" came a much lower voice, coming from someone taller than Monsieur Minh. The man who spoke wore a white handkerchief on his suit's front pocket, and at the tail of his left eye was a long scar that he had gotten from one of the fights at his opium business.

Monsieur Duy.

Tattler often heard stories of him through the housemaids' gossip. Oh, how they all adored Monsieur Duy. They whispered into each other's ears, giggling. *He is the kindest!* they often remarked. Allegedly, aside from the infamous and ruthless opium business,

117

Monsieur Duy also possessed a broad piece of land on the out-skirts of Sài Gòn, which he lent to the rural men and women who lived nearby to grow paddy. There had been multiple occasions when Monsieur Duy absolved the farmers' debt during harsh droughts, giving them grains and sometimes meat so that they could survive the season, earning unyielding admiration and respect from the people. Tattler believed these to be basic human acts, but everyone treated Monsieur Duy like he was a deity.

Still, she supposed those were better than doing nothing. Not once had Tattler heard of the other three men's good deeds.

Both Monsieur Minh and Monsieur Edmond left Monsieur Duy's question to hang, huffing at each other like animals. At last, Monsieur Phong broke the tension, adjusting the black-rimmed glasses that sat on his nose.

"Leave them. I'm heading out for a smoke. Want to join?"

"Yes, let's," Monsieur Duy replied a beat too quickly.

Tattler thought that was the end, so she continued scanning the room for her potential suitor. She didn't realise that someone indeed had spotted her and was now standing just next to her shoulder.

"Blue tunic," the familiar voice commented. "Aren't you supposed to be working?"

Tattler turned to face Monsieur Edmond. His lips were stained red, his breath sour with wine.

"Monsieur . . ." she stuttered whilst her mind scrambled to search for an appropriate explanation that would save her from a beating by Madame Nhu. "I was just . . ."

"Don't worry about it." Monsieur Edmond grinned teas-ingly. "I'm sure you deserve a quick break. I understand, to be honest. This party is such a bore."

Without waiting for Tattler's reply, he tilted his head back, finishing the last few drops of his wine. Tattler stared at the empty green bottle, not knowing what to say.

"I have an idea," Monsieur Edmond continued once he had swallowed the liquid. "Join me in the garden, would you? I could really use some company."

For a second, Tattler couldn't breathe; Monsieur Edmond's piercing green eyes looked so genuine. Subtly, she pinched the flesh on her back to make sure she wasn't hallucinating. When her nerves registered the pain, Tattler struggled to hide a smile.

"It would be my honour, Monsieur."

Tattler dipped her head slightly, like a rich woman accepting an invitation to dance. She followed Monsieur Edmond's outstretched arm, walking out of Madame Nhu's bustling living room. As she breathed in the refreshing summer night air, Tattler looked up at the starless sky and mumbled her gratitude. Hai had secured Monsieur Minh, sure. But Tattler had found herself a far finer prize.

Marianne

Behind the closed gate to the Moutets' mansion, Marianne stood waiting nervously. A cold sweat formed across her forehead, but she hadn't the mind to wipe it dry. Her nerves were thrumming with apprehension, following Leon's cryptic order. Lost in thought, Marianne startled when a black stray cat leaped off a branch from a nearby tree, falling to the ground.

"Goodness," she gasped just as the animal let out a screeching squeal. "Where did you come from?"

Pity filled Marianne's chest—she hated seeing animals hurt. Bending her knees, she squinted to examine the cat for injuries.

"Poor thing." She refrained from patting the cat's round head. She didn't want to get too attached. In a perfect world, she would have taken the animal with her, nursed it back to health, kept it for the house. In time, its fur would no longer be matted, instead a shiny black, yellow eyes bright and playful.

But they weren't living in a perfect world.

The sight of animals—birds, cats, dogs—ignited a vile desire in Leon. He enjoyed their weak cries for help; he liked watching them suffer. He would leave them without food or drink for days, sometimes weeks. Staying in the Moutets' mansion was more a punishment than a privilege.

"Shoo." Marianne stood, her feet thumping loudly to scare the animal away. "I'm doing you a favour."

She watched the cat disappear into the bleary darkness beyond the mansion, then shifted her gaze back to the iron gate, anticipating the blaring headlights of Leon's car. Dressed in her composed, collected housekeeper's attire—a calf-length white linen dress and freshly polished black oxford shoes—she tried to shield her nerves. She understood the subtlety of Leon's request: an incoming *episode*. One that would threaten Edmond's life.

It wasn't supposed to be like this, Marianne shook her head. She didn't want to, but the sentimental side of her always reminisced about those old, golden days.

One sweet and dreamy spring morning when she was twenty-five years old, Marianne was sitting next to her oldest friend, Adeline—who in one year's time would grow to be Edmond's mother. They were lounging in the Moutets' grand garden when Marianne's mother arrived, a sulky young man trailing behind.

Miss Adeline, Marianne's mother had called—unlike her daughter, she never disregarded Adeline's title. It didn't matter that their families were close; the Moutets were superior, one of the few aristocrats remaining after the bloodbath of the French Revolution. *This is Leon. He ran after a thief who tried to steal my purse. Such an honest and brave young man*, she explained. *Could you help him find a job at the mansion?*

Yes, that can certainly be arranged, Adeline had replied, a teasing grin on the curve of her lip. She turned and winked at her friend—Marianne would later mark this moment as the start of Adeline's fairy-tale love story.

She didn't know it would later end in tragedy.

When Edmond was born, Leon was ecstatic, his eyes crinkled with happiness. He fussed over his son, forfeiting sleep to stay by Adeline's side at all times. But then, she changed, pushing Leon away. Adeline loathed Leon's presence, cursing whenever he was near. In the end, just like his wife, Leon blamed their child for the explosion of his marriage. As they bickered and fought, the Moutets' only heir became unwanted offspring, a cloud further dimming his parents' perishing love.

But to Marianne, Edmond was a shining star, her rescuing light from a dark tunnel. Before him, Marianne was lost; she had not understood her life's purpose. Women did not have careers, and she never wanted to get married. Like a gift from the universe, he had arrived, giving her someone to love, to care for, to protect.

She had followed Leon and Edmond when they moved to Cochinchina. *A fresh start*, Marianne had naively thought. She didn't expect to constantly catch Leon outside Edmond's bedroom, staring. He never went inside, only stood with his fingers balled into fists, his breath resentful. Like a faceless spirit, Marianne would crouch in a corner where she was certain Leon could not see her, observing, vowing to do everything she could to keep Edmond from his father's vicious rage.

Even if it meant cleaning the blood spatters off Leon's bedroom walls. Even if it meant gathering sheets and clothes to destroy. Even if it meant aiding him in terrible, unspeakable things.

This reminder helped Marianne hold her head a little higher. She adjusted the collar of her dress, observing her surroundings. She didn't realise she had been pacing amidst the memories, and now she waited for Leon next to the water fountain—one of his most prized possessions.

When he first had this mansion built, Leon had ordered the piece from a famous French sculptor. The man cast, coloured, then carved the details in Paris, before arranging for transportation to Cochinchina on a cartel ship. The whole process took over half a year, all for some vain four-tier fountain with a detailed, lifelike horse head mounted at the top.

Imagine what Madame Nhu will say, Marianne. The thirst she'll feel for something so precious. Something so French. He had laughed when the creation arrived, satisfied with this tasteless rivalry. The sound of his laughter, more like a screech.

A drop of water landed on Marianne's left cheek. She wiped her skin dry with the back of her hand, then stifled a yawn. As if on cue, the front gate creaked open, and Leon's car appeared.

The Moutets' mansion and the Khåis' were within walking distance of one another—Madame Nhu's at the end of Charner Road and Leon's at its head, with no other properties in between. Still, Leon always took his flashy car. A show of wealth and social standing, more than convenience. Once the vehicle came to a complete stop on the neatly paved orange driveway, Leon let out a slight groan and stepped out of the car.

I'm an independent man, he often mocked. *Can't afford to waste my precious time waiting for the valet.*

Now, Leon stood in front of Marianne, shoulders broad, limbs long. At first glance, he looked much younger than his age. His skin was still smooth, except for the laugh lines around his mouth: proof he used to deceive the world that he was a kind, trustworthy person.

"It is so damn hot tonight," Leon cursed and pulled out a black-and-white chequered handkerchief from his trouser pocket, dabbing the sweat on his forehead. The air was heavy with summer heat, but he refused to take off his charcoal jacket.

Marianne watched as Leon reached for the fine bamboo comb from the inner flap of his suit. The silver strands of his hair were still in place, secured in a coif, but Leon was always paranoid about them falling. She had never encountered a man more obsessed with his appearance—Leon needed, under every circumstance, to appear impeccable, hair pulled away from his face, leather shoes shiny, his wardrobe an extensive collection of imported fine wool and luxurious Italian silk.

I must be prepared, Marianne, Leon would say, his voice toneless, he a teacher, she his unwilling student. *Should I ever have a heart attack the same way Khải Siêu did, I will leave this world swaddled in a splendid outfit, unlike him and his shabby bathrobe.*

She never responded, but Marianne understood this philosophy—the more embellished Leon's sheath, the more reluctant the desire to examine the rusty blade beneath.

Somewhere inside the house, the grandfather clock announced the time: 10:00 p.m. on the dot. Marianne had been waiting for more than an hour for Leon to return from Madame Nhu's party, and her legs were numb. She cleared her throat.

"Monsieur, what seems to be the trouble?"

"This young lady here," Leon gestured vaguely towards the car behind him. It was a 1928 Falcon-Knight Roadster in pale green, another of his prized possessions. "She needs a *touch up*."

He looked directly at Marianne then, grinning.

"Monsieur." She dipped her head.

"Send her to my room once you are through."

He staggered towards the white stone staircase, not sparing another glance at the body slumped in the car. Marianne's eyes were alert as they followed Leon's steps, his weakened vigour ultimately showing. He was tense, she knew, struggling to hide the disgraceful wheeze that escaped his decaying lungs.

He no longer looked young for his age.

Behind Marianne, the black iron gate creaked shut.

* *

She was easy prey, the young woman in Marianne's arms. Her outfit was now torn in half, left in a crumpled heap on the ground. Her naked skin brushed against Marianne's, laid out on the bed, waiting to be clothed in a white silk dress. A nameless sensation clouded Marianne's head, but she couldn't stop. Once, she would have questioned why she did this—why she felt obligated to Leon, to their lifelong shared history. But when she realised she was doing this for Edmond, Marianne denied herself the temporary relief of remorse. She didn't care how broken or how rotten these actions made her. None of it mattered, as long as Leon was distracted and Edmond was safe.

"I'll see if Monsieur is ready. Bring her up in ten minutes." Marianne's voice was stern as she spoke to the two valets, waiting in the corner of the guest room.

"Yes, Madame."

She held her breath as she headed for Leon's bedroom; she dreaded being in his presence. As she hesitated just inches from Leon's doorframe, Marianne could no longer remember the young man she grew up with. It wasn't the power or wealth that followed his marriage to Adeline. It wasn't the fact that he was now Marianne's master. No. It was Leon's cruelty, his bloodlust, something entirely new to the person she had once known.

Leon was smoking at the balcony, oblivious to Marianne's appearance, his other hand resting on the black iron rail. A white towel was wrapped loosely around his lower body, and his hair was still wet. Shimmering moonlight perched on the reflection of his damp steps, the marble floor behind him speckled with glassy pools. From where Marianne stood, if she squinted, she could see a bit further on the horizon: amidst the navy cloak of night was Madame Nhu's estate. She guessed Leon was looking at the same thing. He enjoyed such petty acts—comparing his mansion to the Khải's, nodding with satisfaction.

That woman and her many schemes, Leon had lowered his voice to a conspiratorial tone, once, in a chatty mood. *She is a fool, Marianne! Take her house, for example. Why the need for so many timber shutters on her windows? Look around you. Our home is surrounded by nothing but transparent glass. Do you know why? I want to let everyone see what they're missing.*

125

Leon never bothered hiding his hatred, and Marianne never needed the explanation. Like most men, Leon didn't enjoy the company of powerful women.

"Monsieur," Marianne called when she heard the valets on the floor below. "She is ready."

An announcement. She hardly needed Leon's permission on this matter; she had assisted him far too many times already. When the valets appeared, panting heavily, Marianne pointed at the king-size bed in the middle of the room, instructing the young men to place the girl there.

"It's done, Monsieur."

"Good. You may leave," Leon said, his back still turned to Marianne. A cool night breeze arrived, and the gauzy curtains shifted, billowing together, eerie.

Marianne dipped her head before exiting; she didn't want to be in Leon's space another second. She already knew what would come next. When tomorrow arrived, she would return, pressing her lips shut as she dressed the young woman's wound, swaddling it in thin cloth.

Once she reached her bedroom, Marianne closed the door with a force she did not know she had, her hands shaking violently. She dropped to the ground, leaning against the sturdy wood panel, a crutch for her enervation.

Above Marianne's head, she heard Leon's muffled grunting.

She closed her eyes, but she could not escape that room, the horror Leon was certainly inflicting on that nameless, transient maid. It was a lie, what Leon often promised, in his more human moments. He never believed it, and neither did Marianne. His scorching thirst would never stop burning, demanding new victims. There was nothing in the world that frightened Marianne more.

Edmond

Tonight, the mansion was quieter than usual, enough for Edmond to notice a faint sound coming from his father's floor. He intended to step out, trying to decipher what it was, but the queasy feeling in his stomach already returned. He failed to reach the bathroom in time; the normally short distance from his chair, by the writing desk, to the toilet seemed to double. In the corner behind the timber door, Edmond's legs collapsed, and he started retching. When he was done, Edmond wiped his mouth with the back of his hand. For a sliver of a second, he was disoriented. He tried to stand up, to get away from the puddle of his own vomit, but the sudden movement knocked him down, flat on the ground. The room was spinning wildly.

Great, Edmond sighed. Once again, he had drunk himself senseless.

He blinked, and slowly, his surroundings came into focus. Edmond saw the familiar posters of his bed, the curvy legs of his writing desk. He was home, and this was his bedroom. And what was this pungent scent of decay? Yes, the puke. Why had he been drinking so much? What was he trying to run from? Edmond groaned.

This always happened when he returned to this land.

Sometimes, Edmond wondered if the ground where his father's mansion stood was haunted—he felt cursed, every time he came back here. Day after day, the conflict between his true emotions and his mother's lessons tore his psyche apart.

Edmond recalled Minh's remark, just a few hours before. He sensed the shame creeping back, his ears hot, as though his friend were still standing here, repeating the comment.

This had been the dynamic between Edmond and Minh, even from the beginning. Almost twenty years had passed but Edmond could still remember vividly how much Minh had initially disliked him—the nose scrunches, the glares, the obvious annoyance each time Edmond conversed with either Duy or Phong. Minh had never been subtle. Such hostility should have dampened Edmond's determination; after all, no one had ever denied him anything. Why waste his energy chasing after an arrogant boy who clearly did not want to be friends with him?

Still, the more time Edmond spent observing the boys from afar, the more desperate he became. The jovial laughs that Minh, Duy, and Phong often shared slapped Edmond's chest where it was most hollow. Whilst he had everything he could ever wish for, Edmond had never been to school prior to Cochinchina. He'd never had friends before.

In the end, Minh relented to Edmond's constant effort— wherever the boys went, Edmond asked to join. He brought them sweet treats after each weekend he spent at home. He bonded with both Duy and Phong, relying on them to sway Minh's mind. Yet, Edmond could never really say that he won Minh's acceptance, merely his toleration. There could only be one sun in the sky, and both Edmond and Minh shone too brightly.

But when Edmond met the other boys, he was no longer alone, and so it didn't matter that Minh didn't like him. He finally had friends his age, and for this he was incredibly grateful; his mother's warning to stay away from the inferior species retreated to a dusty corner of his mind.

It didn't stay there long.

When the other students started coming to Edmond for permission to do things he hadn't known required his authority, everything changed.

Why me? Edmond asked, his voice innocent.

You're French.

The sentence made Edmond wonder, of course. He was curious if this was how everyone—including his closest friends—saw him.

It wasn't enough, though, to make Edmond believe he was truly superior. No, that came soon after, when he finally noticed the boys' timidity around him, when he returned to Paris that summer to see his mother. She resumed her whispers: France was where *civilisation* lived, and they should never share the same air with the inferior *yellow* species. Her voice felt like a soothing wave, washing over the rawness of Edmond's young soul, shaping his beliefs into her gospel truth.

Spit it out!

His mother's order, sharp like shards of glass.

It was near the end of his vacation, and one afternoon, Edmond came home hungry from playing soccer in the park. He wandered inside the kitchen, the sight of a foreign delicacy near the windowsill capturing his attention. Hungry and restless, he reached for it, chewing without thinking. The sound of the wrapper must have woken his mother because a few seconds later, Edmond heard footsteps descending the stairs, and he tried his best to quickly swallow the treat. His mother stood with her mouth agape at the kitchen doorway, fuming with anger. She had marched towards him, violently tugging the collar of his shirt, dragging him to the toilet. Later, he learned that the biscuits were a gift from an Annamite diplomat, his father's acquaintance, and that his mother intended to throw them in the waste bin.

Spit it out! she repeated. *That filthy, filthy rubbish!*

She forced Edmond's face over the toilet bowl, bunching his soft curls in a lock behind his head, ordering him to puke, slapping his back with such force it echoed through his hollow chest.

Afterwards, his mother made Edmond promise to never touch foreign food again, to hold himself higher. He was superior, for goodness' sake. She sat him at her writing desk, and command he write the sentences precisely one thousand times, so the belief would never leave his mind.

My name is Edmond Moutet. I am French. I am superior to the filthy Annamites.

My name is Edmond Moutet. I am French. I am superior to the filthy Annamites.

My name is Edmond Moutet. I am French. I am superior to the filthy Annamites.

My name is Edmond Moutet. I am French. I am superior to the filthy Annamites.

My name is Edmond Moutet—

He never fully believed his mother's statement, but he never fully dismissed it, either.

Now, as he tried to sit up, elbows scraping against the cold marble floor, Edmond examined the creamy wall in front of his eyes, imagining Minh in front of him. He needed to numb his nerves, his humiliation, Edmond decided. He summoned the last of his strength, stumbling on his feet towards the seven trunks he'd brought back from France. Two days ago, they were full of liquor. Today, one was already empty.

Edmond didn't hesitate, his fingers wrapped firmly around one of the bottles, pulling it away from its kind. *You and me, both isolated*, Edmond thought. *We ought to stay close.* He closed his eyes, welcoming his trusted companion. As the wine crawled through his veins, Edmond felt renewed. His skin felt lighter, his heart no longer heavy. One gulp, and he was a different person. No remorse, no regret. No pain, no ache.

Smiling now, Edmond turned to look at the maid he'd found at the party.

She was sitting on the floor at the end of his bed. A small, timid lump.

Edmond swayed slowly in the maid's direction, his green eyes a darker shade of curiosity. She looked back at him with the same hopeful gaze he had seen a few hours prior—that sparkle reminded him of his pathetic self, a man who loved those he shouldn't, a man who believed this terrible world was good and kind.

No wonder he brought her here, to his father's mansion, to his room, where dreams went to perish. When Edmond saw the maid—a grand ambition for a better, shinier life written plainly across her face—he decided to teach her a lesson.

The silence around them stretched to a century. Edmond remained quiet, considering the maid's cautious expression. He studied her long hair, falling on her slim shoulders, a black waterfall. The colour was striking, highlighting the roundness of her face.

Without taking his eyes off the maid, Edmond walked towards his bed, reaching for the pair of silver scissors under his pillow. The metal felt substantial in his palm, heavy with significance. A sacred thing. Edmond recalled Marianne's voice the day she convinced him to keep them where he slept.

Remember the nightmares? Marianne had asked. *This weapon helps sever the threads that tie you to the vengeful spirits of the underworld. They are the ones who haunt your sleep. You'll be safe now.* Standing in front of her, Edmond was dumbfounded, trying to stifle a laugh at Marianne's adorable gullibility. She had learned of such superstition, she continued to explain, her voice serious, from the lowborn female vendors at the local market. She had ignored Madame Moutet's warnings of *strange yellow voodoo* and befriended them anyway. Edmond had pretended to listen intently, to drink in her every word, because Marianne was one of only two people in this world who he truly loved and trusted. Later that night, before he fell asleep, Edmond placed the pair of scissors under his plush pillow—he hadn't the heart to confess to Marianne that *he* was the vengeful spirit she had been desperate to avoid.

Now, that same holy weapon felt hot in Edmond's grip. He passed the pair of scissors back and forth between his hands. Taunting.

"What are you willing to lose to change your life?"

The sound of his voice was dense with phlegm, and Edmond wasn't pleased. He flooded such nastiness away with two full gulps of wine. Which nastiness he was trying to rinse, the mucus inside his throat or the guilt at the bottom of his pulsing heart, Edmond didn't know. He decided to leave that question for a sober Edmond, who would later wake to a throbbing hangover.

"Anything you ask of me, Monsieur," the maid replied swiftly. Her dark brown eyes were full of determination.

"Very well." Edmond nodded. "Just what I like to hear."

He moved in her direction, the pair of scissors balancing on his four fingertips as he outstretched his arm.

"Here. Cut your hair."

"Monsieur?"

"Come now." Edmond pasted on an expression of disbelief. "Don't tell me you changed your mind."

"I'm afraid I don't follow." She held his gaze, never looking away. Had the circumstance been different, Edmond felt he would have liked her. A strong, courageous young woman.

"Think of it as a test. A kind of proof, if you will. To show me how serious you really are about leaving your old life behind."

He smirked as the young maid stared at the two silver blades, undoubtedly considering her options. Across from her, Edmond remained tall, his back straight, arms crossed in front of his chest, throat hot from alcohol. The taste of the wine changed him, turned this moment entertaining, instead of wicked and mean.

Finally, the maid spoke, her voice quivering. "Yes, Monsieur."

She twirled the locks between her fingers. Swiftly, she sliced them to half their original length.

Edmond briefly looked down to where he was standing, three empty bottles next to his bare feet. He should have felt disoriented; he should have been drunk, or high on the pain he had forced upon the maid. But he wasn't drunk or high, and now he could feel his sunken cheeks flaming with shame.

In the end, he couldn't watch as the maid's hair grew shorter and shorter whilst her sobs grew louder and louder. He needed more alcohol before he could look at what he had orchestrated. Edmond wished he was either plainly vile, like his father, or fully kind; this murky shade of grey was a path he hated navigating.

At last, though, when the liquor had finally hypnotised his nerves, Edmond regained his composure as he guided the maid towards a shiny mirror. She was heaving uncontrollably, and he stared in fascination at the tears that congregated on the edge of her round chin. Her hair was now spiky atop her head, the physical evidence of her foolish bravery, her undying faith.

"Painful, isn't it? The price we have to pay," he said, patronising. "It's only getting harder from here, my dear. You can only stay if you have the stomach for it."

With that, Edmond smirked, returning to his bed after drowning the last of the fourth bottle. The maid bellowed in utter desperation when she glimpsed her feral reflection in the mirror on his wall. He closed his eyes, letting his body settle on the mattress. His job was done, Edmond thought. He had taught her a lesson. Whether she stayed here or fled, he no longer cared. He rolled to his side, his back now facing her. Arrogant. Unafraid.

A second before he fell asleep, the old Edmond, the *real* Edmond resurfaced. Quickly, a flash, just long enough for the whisper to drown in his pillow—two words the maid would never hear.

"I'm sorry."

THAT NIGHT

Timid footsteps filled the airy dining room.

Eighteen people stood side by side, awaiting instructions from their master. A deafening silence swaddled their senses, until suddenly, a crow gave a cawing sound somewhere deep in the pine forest. A croak, confirming: death was nearby.

The noise startled Duy, sending chills down his back.

He had no choice but to continue his investigation.

Five minutes earlier, Duy had sat in this same spot, dreaming of the amount of money he would pay to pretend that his problems didn't exist. He wanted to point an accusatory finger at his own soul, scolding its ever dissatisfied complaints, and its stupidity, for not knowing how good his life had been. *You have never really grown,* Duy frowned. Like the child he once was, who threw a wild tantrum after his untouched toys had been taken away, Duy only treasured his good fortune when it became clear it couldn't last forever.

Five minutes earlier, Duy had also fought the urge to press his ear against the wall, to listen, guess what the other two were doing. It had been ludicrous, this action. It had only further highlighted his distrust in his very own friends. Leaning back in his chair, Duy was desperate for the oblivion of sleep.

He had sighed; a vague thought brushed his consciousness, and he had hated himself for considering it. What would become of them, of their friendship—their brotherhood—if he conceded to such a suspicion?

Five minutes earlier, Duy had suppressed his mind to a cramped and artificial box of calm, and decided to pursue another possibility. An absurd possibility but a possibility nonetheless: he rang the bell, rounding all the maids, housekeepers, and cooks into the main dining room.

Now, the servants positioned themselves in a straight line in front of him. It was the middle of the night; the sheen of sleepiness had yet to lift, their feet naked and vulnerable atop the marble tiles. The housemaids, young girls, were the most frightened. They glanced at one another, worried, afraid. They hadn't a clue what had happened, and they dared not ask.

Duy briefly considered a good old-fashioned beating. He wasn't one for unnecessary violence, nor was he one for injustice; pain was a powerful emotion, cornering people into admitting even mistakes they did not make. He settled on prolonging his silence instead, sitting with his long legs crossed. The slight curl of his hair—normally pushed to the back of his head and secured by a hefty amount of gel—now drooped down his forehead. Exhausted. Defeated. Duy tapped his fingers against his knees, a dance to buy his mind an extra sliver of time—partially because he wanted to create suspense and partially because he didn't know what to say. Duy was following the wrong trail, he knew, but knowing was only one thing. He would only abandon this route once he found physical evidence to prove it completely illogical.

Nothing was more stubborn than a man in despair.

Folding his fingers into his palms, Duy remained still as a statue. Quietly, he studied his servants.

He started with Old Ba, the butler who had been working for his family since before Duy was born. Old Ba stood in the middle of the line, directly in front of Duy, an honest man with nothing to hide.

The warm, sincere expression on Old Ba's face reminded Duy of that summer vacation when he was ten years old. Dutifully, Old Ba had followed his family to Đà Lạt to take care of him. Back then, Old Ba wasn't Old Ba but simply Ba, a middle-aged man whose skin hadn't yet sagged, whose unkempt goatee hadn't yet turned silver. The trip started as boring as any, until the group of four boys gathered inside this very room, giggling as they tried to eavesdrop on the adults in the living room next door. It was improper, and afterwards they were made to stand in a straight line, very similar to the line the servants now assembled. Looming over them, Edmond's father demanded to know whose idea this was, in the scary voice he only ever used for discipline. The boys all avoided looking at the imposing man, his broad hands holding a black leather whip—they all shook their heads. They bonded over this small secret, so even when their calves turned red, the boys did not cry.

The next night, Edmond suggested visiting the cemetery at midnight; the spooky stories and legends piqued his curiosity. They would have gotten away with it, if not for Ba and his unbearably annoying habit of telling the truth. He reported the incident to Madame Mai when she ordered him to check on the young master's bedroom, and once again, the boys were scolded. They didn't mind; their friendship only bloomed brighter.

Now, Duy needed that honesty. A final wake-up call to end his wishful delusion.

He breathed out at last.

"You will tell me—and you will tell me now—of your where-abouts from nine o'clock tonight."

Just as Duy had anticipated, it was Old Ba who summoned the courage to respond.

"Monsieur, you ordered us all to retreat early for the night so that you and the other masters would not be disrupted. We were all asleep in our quarters since seven. I counted the heads myself."

The earnest answer he had expected—Duy wanted to shout.

Pressing his lips tightly, Duy bit back his fury. He knew, as he had known from the beginning, that there were only four of them in the room, that the servants' quarter was always tightly packed with restless bodies, that it was impossible to move even a finger without waking everyone else. Duy also knew that he was not really angry at the butler; rather, he was outraged with his pathetic self, his own wilful refusal to follow the most logical explanation.

He waved for the servants to retreat back to their quarter, instructing them to stay until they were told otherwise. The sound of their gentle footsteps disappearing into the gloomy night was like a foreign lullaby.

Duy couldn't help it. After the servants had exited, he began to weep, his tears heavy with a mixture of fear and resentment. The little boys in his memories seemed fictional, like characters from a tale Duy had been using to lure himself to sleep, their loyalty towards one another a figment of his imagination.

Once the pain eased slightly and Duy could breathe again, he turned and searched for the clock, hanging near the timber door, wondering how much longer until the governor arrived. Very soon, Duy guessed. The governor was currently on holiday, staying in his own vacation mansion in Đà Lạt, not far from the Caos'. He didn't have much time, and he needed to make his moves carefully, as he would a game with his chess master. The most important game of his life.

He heard someone approaching.

Phong.

Duy locked eyes with his friend, wanting to say something, anything. But the words refused to come. The two men stood in silence for a second before Phong opened his mouth, his voice sombre, his expression impossible to read.

"You need to come and look at the body."

Duy nodded and followed without protest, ignoring the morbid thought: perhaps it would be better if the body started its decomposition process now, way earlier than scientifically possible. They would have a missing person's case, instead of a gruesome homicide.

Despite himself, Duy wished Edmond would disappear—his body vanishing forever into thin air.

THREE DAYS PRIOR

Madame Nhu

She had to do it for her family.

Long after the last guest had gone—long after the suffocating feeling arrived, like she were lying within the walls of a coffin—Madame Nhu finally accepted that she wasn't going to fall asleep. She crept out of her bedroom and followed the wooden staircase that connected the upper floors to the altar room. When she first entered, the sky from the small window facing west remained an obscure dark grey, no longer midnight, but not quite morning.

Now, Madame Nhu kneeled with her forehead resting on the cold tile floor. Her god asked no question, but Madame Nhu still explained, trying to convince the divine, trying to convince herself.

"This is all I have ever known."

Madame Nhu's voice trembled in her throat. She didn't know why she felt guilty; after all, she had made the decision based on the lessons she'd been taught since birth. It was true, what Madame Nhu was whispering, the sole defence behind her actions—the elite should only ever marry the elite.

The altar room dimmed down to a stale, condemning silence. Madame Nhu's eyes were teary from the acrid smoke, twirling from the burning incense. Three sticks stood inside three copper burners, their bellies round, prepared to digest her sins. Gently, Madame Nhu pulled her forehead from the cold ground and sat upright, looking straight at the inlaid wooden altar cabinet. It wasn't exceptionally tall, but Madame Nhu found it staggering enough. How she used to adore its decorations—mother-of-pearl birds amongst blossoming trees, inlaid on its two doors, with peaceful waterfalls running up the side panels. Behind the cabinet, high on the wall, was a scroll, which read *everlasting happiness* in cursive hanzi characters, the golden frame around it ornate with detailed carvings of cranes flying towards the sky. Everlasting ambition. Everlasting desire.

It was gone now: the hope Madame Nhu had felt when she first ordered the servants to place the cabinet inside this room, when she herself placed the golden Buddha statue, and the golden candle holders in the shape of flying dragons, and the photo frames of her parents-in-law and her late husband atop the rosewood surface. Once, this room had been her solace, where she came for every solution and validation.

Now, she did not know if she could forgive herself.

"I beg your forgiveness, Buddha."

Madame Nhu closed her bloodshot eyes, clasping her hands together in prayer, hoping her sins would be pardoned by the divine.

She was roused from her pursuit by the violent sound of cursing. Minh. She sighed. He was standing in the front yard, roaring. Clumsily, Madame Nhu got to her feet and took off the string of beads around her neck; the wooden spheres were so different from the luscious pearl necklace she had worn the night before.

Closing the door behind her back, Madame Nhu followed the five flights of stairs down in the plain black rubber sandals she only wore at night. Her party gown was replaced by an embroidered silk top in deep yellow mustard and silk trousers in black; the darker shades did not compliment her face. She looked paler, older somehow, as though last night's scheme had taken a decade off her life.

Once she was outside, Madame Nhu realised she hadn't been in the altar room for long; the sun had yet to make its appearance over the horizon. Quickly, she made her way to the line of tall banana trees, using their low and giant leaves to conceal her presence. She needed a moment to prepare herself before facing her child. The scene in front of her was horrifying—Minh was unleashing his wrath on the servants. Madame Nhu clenched her eyes shut when they cried out, as if by doing so she could successfully deny her involvement.

"Where the fuck is Hai?" In the middle of the yard, Minh screamed.

Madame Nhu flinched when Minh spat in the face of the old butler. The elders were always wise; she remembered constantly teaching him so. She had taught Minh to respect the old man, but it seemed now that her lectures—like all her other efforts to contain Minh—had been in vain.

Madame Nhu stared at her son, shivering. It was as though a monster had swallowed Minh whole and was now wearing his skin. His hair was dishevelled, his shirt half-unbuttoned, lurid red rashes marking his body. She couldn't tell if she knew him at all.

Maybe she never had. As a baby, Minh's fussing and crying constantly filled her soul with dread. A prophecy, perhaps. Even now, Madame Nhu couldn't guess what Minh was thinking.

The wind rose, wafting the repugnant stench of liquor. Madame Nhu grimaced. She never understood the appeal of drinking—why anyone would voluntarily surrender their sanity and coherent thoughts was beyond her. *Wasn't it clear*, Madame Nhu wondered, *that the more rationality it consumed, the more control it craved?* To a vulnerable woman such as herself, intellect was her most prized weapon, and also her deadliest. She would die before giving it up.

"Monsieur, I really do not know."

Madame Nhu heard a juvenile voice, bellowing in anguish. It was Ti, the young valet, lying on his side. His arms were wrapped around his abdomen, and his face was smeared with tears and blood.

His sobbing did little to soothe Minh's rage; Minh was no longer beating this servant for information; instead he was using the young man's body as an outlet for release. His shirt turned transparent from sweat; the black mole below his right shoulder blade was showing. His breath was now short and urgent, but he showed no sign of stopping. Minh stomped once more on the poor boy before Madame Nhu finally intervened, the faint cracking sound drawing her out of hiding.

"You lot," she said to the terrified servants. "Scram, now."

She kept her voice loud, to mask the pulsing fear.

Turning to face Minh, Madame Nhu tried her best to hide the quiver in her voice. She struggled to form an authoritative sentence and, in the end, settled for a short and direct question.

"What has gotten in to you?"

"Ah, mother dearest," Minh retorted, his words a mockery, devoid of affection.

He didn't even look at her.

143

Madame Nhu kept her distance, searching his distorted face for a flickering sense of familiarity. She found nothing.

"I find it rather hard to believe . . ." Minh continued before pausing for a second to vomit over the grey cement of the Khải's front yard, his body folding to half its normal length. Madame Nhu's eyes widened as Minh wiped the corner of his lip with the sleeve of his shirt, remembering her fussy son and his pedantic hatred for such acts of filthiness. She felt a pang of sadness, echoing from the deepest part of her soul. Had Minh really changed so much, or had she failed him as a mother?

Minh shifted left and right, searching for balance on his unsteady feet.

"I find it hard to believe," he continued, "that you don't know where my wife is."

"Don't be ridiculous!" Madame Nhu snapped; her head throbbed as she raised her voice. "She is not your wife. There has been no proper wedding. The girl's family doesn't even know of your silly little courtship. That wretched woman, she doesn't deserve you. You were so drunk, I bet you didn't notice. She left with Monsieur Moutet."

It was the script she had prepared last night, now delivered with a forced look of triumph.

"Ed?" Minh's tone was full of surprise, though his fingers were already balled into fists, ready to strike.

"No. Monsieur Moutet—Leon Moutet. Don't you dare get on his bad side, Minh. I mean it."

"Did you *sell* my wife to that monster?"

Minh was roaring once more, his brawny hands reaching to squeeze Madame Nhu's frail shoulders in fury.

"Have you gone completely mad?"

144

Madame Như struggled to free her body from his grip, her face darkening with fear.

"I simply introduced her to Monsieur Moutet upon his arrival, out of *courtesy*. On your behalf? Yes? He might have charmed her into following him home. Who am I to know? My dearest son, women are opportunistic beings."

She went on.

"And you are clearly too gullible. She has you eating grass out of the palm of her hand."

As if to intensify the dramatic effect of the story she had spent all night anxiously weaving, Madame Như shook her head, exclaiming her disdain by smacking her lips together.

"You are lying!" Minh spat at the ground, his finger trembling slightly as he directed it at his mother's face, an act of barbaric disrespect. "Hai would never do that to me. She doesn't care about money or reputation or any of these vain things you are always obsessed with. This is your doing, I *know* it."

Minh glared at his mother, the red veins in his eyes like puppet strings, pulling Madame Như's son further and further away from her.

"Where has your sense gone, you pathetic boy?"

She wanted to raise her hand, to give Minh a slap on his defiant face, but she stopped herself. He was no longer a child, and he was now immune to her pointless, ineffectual beatings.

"I could never, *ever*, make the Moutets do anything. You of all people should know that. If the girl were to leave with Monsieur Moutet, she left *willingly*."

Madame Như panted, trying her best to hold the last few words in her mouth. She needed Minh to believe that he had been betrayed, not by his own mother but by the lowborn Hai, the greedy, manipulative woman who jumped at the first chance to be with the indestructible Leon Moutet, who got everything he wished for, no matter the cost.

Madame Nhu eyed Minh cautiously, scrambling for more convincing details. To her surprise, though, Minh stopped arguing. Slowly, the anger evaporated, leaving his face white, his eyes empty. He was completely heartbroken, Madame Nhu realised, sensing an ache inside her chest.

That wouldn't change her mind, however; she knew her family would be better off this way.

Tattler

Tattler found a spot on the ground, next to the most elaborate four-poster bed she had ever seen—the one she used to admire in Madame Nhu's bedroom now seemed laughably inferior. She leaned her head against one of the pointy corners, exhausted. She hadn't moved an inch from this spot since the night before.

The four elongated posts of Monsieur Edmond's bed stood proud and tall—their bodies were scarred with straight lines and geometric shapes, a testament to the sculptor's talent as well as the hefty price of the piece. Gently, Tattler traced her fingers along the cloud and clover indentations, marvelling at the precious mother-of-pearl flowers winding up the side panels. They caught the soft, warm light from the lamp atop the writing desk, glinting a flash of rainbow. The colourful hue reminded Tattler of the fish scales she often washed off the dingy kitchen floor after the chef finished preparing Madame Nhu's meals. A shade of opulence that Tattler had always wanted to wear, but never could. The desire was like a bubble of soap; each time she tried to touch it, it would burst.

Tattler considered the perfection of the carvings and felt the urge to leave her greasy fingerprints—proof that she had been here. An act of rebellion, after all Monsieur Edmond had put her through.

Absentmindedly, she tried to run her hands through her hair, to brush it out with her fingers. Her heart lurched as she touched empty air, remembering that her hair was clipped short. When Monsieur Edmond handed her the pair of scissors, of course she hesitated. Women in her culture didn't normally cut their hair. A symbolic rather than a practical thing, really. They treasured those long strands, growing them out from the moment they were born—an embodiment of a bond with their ancestors. But her mother had sold her to the Khảis; the bond perhaps had long been torn. What of a little more hair, in exchange for a different life?

Such was the thing with hope, Tattler would later realise. It was cruel, the future's unpredictability. In that moment, kneeling in front of a powerful man, she had failed to make the right decision, and even now, she couldn't tell whether she had chosen wisely—deciding to stay here, in his bedroom, ignoring Monsieur Edmond's ominous warning, betting on his vague promise of a different life, clinging onto the last shred of hope that she had successfully proven herself.

"Ah."

From where he lay, Monsieur Edmond mumbled incoherently. He wasn't a sound sleeper, alternating between babbling and snoring. She had never seen a person drink so much, not even Monsieur Minh. She slowed her breath, watching Monsieur Edmond's chest rise and fall, analysing the creases and folds across his forehead. What was he dreaming of? She couldn't imagine a man like Monsieur Edmond, harbouring her own common despair. What had he mixed into his liquor? Something stronger than wine?

She fixed her gaze on his sharp jawline, imagining a blade so pointy it could stab straight through her hope, her desire. Now, she was nameless, like the time before the servants at the Khảis' mansion started calling her Tattler—her life a series of hand-offs, passing from one master to the next.

The realisation drained her pride. Exhausted, she fell asleep on the hard and unforgiving marble floor. Tattler used her bony left arm as a pillow, her forehead creasing with stiffness and fright. Her body curled into a foetal position, helpless, afraid. As she began to breathe softly, her muscles refused to relax. This happened sometimes, before she fell asleep: Tattler was transported back to the beginning of her story.

Tattler was born in a small village, so small no one bothered giving it a name. It was nestled at the edge of Củ Chi, a rural district further down south of Sài Gòn, where most families were just as poor as her own, where the only way to survive was through working in the Khải' paddy fields.

The fields were a vast, luscious green carpet, always filled with the fresh, intoxicating scent of young shoots. Day after day, farmers would arrive before sunrise, their bare feet submerged in muddy water, their backs permanently curved. Above the pale yellow of their conical hats, birds would form a line in the vast blue sky, their chirping softly cradling the workers with sympathy. The farmers would grow and harvest rice for the masters—the Khải. They would pay ground rent on a monthly basis, with hardly anything left to call their own. Tattler never managed to fully understand those predatory requirements—shouldn't they at least be entitled to the rice that *they* reaped and sowed? When she voiced her confusion, however, Mother simply said she was too young to understand. Her tone was clipped, as though she feared others might discover what she really thought of her masters. So Tattler stopped asking. It was a long time before the world finally revealed its true self—where the wealth of the elite rested entirely upon the exploitation of powerless farmers, like Tattler's parents.

Life would have passed them by as such, difficult but bearable, had it not been for *that* year. They faced the harshest drought, hardened land, and withered fields. Tattler was thirteen when it happened, with a frame smaller than most kids her age, her bones more prominent than her flesh. A walking skeleton.

One morning, she woke with a great sense of disorientation, the hunger catching up to her weakening body. Tattler gave herself a moment, before sitting up. Her head immediately turned in search of her father in his usual spot, with his back flat on the splintered panel and his mouth agape, oblivious to his own family's suffering. In that moment, looking at her father, at his failure to protect the people he loved most, Tattler sensed a feeling she was too young to have. The feeling was so intense, so vile and dark, it scared her. She shook her head to waft the thought away and noticed the strange air inside her family home. A smart and observant child, Tattler knew instantly that something was wrong.

From the corner of her eye, Tattler noticed a small lump sitting in the dark shadow of the room, weeping, sobbing uncontrollably. She blinked and the image came into focus—her mother was crying, holding Tattler's oldest brother in her embrace.

Her *dead* oldest brother.

He had passed away overnight, a fifteen-year-old boy who never knew the world beyond this nameless village. The famine finally took Tattler's family as its victim, and they were helpless to stop it.

Tattler loved her dear brother. She had shared a decade's worth of memories with him, and now, he had simply stopped breathing. He had gone, without saying goodbye. She knew what death was, what it meant, but she was not prepared to deal with it. Nothing made sense, not to an overwhelmed child, except seeking a place to hide.

When Tattler was certain her grieving mother couldn't see, she snuck out of the house. Her surroundings were hazy as she stepped outside, and Tattler was afraid. The vengeful ghosts from the stories the children in her village liked to tell added a thumping fear to her chest, but she walked anyway. Tattler walked and walked, with no destination in mind, allowing her feet full control, the brown dirt road parched beneath them.

Finally, she came to a stop, in front of the imposing strychnine tree. The tree was rumoured to be older than the village chief, its trunk thick and daunting. Its existence was like a marker, informing Tattler that she made it to the communal house.

Tattler tilted her head back, admiring the terracotta and curved roof, the majestic dragon carved in the centre, its front nails flanking the sun. The village used to hold special gatherings here, but no one came as of late; much of the village had passed away from starvation. Celebrations, happiness—they were all in the past now. Tattler felt hot tears prickling, and instinctively, she clasped her hands together in prayer.

Dragon Lord, please cease your roaring fire and grant us one drop of rain, she pleaded.

There was no answer from the divine. Suddenly, Tattler felt extremely tired; her legs collapsed, folding inwards. She sat with her hands tucked underneath her bottom and her back against the tangled roots of the old tree. Not the most comfortable place, but a place to lean on all the same.

The air felt so still—half the people she knew had passed away, and the rest hadn't yet woken up. Even the growling of her stomach no longer sounded as loud, and the excessive crying of the local infants had already faded. Tattler was ready to close her eyes, to revel in the complete silence of her own company, when her tiny fingers brushed something dry and brittle. The light brown seeds of the strychnine tree. She looked up to its layers of leaves, the many different shades of green, swallowing her saliva at the bright orange clusters of fruit hanging on the branches. Their bodies, as small as longans, seemed so juicy and inviting. Tattler wanted to climb the trunk, to stretch her scrawny arm towards the food. But she knew the legend of the poisonous plant, the warning from the elders to stay away from it. Fatal toxin, they called it, but Tattler couldn't agree. How fatal could it be, really, when half her village had already died from hunger?

Still, Tattler didn't tempt fate, not when it had proven to be so fragile, fickle. She stood up and headed towards home, trying to forget the image of the succulent fruit.

She reached the narrow alleyway—a shortcut leading to her parents' humble house—before she could finish counting to ten; her body was desperate to escape the putrid air, dense with the scent of dead bodies. Once she successfully left the smell behind, her stomach growled even louder than before; the unplanned sprint took more energy than she could afford. She tasted her bitter hunger, as more saliva gathered in the corners of her mouth. Tattler licked her lips, dreaming of the diluted congee that her mother used to make. It had been nothing more than a saturated concoction, mixed from ten parts water and a half part rice, and it tasted so bland. That day, however, she thought of the food that she used to hate with a desperate yearning.

Mother, I'm home.

Tattler called to an empty space; her father had lost the ability to acknowledge movements around him—the alcohol was destroying his organs. When her mother finally appeared, her face was smeared with sweat and tears, her eyes puffy and her voice hoarse.

Your brother . . .

She couldn't finish the announcement.

I know.

They weren't able to say much else; a strange vehicle stopped outside of their dilapidated house, interrupting their shared grief. In that moment, the ache somehow doubled across her mother's face. She handed Tattler's baby sister over, rushing outside, both knees scraping the rough ground.

Grant me some mercy, Madame, please. Give me another week, please.

Her mother cried and pleaded, her body a pitiful clump at the strange woman's feet. The tears on her weathered face had yet to dry from the loss of her firstborn, but life gave her no rest.

From inside, Tattler winced, feeling a jab in the middle of her heart as she witnessed her brave, hardworking, kind-hearted mother at her lowest—on her knees with calloused palms rubbing, words lost to her wailing. Meanwhile, that strange woman stood proudly, wearing an alluring black aodai, the extravagant outfit Tattler heard about so many times before. An outfit for the rich people who lived in the city.

Stop it this instant, the woman snarled. *I have given you enough time. There is a limit to my generosity. Either you pay the ground rent now, or proceed with what we agreed upon last month.*

The mention of money stifled her mother's sobs. Slowly, she got to her feet, walking back inside with her shoulders drooped. Defeated.

Come.

She waved Tattler over, her face deformed, eyes black with penitence.

Obediently, Tattler moved.

Did I do something wrong? Tattler asked as her mother cried louder.

You are going on a trip. Her mother smiled; perhaps she was trying to ease her own guilt. *The lady standing out there is Madame Nhu. You are going to live with her.*

Tattler couldn't find a response, her mouth hanging agape as she tried to dissect her mother's words. She didn't understand, her ears hot with terror, her mind frantic with concern.

You needn't worry, her mother continued, pretending she didn't see the shock written plainly across her daughter's small face. *You will no longer be hungry or in pain. You hear me? You will have a great, great life.*

Before Tattler could protest, she felt her mother's scrawny hand from behind, nudging her towards the other side. A different world, a different life.

Tattler walked in a daze, coming to a stop in front of her new master's fancy car. Its coat was shiny and black, its headlights round and as bright as the stars Tattler sometimes spotted in the infinite night sky. The vehicle looked so similar to a horse carriage, but instead of a horse, it was driven by an old man. Next to him, Madame Nhu leaned against the car door, looking bored and out of place. Her neck was heavy with gold chains, her wrists jiggling with multiple bracelets, her skin smooth and pale. On her red lips, she wore a cold smile, like a crescent moon covered in dark blood. She barely glanced in Tattler's direction, shrugging noncommittally.

This will have to do.

That was the first time—but far from the last—that Tattler was referred to as an object. A *this*, not a person. Her existence, her worth, equivalent to the fish and meat being sold at the local market.

Come.

Madame Nhu gestured towards the interior of the luxurious car. The same word her mother said a few minutes ago, but it sounded so foreign coming from the powerful woman. Icy, distant.

Tattler faltered, wanting to run in the opposite direction—but in the end, she followed her new mistress's command. Perhaps even as a child, Tattler understood that people like herself and her mother hadn't any choices, only orders to obey.

Inside Madame Nhu's magnificent vehicle, Tattler pulled her knees to her chest, trying to hide on the black rubber floor. From the corner of her eyes, she saw Madame Nhu on her plush leather seat, mouth twitching in disgust, worrying that Tattler would spoil her precious car with mud and fleas.

When she first felt the wheels moving, Tattler turned her head to look at her mother for the last time through the car's rear windscreen. She couldn't see her mother anywhere, and Tattler started to cry. The last things Tattler saw from her life as her mother's daughter were the imprints of the tires, taking her away from all she had ever known.

"Wake up."

Now, Tattler woke to a dull ache in her lower back. Slowly, she blinked. It was Monsieur Edmond, looming over her. He gestured for her to sit up before squatting down on his heels, facing her. He stroked her round chin with his fingers; the sharp nail on his thumb left a long scratch on her skin, but she didn't wince. Monsieur Edmond considered Tattler and smiled, but his expression was unkind. His breath was already sour with wine, and Tattler bit the inside of her left cheek so she wouldn't scrunch her nose.

"I trust you've had a good sleep. Now, let us have some fun."

Tattler's heart plummeted. Just as she had all those years ago, driven away from home for the last time—Tattler felt afraid.

Edmond

Edmond stood at the door to his bedroom, his arms covering his chest; the dirty, wrinkled suit from the previous night had been replaced by a white linen outfit. His hair no longer resembled a bird's nest after a horrendous storm; now it was clean and slightly damp from his bath. He smelled of fresh soap and fresh clothes, the putrid scent of his vomit, gone.

He supposed he looked much more presentable, though in truth he didn't think it mattered. This was a façade he presented to the world. Who he really was, he no longer knew. He had spent so long running from his demons, Edmond had lost himself.

He counted on his fingers, estimating the days of work he had missed ever since his return to Cochinchina. It was adorable, really, to refer to the little, insignificant things that sometimes required his attention as work.

Unlike the Caos' opium empire and the Khảis' rubber plantation, the Moutets' definition of business seemed rather embarrassing. They didn't build anything with their own hands; their whole livelihoods relied on his father's skin colour. Whilst the Caos, the Khảis, and even Phong's father fought hard for every centimetre of the ground they possessed, the Moutets had everything handed to them. Edmond hardly ever attended meetings, or handled disagreements between workers; his only job was to acquire land, then sell it for triple the price, or rent it to the middle-class Annamites who had enough money for a small farm.

Had it really been that easy for Edmond? Was it true, what his mother had claimed? Was he actually superior to them all?

Edmond thought back to the winter when he was ten, when his mother first came to this colony. His father had refused to send

Edmond back to Paris that year. After a few disagreements, it was settled: she would come during the colder months when the air was less polluted. *Fewer people in the streets.*

Her presence was kept a secret—in his mother's eyes, the trip was a smear of shame to the aristocratic name of Adeline Moutet.

When she arrived, before her feet even touched the ground, she had gingerly announced that five of her suitcases were full of money for an aircraft.

That stupid emperor. I ought to show him that his royal blood could never compare to the French, Adeline declared flatly.

Back then, the only person who had access to an aircraft was Bảo Khánh, the emperor of Annam, father to the future king, Bảo Nam. Edmond couldn't understand it, his mother's determination; he was far too young. The outrageous purchase was a way for Adeline to show she had more resources than the royal family could ever dream of. And that was true. Mother snapped her fingers, and the next day Edmond was taken to see the vehicle—a two-seat, two-propeller aircraft, worth roughly four million piastre, the equivalent of twenty kilograms' worth of gold.

They took the aeroplane to the hunting ground, where their family came to meet the emperor. The valet was sweating in one of the seats, trained to fly a plane only once before. His mother wasn't anxious, however; she held Edmond in her lap, playing with his soft blonde hair. Somewhere down below, his father was taken to the meeting by a small car.

The flight didn't take long, and Edmond was on his feet before he knew it.

This way. His father appeared a bit later, beckoning for Edmond to follow with a cold voice.

Obediently, Edmond trailed his father's footsteps, looking up to see the emperor coming from the opposite direction. He walked leisurely, dressed in the typical hunting attire that both Edmond and his father were wearing—black rubber boots that reached their knees, creamy beige corduroy suits and duck caps with folded ear flaps in khaki. An ensemble of brave men, well-equipped to slaughter some ducks.

His mother, though, strolled silently behind, looking out of place. She graced the men with her presence in a trendy black pencil skirt, silk burgundy blouse, and a caramel velvet opera coat. The weather was bitterly cold, and that made Edmond's mother seem even more ethereal—her cheeks flushed pink, her lips a bright shade of red. A true beauty.

There were some shooting hounds running towards the wood to collect the injured ducks, polite laughing from the emperor, and some intricate political agendas Edmond was too young to comprehend. Overall, the whole trip was unremarkable, and Edmond knew he wouldn't have remembered any of it, had it not been for his mother's reaction after they parted ways with the emperor, who had accidentally brushed his mother's index finger on his way towards his car, leaving her utterly speechless.

In the plane, on their way back to the mansion, his mother shrieked, demonic and deafening, rubbing the skin on her left hand profusely. Edmond was petrified, staring at the red and purple bruise his mother was inflicting upon her own body. When they reached the black iron gate to their house, he rushed after her, following her to the bathroom, standing in the corner as his mother heaved over the toilet bowl. Had his mother been poisoned by the emperor's quick touch? Edmond was confused.

Stay away from those rats! They're not your friends.

His mother turned to him and sneered. In that instant, she no longer looked like the beauty from earlier, tears rolling down her cheeks, smearing her powdered face, blurring her features. A line of snot dripped from her flared nostrils, a string of bile escaping the corner of her red painted mouth.

Edmond didn't know what to think, witnessing his mother's hatred. He felt strangely protective of her, the woman who had mostly been absent from his life. Anything to keep her happy, to keep her close, right next to him. Edmond wanted to hug his mother tightly, to ease the pain she carried, but staying away from his friends? Edmond was perplexed.

What have they ever done to you? Edmond wanted to ask his mother, but the words refused to come.

Later that night, Edmond sat with his legs crossed on top of his bed, considering his dilemma. He thought of his friends, the only friends he'd made in this foreign land, the few who took him in and accepted him like one of their own—Duy with his teasing eyes and quick wit, Minh with his stubbornness and strength, and Phong. Everything about Phong. Together, the three of them showed Edmond a life outside of the enclosed bubble he had been living in prior to moving here. How could Edmond ever leave them?

But then the images of his mother came rushing in, making Edmond wince. He shut his eyes and scrunched his nose, clasping his hands together, begging them to go away. He was so young, a confused child. No one would get it, not even Marianne. This left Edmond only one choice, and he moved towards his window, looking out at the navy, starry night.

Help me. Please, make Mother like my friends, Edmond said aloud, trying to negotiate with an imaginary deity. *I'll do anything.*

Give one up. Don't be greedy. You can't have them all. The deity replied, Edmond pretending that his offer was considered.

Minh, Edmond replied, an answer with no hesitation. He gasped, his heart banging against the wall of his chest. He didn't really mean it, did he? How could he? Minh was one of his best friends.

For the next few nights, Edmond couldn't sleep, worrying that the second he closed his eyes, some external force would arrive and take Minh away, all because of him and his stupid wish.

Of course, now Edmond knew. No one had been listening—no one had harmed Minh. He was still scared of his rapid resolution, though. Would he really sacrifice Minh, just to ease his own suffering? And why was Minh the first person he picked?

Edmond shuddered; he'd been asking himself this question for as long as he could remember. His throat suddenly itched—his body's signal. It wanted wine, wanted salvation. Edmond hoped the alcohol would be sterile enough to cleanse his vile memories.

Gently, Edmond moved inside, closing the door, sealing his bedroom shut from the outside world. Earlier, before sunrise, he allowed one housemaid to enter and clean his vomit from the day before. The girl walked in, with a bucket of water in one hand and a damp towel in the other, pretending to not see the human lump at the foot of Edmond's bed. She kneeled next to the reeking puddle, scrubbing the floor with intense focus, not daring to utter a single question about the hairless creature her master was keeping. Seeing this, Edmond scoffed. How heartless people could be when their own lives were on the line.

The space smelled much better than before, fresher and brighter with daylight streaming through glass windows. Edmond ignored the bowl of fruit that Marianne had prepared, leaving it untouched in the middle of his writing desk. His favourites, oranges and bananas, now only a faint memory on his tongue. He drank so much he forgot to eat. The way Edmond walked these days almost felt weightless.

He stared at his precious tan leather trunks, two of which were now empty. Reaching inside for a bottle, Edmond's grip tightened. The alluring red fluid, his favourite sight. His saviour.

Edmond ignored the cupboard behind his back, full of fine crystal glasses. He saw no point; it was faster this way. He tilted his head back, his throat welcoming the burn. His eyes closed, relaxing.

Gulp after gulp, Edmond consumed the wine like water. Before he knew it, he had already emptied three bottles. Edmond knew what would follow, but he couldn't stop.

His alter ego—a different Edmond, changed by wine. Subtly, his composure shifted. Edmond stood a little taller.

Finally, he eyed the young maid, still sleeping on the ground with her brows knitted together in fright and confusion. She no longer resembled a woman; her short hair reminded Edmond of the boys Marianne sometimes hired to polish his leather shoes.

He didn't understand at first, why she chose to stay. When Edmond first woke, he had expected to find the room empty. He was stunned, astonished, really, seeing the maid's tight grip around the foot of his bed, refusing to let go. It seemed useless, his warning last night. Either she didn't believe it, or she didn't care. She must have thought Edmond would give her everything—title, security, wealth—after she passed her tests. She must have thought it would be worth it, the dignity she sacrificed for a *better* life. "Foolish creature," Edmond hissed. She knew nothing of this material world, yet she romanticized and desired it anyway.

Using his left foot, Edmond nudged the maid's back.

"Wake up," he commanded.

She stirred and sat up; her eyes clouded with fearful reservation as he sat on his heels, his thumb fondling her round chin, announcing her next lesson. She watched in silence as Edmond pulled out two more bottles of wine; both had been previously uncorked by a servant.

"You see," Edmond began. "In *civilised* culture, you need to learn how to drink. I presume you've never tried wine. Yes?"

"No, Monsieur. I have never." She dipped her head.

"Cheers, then." He handed her a bottle, clanking his against hers. This time, Edmond didn't tilt his head back, waiting for the maid to swallow her drink. How strong her determination was, he wanted to see.

It seemed the maid understood Edmond's intention because she didn't even hesitate.

She drank.

Edmond laughed, his eyes widening with surprise and excitement. He didn't expect such high spirits from a maid who had just yesterday cried senselessly over her hair. His amusement didn't last long, though—she couldn't keep the liquid down. In mere seconds, the maid folded over, dry heaving onto the shiny white marble floor. Miserably, she glanced up at Edmond, a string of saliva drooping from the corner of her mouth.

Edmond was startled. How similar the girl now looked to his mother, all those years ago.

"I beg your pardon, Monsieur," she panted. "I couldn't do it. Please, forgive me."

She was still begging and apologising, but Edmond could no longer hear. He was drawn to her, shortening the gap between them. *Stop it*, he commanded himself, but his body refused the order. His right hand lifted, the blow hot as coals against her already burning cheek.

Then, he grabbed the back of her tunic collar, pressing her face just inches from the surface of her own vomit, the same way his mother held his head over the toilet bowl. How similar, the burgundy puddle and his mother's lipstick.

"Eat it."

Edmond did not recognise his own voice.

"Monsieur, please," the maid begged, sobbing now. "What have I ever done to you?"

He couldn't answer. How could he tell her that the only thing she had ever done was remind him of the person he was?

"Eat."

He repeated with his eyes closed as though he had been hypnotised, controlled by some evil force.

"I can't," she cried again, her voice louder, but Edmond had already stopped listening.

"You are nothing," he roared. "You are nobody. The lot of you, crowding this already scarce land without contributing anything worthy. Why don't you do us all a favour and disappear?"

"Please forgive me, Monsieur. I was wrong. I get it now. I know my place. Please."

The maid was frantic, clutching her hands in front of her chest, praying for Edmond's mercy. Perhaps the sound was deafening enough. Perhaps his alter ego decided to flee. He didn't know the reason, only that he suddenly became himself again, a man who ran an endless circle. A loop of guilt and shame Edmond didn't want to confront.

He thought then of the person he loved most. How simple and effortless it would be, to succumb to that feeling. He never wanted this battle, never wanted to fight his heart. Edmond blinked: the young maid was no longer herself but instead was a product of his imagination. Edmond could no longer think straight. The love of his life was standing in front of him, condemning his ruthless actions.

You can't hurt others to numb your suffering.

Edmond blinked again. He didn't have the courage to respond as Phong's phantom vanished. The words lingered, beating against the walls of Edmond's skull.

You can't hurt others to numb your suffering.
You can't hurt others to numb your suffering.
You can't hurt others to numb your suffering.
You can't hurt others to numb your suffering.

Edmond was pleading, *Stop it. Please*, but the voice persisted. He couldn't hear anything else.

His body no longer felt like his own, borrowed, possessed. He lunged for the pair of scissors Marianne had given him. He wanted to sever the tie between him and his demons: holding the blade with one hand, Edmond started slicing his other arm, watching his skin flay open as his veins ruptured. The maid opened her mouth, perhaps to scream, but there was no sound. His white shirt stuck to his skin, drenched in a violent shade of rouge, the floor under his feet a pool of crimson blood, yet he felt no physical pain.

The last thing he saw before he finally collapsed was the horrified look on Marianne's face as she rushed inside. She said something that he could not decipher—a reflex, as Edmond let the pair of scissors go.

You can't hurt others to numb your suffering.
You can't hurt others to numb your suffering.
You can't—

Phong's voice continued until Edmond's world turned black.

Marianne

A scream, followed by a wail.

The housemaids were running across the room in distress; their fingers curled tightly around piles of blood-stained linen cloth. Their mistress was bleeding far too much. Marianne remained by the pale blue canopy bed, where she offered Adeline a hand to hold and squeeze. She looked down at her friend's pallid face, splotchy with beads of sweat, feeling her own heart clench.

How delighted Adeline was, the pleasant spring day when she realised she was pregnant. How she cherished the child growing inside of her. Marianne remembered this, as Adeline let out another scream and turned to face her.

Get this thing *out of me!*

The birth, until that moment, had been a gut-wrenching forty-eight-hour journey. The doctor decided to perform an emergency delivery when it became apparent that the baby couldn't breathe. There would not be any anaesthesia, Adeline was adamant, and so Marianne stood watching as her best friend's belly was sliced in half, blood gushing out. Adeline panted, crying and screaming before withering to a pulsing lump on the now crimson bed. After, when the most brutal part had passed, Adeline was too traumatised, only glaring at the slippery infant in Marianne's arms, shaking her head when Marianne asked if she wanted to hold the child.

It killed me, Adeline said one morning, a few weeks after. *And now, whatever is left, it keeps on taking.*

Slowly, Adeline turned her head, looking, for the first time, at the boy's wrinkly face, still slightly purple from the complicated birth. She wept. The milk in her chest refused to come.

Later, as Edmond grew up, Marianne knew that Adeline had changed. She was convinced that the birth of her son had been cursed by *that oriental voodoo from those strange women*, who stared at Adeline's foreign beauty the one time she visited China. On brighter moments, Adeline spent time with Edmond, always warning him of *those people's savagery*. Most days, though, she burned hot with seething hatred towards her husband, then her son. What she would have done to that small, defenceless child— Marianne didn't want to entertain such a thought.

The months and years after he was born bonded Marianne to Edmond. She vowed to keep him safe—even if it meant taking him away from his own mother. Perhaps the gods truly listened because not long after, Leon and Adeline's marriage reached its imminent expiry, and Marianne was relieved. Her chance had come.

Look at you! Adeline sneered that final night, her finger pointing directly at the bags under Leon's eyes. They had been arguing again—Adeline had decided Leon should stay home, instead of accompanying her to a charity gala. *You look disgusting. You would be nothing without my family's money.*

She had blazed out the front door, her orange gown seductive, her signature red lipstick bright and bold. Adeline wanted to spend time with her younger lover, Marianne knew, an open secret Leon had caught onto.

Later that night, Leon knocked on Marianne's door, his hair ruffled, his face purple with chagrin. *I'm leaving for Cochinchina, and I'm taking Edmond with me. You should come. Edmond will need a nanny.*

Marianne was devastated—she knew Adeline needed help, *her* help, but the innocent boy needed her more. So without any hesitation, Marianne nodded. She packed all her personal belongings in under an hour.

The journey across the continents to the foreign colony, her effort at filling the vacant space Edmond's parents had created: Marianne could see it all as she stood breathless in front of the pool of Edmond's blood. She felt pain running down her own limbs, as though it had been her own arm that Edmond had slashed.

For what felt like a very long time, Marianne couldn't move. Her icy blonde hair was bunched together in a low bun, tight enough to make her temples ache. Her white dress was ankle-length, pristine and free from wrinkles. Her oxford shoes matched Edmond's in their shine, their laces fastened into two orderly bows. Marianne's appearance was neat and tidy, but she was beaten, exhausted. Her body felt heavy with the secrets that she kept, and now, on top of them: the guilt.

When it finally seemed she could no longer bear the sight, Marianne summoned her stern, rational voice, calling out in the corridor to no one in particular. It didn't matter; the servants all listened to her.

"Get me the valet this instant! And bring the first aid kit!"

A few seconds later, the old valet appeared by the bedroom's door.

"Good Lord! What happened?"

"Don't." Marianne shook her head. "Don't ask any questions. Help him. Please."

"Of course." The valet regained his composure almost immediately, already rolling his sleeves whilst making his way towards Edmond, giving Marianne the space she needed.

With shaky hands, she untied the towel around the belt loop of her dress and dropped to her knees, cleaning Edmond's blood. The least she could do. Her stomach churned, but she didn't hesitate. She let the towel submerge in the liquid and started cleaning. Her shoulders rose and fell as she breathed through her mouth;

Marianne refused to take in the scent of Edmond's pain. She scrubbed and scrubbed, as though she had been hypnotised, ignoring the whimpering girl that sat in a slump in the corner. Inside her ears, a violent buzzing, but Marianne kept going. What other choice did she have, really? Had she stopped and attempted to calm her nerves, she knew she would have cried. She couldn't even look at Edmond, now lying on his bed, his mangled arm wrapped clumsily in gauze. A stranger Marianne barely recognized.

She panted until the floor was clean, though Marianne was certain that if she ever dared to press her nostrils close, she would have been able to detect the nauseating copper scent all the same. Some things simply refused to perish.

Marianne turned to the young girl in the corner, stunned by her spiky hair. Did Edmond do that? Suddenly, she was frightened. The girl only lowered her head, avoiding Marianne's gaze. Her blue tunic was badly wrinkled, and she smelled of vomit and fear.

"Follow me," Marianne said curtly, walking out of Edmond's room. She gestured for the old valet to go ahead, then locked the door from the outside when she was certain that he was out of sight. The brass key felt heavy in the front pocket of her dress.

"Ignore his orders," she said to the few servants who passed her in the corridor. "I will take responsibility. Under no circumstances should any of you open this door. The young master needs his rest, and he needs to be alone."

"Yes, Madame."

Marianne was no madame, but the servants didn't know that. They feared her the same way they feared Edmond and Leon, and she let them. Their fear pulled her closer to Edmond, somehow, like she really was his mother.

The young maids were dusting the photos and the flower vases in the hall—their mumbles vanished once they saw Marianne coming. On a regular day, Marianne would stop to examine the quality of their work. Her index finger would trail the shape of a straight line over each surface as she checked for remnants of dust. But she hadn't the time today. She was tangled in her own guilt—how she resembled Edmond's mother, the woman who neglected him.

She jogged past two flights of stairs, down to the basement where the servants' quarter was. She stomped against the marble steps, hoping the sound was loud enough to scare her painful thoughts away.

They came anyway.

It's your mother's teaching, isn't it? She imagined asking Edmond. A redemption, as though a useless question could help Edmond now. But what else could she do? Edmond was stubborn, and he never came to her for advice. It was natural, her reluctance. But she supposed that was her first failure.

And then, the second. The alcohol. She knew this, too, but she hadn't done a thing about it.

Oh, how the alcohol changed him. Whenever Edmond drank, he became a different person, one that even scared Marianne sometimes. *How much did Edmond hate himself,* Marianne wondered, *to keep drinking like this, to voluntarily become this other person, so spiteful and cruel?*

Marianne pointed at the wooden door to the servants' washroom, the quiet maid still trailing behind.

"Go in there and clean yourself up."

"Yes, Madame," she answered, her voice hoarse.

Marianne slumped onto a creaky, wobbly chair, drained and empty.

Looking down at her trembling hands, Marianne noticed a dry streak of blood on the tip of her index finger. Undoubtedly

Edmond's. Her heart sank. She closed her eyes and tried to peel it off.

She started picking at the surface, working her way down around her nail bed. Marianne did not stop until her cuticles bloated red.

That is disgusting! Marianne, stop it this instant!

Her mother's booming voice. She had always scolded Marianne whenever she caught her daughter in the act of picking her nails. *Unladylike*, she exclaimed, and now Marianne realised that she always heard the scowl whenever she felt like a failure.

She had failed Edmond; she couldn't deny it any longer.

The door creaked as the maid re-emerged from the washroom, startling Marianne.

Like a terrified, badly wounded animal, the young girl stood with her toes curled inwards, asking for protection, her fingers tensing around the edge of her tunic. She dipped her head and kept it there, not daring to look up. The sight unsettled Marianne—she didn't know what to do. She had never been in this position before. She thought it was wise to prolong her silence, reaching for the small purple wallet she kept in the square pocket of her dress, pulling out a few crinkly notes. It wasn't much, what she was about to offer, but it was something.

She was ashamed of what Edmond had done to the girl, and the act of throwing the money in the maid's direction seemed utterly barbaric. She breathed out, calling the maid over. Folding the money into one neat pile, Marianne placed it in the young girl's hand.

"Leave. Forget all about this."

Marianne wasn't a woman of faith, but here she sat, attempting to atone for Edmond's sins.

"I'll stay, Madame," the girl replied much too soon, leaving the cash on the table next to Marianne.

Marianne wondered if she misheard the words; her Vietnamese wasn't excellent, and the girl's dialect wasn't easy to decipher. She stared at the maid, whose lips already merged into a straight line, determined.

"What are you talking about?" Marianne finally managed.

"Please, let me stay here and serve you. I have nowhere else to go. I have followed Monsieur Edmond here, my old master wouldn't dare take me back. And out there . . ."

Out there was far worse than anything Edmond could have done—words that the maid needn't say aloud. She had no home to return to. No shelter to seek. To a young, poor woman with no family, the freedom Marianne offered wasn't an escape, but a punishment.

It was familiar, the loneliness Marianne heard in the young maid's voice. Her stern façade faltered, and she heard herself agreeing.

"Stay here, then."

Phong

Phong studied the world outside the car window.

It was still early, but the streets were already bustling. The people who worked at the cafes and the Chinese tea houses nodded at one another, crowding the sidewalk with stools, chairs, and tables. What they were saying, Phong couldn't tell, but they looked happy and content. *How are the kids*, Phong imagined the conversations between two workers. *Good, good.* A laugh, a pat on the back. *I have to go now.* An urgency to attend to the little stall, before the owner noticed. Hastily, Phong lowered the window—he wanted more mundane conversations; the barrier that separated him from a world that wasn't his shrunk to half its actual height.

The smell of rich bone broth filled the car, boiling inside tall, crusty inox pots, warming his nostrils. Phong could picture plump pork hocks and chicken frames floating with charred ginger and onions, the remnants of flesh fragrant with fish sauce, salt, and pepper. He ordered the valet to stop the car, turning his head in the tea houses' direction, staring from a distance at the white bowls, filled to the brim with equally white noodles, thin slices of fish and chicken, vibrant green onions, and fresh cilantro. He wasn't hungry, but the line of cheap food made the corner of his lips damp; he failed to remember the last time he ate such a humble, comforting dish.

"One fish noodle soup," said a short man, his right hand raised to capture the waiter's attention. Phong watched from the car with fascination, a peek into a life he would never lead. The man wore a white shirt, slightly torn, with an open collar, his balding head hidden by a beige trilby hat, his ashen feet barely visible beneath the legs of his trousers, which were far too long.

The small tea house was already at full capacity. The builders and plumbers from the construction sites nearby had arrived, searching for something quick and cheap to fill their stomachs.

"Waiter! One pate chaud and one soux cream!" Phong heard another man calling, the butchered pronunciation raspy in his throat. An Annamite gentleman trying to adapt to the French palate.

"Never mind, go on," Phong called to the driver, this time rolling his window up.

As his world returned to its usual silence, Phong couldn't keep his mind from wandering. He thought of his twenty-first birthday, his mother's death anniversary, the one and only time his family—his cold-hearted father and the six women he had remarried—sat down for lunch. In the middle of the table, there were two dishes full of pate chaud, and Phong was childishly giddy. Across from him, his father must have seen the hunger inside Phong's eyes because he was stern with his order.

No Western food! Damn it! He exclaimed loudly as his two fists banged against the timber tabletop. *Throw that shit away!*

His late mother never had the chance to indulge in foreign treats—as the people left behind, Phong's family were only allowed the food that Madame Lê had liked. His mother's body had long been surrendered to dirt and time, yet it still felt as though she'd never left the Lês' mansion. The meal quickly concluded with boiled eggs and rice.

Later that day, as Phong sulked in his bedroom the same way he did every year on his birthday, his father sent the butler with an order.

Monsieur Lê requests your presence in the study room, Monsieur.

Phong waved for the butler to leave, then lingered at his own door, unsure whether he should follow. He had seen the look on

173

his father's face during lunch, certain that the old man was drunk. His father would never ask to see Phong otherwise.

When he first entered the study, Phong was overwhelmed. As he initially expected, his father had soaked himself in whiskey, though Phong hadn't anticipated the presence of pipe tobacco, too. The space was foggy, like an early winter morning, and perhaps this was the reason behind his father's summon. Under the veil of vapour, the son he despised no longer looked so real.

Phong sat in front of his old man, silent as he stared at the hand-carved wooden smoking pipe; the left corner of his lips fluttered with a faint smirk. It amused Phong, his father's blatant hypocrisy. His father was proud of his traditional values—the way he dressed, the furniture he purchased—yet there he sat, refusing the rustic bamboo pipe customarily used for smoking, consuming tobacco from a more expensive device instead. Conservative or not, it seemed to Phong that his father only adapted what felt convenient.

Here. His father said suddenly, offering Phong a smoke.

Stunned, Phong didn't blink, hesitating before taking the pipe in his hands. He inhaled deeply, allowing himself a second of instant relief; the vapour temporarily filled the vast space that sat between father and son. After an uncomfortable silence that aged him like a decade, Phong breathed out.

What did you want to talk to me about, Father?

His father didn't respond immediately, his eyes lost under the hazy mist. His gaze had been so fierce and focused, Phong shuddered when he pictured the soul of his dead mother hovering behind his straight spine, her face half consumed by bugs and worms, the other half human and full of condemnation.

At last, his father cleared his throat, his words jumbling at the tip of his tongue.

You know, those women . . .

His sentence was interrupted by a coughing fit, murky drop-lets of his saliva landing on the surface of his otherwise immaculate table.

Phong watched the scene with no concern; coldly, his hand moved towards the crystal jug of water on his far left, pouring the smooth liquid into a glass. He pushed it in front of his father, then leaned back in his chair. Amidst the chaos, Phong considered his father's face. The man had gotten old, his small body more shrunken than ever. The thin brocade shirt in austere black dark-ened his father's expression; his square jaw seemed even sharper without fat and flesh hugging the bones.

After the coughing stopped, his father pushed the glass aside, reaching instead for his flask of liquor.

For a very long time, the unbearable silence continued; the only sound inside the inky study came from the two men's soft breaths, then from his father's bony fingers rummaging through the envelopes and files in the top drawer of his pedestal writing desk. His father refused to continue his half-told story—at least not until he found what he had been searching for. An old photograph of Phong's late mother. When he finally spotted it, hidden carefully under multiple layers of mail, he slid it across the desk, allowing Phong a glimpse. His mother's short life, her essence, reduced to a small square portrait in black and white, with dirty, yellow edges.

Phong leaned forward; his late mother's face hypnotised him, the mystery of who she once was drawing him close. He reached for the picture, holding it tightly in his right hand, a picture he'd never seen before. His mother was young, eyes squinting in the middle of a jovial laugh.

Those women I remarried, his father resumed, *they look like her, do they not?* His tone was flat and firm, a fact rather than a theory.

I chose them, he said quickly. *Because in a way, they help me keep your mother alive.*

Phong hadn't a clue what to say in response to such a jarring confession, so he pressed his mouth shut. He fell again to the back of his chair, letting the wooden panel groan as it absorbed his weight. He tried to recount the miserable lunch earlier, realising that he, too, had always sensed a faint familiarity when he looked at them. So faint, Phong hadn't been able to put a finger on it.

The familiarity came from the women's distinctive features. If Phong closed one of his eyes when he glanced their way, he would have seen his late mother's upturned nose on his father's second wife, his mother's slender neck on the third, his mother's hairstyle on the fourth . . .

So that was the real reason his father continually remarried. It wasn't because of love or loneliness; he was expanding his collection of women who resembled the one he adored.

Phong let out a muffled sigh thinking of his father's grief and his strange, cruel attempt at preserving the past.

I suppose you have heard the rumours, his father said levelly, disregarding Phong's discomfort when confronted with gossip of his father's impotence, how he hadn't been able to produce another son or daughter. *I assure you, I am not a man without compassion. Boys and girls, they are all secured good livelihoods at the Khải' plantation.*

A confession Phong hadn't anticipated. He didn't know what to feel, how he should have reacted. In that instant, Phong could only imagine the blank faces of the stepsiblings he never met, never even knew about prior to this conversation. How devastatingly similar their fates had been to that of their mothers—ghosts, denied of their titles.

Why, Father? Phong asked, the question biting.

They are not your mother's children.

176

His father replied, again, almost too quickly, too truthfully. Phong knew he carried no regrets.

Now, in the back seat of the car, Phong scoffed at his own hypocrisy as the memory dissipated. Three years had passed, and not once had Phong been able to gather the bravery to ask Minh about his stepsiblings, now living and working on the Khảis' plantation. The last, flimsy chance Phong had at a family.

"Monsieur, we have arrived."

The valet spoke loudly, oblivious to Phong's desperate yearning.

He nodded his acknowledgement. The old driver's arm was gesturing towards the façade of Le Grand Hotel. It was a three-story building, its height average, its land imposing. There were ornate balconies in the front, with small baskets of pink and red flowers hanging firmly from black iron rails. Poetic and whimsical. The staircase led to the entrance, where a butler awaited, the walls, all drenched in blinding white paint, the carpet a bold maroon— its vivid colour accentuated the succulent green of the carefully pruned bushes. Phong counted five decorative chimneys, scattered along the edge of the bright yellow roof, a textbook display of French architecture within Annam. Briefly, he wondered how much effort it required to maintain something so useless—before laughing at himself. He was wearing an Italian suit when a plain, cheap tunic would do.

Phong wasn't in a rush. After all, Duy wasn't a stranger to his tardiness. He spared another moment, taking in his surroundings. The sidewalk in front of Le Grand Hotel was free of the working class, the grey cement a resting place for two stone guardian lion statues. Their eyes were sharp, their mouths half-open, striking.

The establishment was positioned at the junction of Grande Rue and Avenue Hugo. Before the French arrived, these streets had worn the names of the heroes of his country—those who defended the nation with paramount bravery—like a badge of honour. Now, since the French occupation, memories of those heroes and that golden past were wiped off the monumental street signs, like they had never existed at all.

Phong felt a wave of sweeping shame. Try as he might, he could not remember those heroes' names. Maybe he was a traitor, too. Phong no longer wore traditional costumes, and he frequented French bars and clubs more than he did the Annamites' institutions. Whilst he did not want to erase the markings of his true identity, he was determined to expunge himself from his father's traditional beliefs and values. Phong didn't want to uphold the same faith, or become the same person, as his abusive old man.

Stepping from his glossy black car, Phong shook his head; he had spared his father too many thoughts today. He looked down once more at his Italian leather shoes, whistling a soft tune of approval. Then he adjusted the cuffs of his crisp shirt and entered the upscale part of the world, through the door of Le Grand Hotel, where his people remained nameless.

Duy

Duy sat in the corner of the hotel's restaurant, his square chin resting in his palm. His eyes darted back and forth between the vacant space on the table—empty still, his hot black coffee not yet delivered—and the tan leather watch on his wrist. As each minute ticked by, his irritation grew. Phong was always late.

It was early in the morning. Early for Duy anyway—he normally didn't wake before lunchtime. This disruption of his daily routine made Duy's head throb, but he and Phong always met at this hour, rain, hail, or shine. It was strange, this ritual they had formed awhile back—a meeting, just the two of them, the day after any party or event. Minh and Edmond never understood the hatred their other two friends harboured for elite society, refusing to join, leaving Duy and Phong alone to discuss their shared eccentricity. Together, the two men would sit and entertain their tired minds by mocking the pretentious functions that they, too, had been a part of.

Duy tapped his shoes restlessly against the glossy white floor, shifting uneasily on the edge of his seat. The walnut chair was unwelcoming; the thin, flat cushion failed to mask the stiffness of the surface. They looked stunning, of course—a fine combination of nostalgic, vintage aesthetic and sleek, modern appearance—but he also knew that the hotel only chose such furniture because it was cheap. Anything to help reduce their expenses, Duy supposed.

He eyed the minute hand on his watch again, annoyed. Another five minutes had passed, and Phong was still nowhere to be seen. Duy sighed—he needed a distraction, anything to keep his mind from straying back to Master Cần's funeral. Inside his suit jacket lay the torn piece of paper from that night. Those two

179

words—*too late*—patronised Duy. An incoming typhoon, eager to obliterate.

The slender waiter in the red velvet bow tie made his way over, holding the black cup of coffee on a dark wooden tray. He gave Duy a polite, sincere smile before crouching down to place the steaming cup on the table.

"The finest coffee from Buôn Mê Thuột, Monsieur," he said, his expression one of pride.

Duy wanted to ask whether they had sent someone racing all the way back to the coffee farm to fetch the roast, for he had been waiting for at least half a year, but then decided against it. It wasn't like him to be difficult. That role had always been reserved for Edmond, and Edmond only.

Besides, he was thankful for the interruption.

The bittersweet scent of coffee filled his nostrils, waking the last of Duy's sleepy cells. He signalled for the old driver, who had been standing on guard quietly, to hand him his brown leather briefcase. Duy undid the clasp and peered inside—for a second, he was stunned by its contents, a reminder of the meeting he was to have with the governor later that day.

The governor was a short, fat man in his early seventies, with a surprisingly clean face and a nasal voice. Inside Duy's briefcase sat a rather thick envelope—the monthly payment the Caos made to have the governor turn a blind eye on all of their *activities*. Duy thought of that imminent hour-long meeting and felt his stomach clench. An entire hour of pretentious laughter, the booming sound a slap against all honesty. And the condescension—oh, how he hated that. The condescension that laced the governor's sentences as he remarked on the young king and the royalty's failures, on the outdated ideology the stupid Communists in the North still believed in and followed blindly. The stories about rebellion, too;

the governor loved to flaunt his power, to entertain himself and to threaten the Annamites like Duy. Behind the words, Duy would see the young men and women in Hà Nội, captured and tortured in prisons for fighting the new system, for trying to unite their now heavily divided nation. The gruesome scenes of suffering would be turned into entertaining anecdotes the cruel tirailleurs liked to tell during parties, pride beaming across their idiotic faces.

Duy loathed it all: the predictability of it, his contempt for this poisonous society, as well as his cowardice. And so, he hid.

He reached for the chessboard behind the white envelope. His life might have been decided for him even before he was conceived, but within the world of chess, one right move could hold a universe of possibilities. The fate of every single chess piece was his to manipulate.

Suddenly, the harsh lines disappeared from his face. Duy felt his jaw unclench, his shoulders relaxing, his chest rising and falling calmly. As he placed the chess pieces in their correct starting positions, the hatred he'd felt earlier vanished. He was in control again.

Moments like this, Duy wondered. Would he truly care for a life of freedom, without fine wine and imported whiskey, without servants to take care of his menial daily tasks? He scoffed as he stared at the hand-carved chess pieces. They were made from the most expensive materials—black lacquer, mother-of-pearl, buffalo horns and bones. Their true value was precisely the kind of extravagance Duy was always so quick to deem unnecessary. He might argue that he was different from the pretentious people around him, for he hadn't the need to flaunt his wealth. But he was one of them all the same, his indulgences something only people in his position could ever afford.

At the sound of footsteps, Duy put the pawns down. He rolled his eyes at Phong's leisurely manner, no guilt or remorse.

181

"What if I were a patient in dire need of medical attention?"

"Then that would be unfortunate, considering I don't know enough to give a proper prescription."

Phong's voice was flat and cold as water washing over rocks. They grinned at one another, greeting. Duy understood why Phong wished to remain an opium addict—it was easier to succumb to the wicked relief the substance offered, much easier than to spend his life trying to please his father, knowing nothing Phong ever did could make him proud, not even to follow in his footsteps and become a renowned chemist. But that conversation stayed neatly tucked under a pile of things they would never touch. Phong pulled out a chair and wiggled two fingers in the air, signalling for the waiter.

"Black coffee for me."

He tossed the order in the air, not caring whether the young boy heard. Phong was agitated.

"What's with you?" Duy asked after the waiter left, his eyes narrowing. "Right. When was the last time you smoked?"

"I'm fine."

Duy had heard this same statement so many times over the years, he no longer believed Phong's words. The statement that was devoid of facts, a mask Phong felt he needed to wear.

"Ed left with some maid at the party. Minh was wasted," Duy began, once again ignoring Phong's obvious discomfort. His tone was clipped, like he was reading a business report at the weekly family meeting.

"Ed left with a maid? Like a French maid?" Phong asked, surprised.

"No, a girl from Minh's estate."

The comment caught them both off guard.

It was never a secret, but rather an unspoken fact, that Edmond hated the association with anyone who wasn't French—aside from

Duy, Phong, and Minh. Even then, there had always been an imbalance of power, felt but never discussed. It was almost comical at times, for how powerful could these four men possibly be when they avoided all important conversations? What was the difference between men like them and the turtles who retreated to their sturdy shells upon sensing danger? Duy couldn't answer for the others. He supposed he couldn't really answer for himself.

Duy recalled the tantrum Edmond had once thrown after losing a game back when they were children. They were seven or eight years old, maybe a year after Edmond first arrived. In Duy's memories, it was Edmond who attempted to hit Minh, to spit at the game's setup and push Duy off his seat. Edmond's face and neck were red with shame from losing and exhaustion from screaming; the snot dripping from his nose reminded Duy of a sick donkey. Duy was teasing his friend when their parents emerged after hearing the sudden commotion. The adults surrounded them— Edmond's father said nothing, his glare, intense with blatant disapproval, on his son, who had been kicking convulsively on the ground, like a dying fish gasping for water. All the other parents, however, rushed over to Edmond, cooing over his imagined injury. In the end, Madame Mai was the first to break from the crying prince to find her own son and whisper in his ear: it was important to let Edmond win because he was *different*, and his *differences* required sensitivity and protection by his close friends. Duy nodded his agreement, though he did not understand his mother's words; he simply wanted to resume playing, to finally win—he had just discovered a rather smart strategy. He hadn't realised until much later, when his height had doubled and his mind thickened with discreet wisdom, that he would never have the chance to employ his clever tactics; Edmond's French hands were always supposed to be the fastest, no matter the circumstances.

Days passed, months folded together, and years bled to decades. They grew up side by side, yet the memories from that day always haunted Duy's mind, daring him to question whether they were close because they had no other choice. After all, it was expected that the elite families would stick together, the way bees circled a hive. He wondered if they were truly friends, in spite of Edmond's *pedantry*. He failed to catch a definite answer, no matter how hard he tried.

Duy shook his head, steering his thoughts in another direction. The coffee felt cold when it touched his tongue, but he didn't mind; he and Phong resumed their gossip quietly, and when they grew hungry, Duy ordered them a plate of pate chaud. In this establishment, the cost of the basic fried pastry doubled, compared to the cost of the pastries from the stalls just outside the door. It didn't matter, of course; money was never a problem. Phong didn't say much, silently munching on his favourite dish, and as per usual, Duy pushed the last piece in Phong's direction. He had been doing this ever since they were kids—the tendency to favour Phong, the complete trust that Phong would always have his back. They were brothers, each other's family.

He would do anything, Duy thought to himself, to ensure Phong's safety.

Hai

Warm, golden sun fought its way through the glass panel, lighting up the room. Outside the closed window, birds were chirping loudly. *Look at us and our freedom*, the animals seemed to mock. Inside, Hai wanted to scream. When she was younger, she used to believe monsters hunted only when darkness arrived. But now, the day was bright as ever, and she was not safe. Wherever she was, the door was sealed shut, the space eerily still. A wave of panic rose from the pit of her stomach—she was confused, anxious, and scared. She wasn't chained down, but Hai knew she was being held against her will; her mind was frantic with broken recollections, her lower body aching. She longed for those blissful few seconds from earlier, right after she opened her eyes. That fleeting moment of nothingness, of utter oblivion.

A while ago—Hai couldn't be precise, minutes had melted into years—a fair-haired woman with beautiful, strange blue eyes had come in and guided Hai to a seated position. She was propped against the chalky white wall with a plushy pillow behind her back. Cautiously, her eyes followed the foreign woman's movements, how she avoided Hai's gaze, how a thin strand of blonde hair trickled down the left side of her large face. Hesitantly, Hai wanted to ask where she was but thought better of it—the woman would not know her mother tongue.

The woman was already gone, and Hai was alone, left to wither by herself. Another moment passed, without any noise—did no one else live here? Her mind was slow, her energy depleted; she couldn't think clearly. Her throat was scratchy, and her stomach was grumbling violently; her limbs felt tormentingly redundant. She wanted so badly to rise to her feet and fill the gaps in her fractured memories; the thumping of her heart made a loud, begging sound. What had happened? How did she get here?

Perplexed, Hai tried to go back to the beginning—the party the night before. She closed her eyes, bringing herself back to the scene. There was an overwhelming feeling, bubbling in her stomach—so many strangers. They had all gifted her identically strained smiles, their noses like hunting hounds, sniffing her out as the outcast. Still, Hai offered them her hand the way Madame Như had taught her, her eyes crinkling as she laughed along to jokes she did not fully understand. She remembered Madame Như's cold fingers, lacing through her own, as she was introduced to the silver-haired man.

Monsieur Moutet. This is my son's good friend.

Monsieur Edmond's father, Hai thought, not noticing the subtle hint in her master's words. The brief but wicked grin across Monsieur Moutet's face, also left unseen.

Splendid! Monsieur Moutet beamed, delightful. *I have a fine bottle of wine in the back of my car. Such good and happy news—we must toast!*

He winked at Madame Như, then excused himself. When he finally returned with two full glasses of wine, Hai was reluctant. She never liked the burn at the back of her throat, but she didn't know how to decline the offer without offending the powerful man, either. She felt a slight pinch of encouragement from Madame Như on her lower back—Hai had no other choice but to relent and accept the drink.

After that, her memories turned hazy. She was guided to the smoking room; she was sure of it: there were the distinctive velvet sofas in strange yellow mustard in one corner and Madame Như's precious paintings on the wall opposite. The last fragment Hai had of the night was a walk through the candle-lit corridor.

Where . . . Hai had asked weakly, but she received no answer.

Now she was here, in a quiet, foreign room.

Hai skimmed her surroundings, hopeful for the sight of something, anything, she recognized. Hai felt suddenly jealous of the animals in the circus; their cages were obvious, with foreboding black wires, signifying their captivity. What had she here?

A chandelier.

A chandelier, made of flashy brass, with luminous decorative crystals that looked like tears, their bodies so pellucid they flickered and gleamed. Despite the morning sunshine, the many bulbs stood proudly and shone vividly. Such brightness worried Hai. She knew that she was no longer inside the Khải' residence; Madame Như would never permit such a waste during broad daylight.

The rest of the room was plain and simple. The bedside tables were left bare—no photo frames, no family portraits. Finding no useful discoveries, Hai sighed and started examining her body: she was no longer wearing the beautiful five-piece aodai with the significant meaning Madame Như had explained. She was wearing a short and thin, almost transparent nightgown, as though she was about to fall asleep in Monsieur Minh's arms. Except he wasn't here, in this foreign space. He didn't barge in, searching for her. Hai's heart fluttered with a rising panic. The realisation was sudden: she needed to escape.

Hai tumbled out of bed, frantic. Instead of landing on her two feet, though, she heard a loud thump.

She couldn't stand.

Running down her legs, now, was a spine-snapping pain that blurred Hai's eyes with tears. Her body was tense and hot with nerves, beating against flesh and bones, and her heart pulsed a frantic, terrifying rhythm. The abrupt and unexpected sensation almost made Hai whimper, but she bit back the urge and chewed the side of her cheek raw until she tasted her own blood.

As she feared, her fall was loud. Like a decaying corpse, attracting vultures. The door swung open within seconds, and the foreign woman returned, holding a stack of white cloths and a copper basin. No physicians followed.

The woman said nothing as she eyed Hai lying prone on the floor. She was a large person, the foreign lady, large enough to easily scoop Hai up in her long arms and drop her back on the plush mattress. They sat together in silence as the woman started to undress, then redress Hai's wound. Hai could see that she was bleeding; her eyes widened in disbelief at the sight of fresh blood impaling layer after layer of cloth. Her stomach churned, her muscles twitching when she saw the deep slash under the gauze, slicing across her thigh; the back of her throat was blocked by a loop of fear so large she could hardly swallow.

Hai winced, the hiss escaping through the gap between her teeth. The woman's face betrayed nothing. Her fingers were quick and her knots were precise. Knowing. She had been doing this for a long time. Hai closed her eyes for a brief second, and behind her eyelids, she saw the featureless faces of other girls wandering in her vision, girls she had never met but knew with certainty had lain in this very bed, perhaps even sat in this exact position, their legs also swaddled in thin cloth. How many, she wanted to ask, but she was too afraid.

"Madame," Hai blurted out at last, her own voice foreign, battered by hesitation and worry. "Could you please tell me where I am?"

The urge rose like a tidal wave. She needed to save herself.

The woman acted as though Hai had not spoken, her attention focused solely on cleaning the mess that oozed out of Hai's wound. The question hung heavy in the air, unanswered and now laden with the rusty scent of fresh blood.

"I wouldn't be asking a lot of questions if I were you," she interrupted when Hai opened her mouth again, her voice clear with a strong French accent.

"Just . . ." The woman faltered, considering her words, then lowered her voice to a whisper, nearly ashamed. "Just do whatever he wants. It's easier that way."

Footsteps against the marble stairs.

Whilst the woman remained calm, Hai's body jolted with fright.

Hai knew what such a sound—loud and deliberate— signified. Such was the sound of authority. This was the person who had been holding her here.

The woman stood abruptly. The dirty gauze sank beneath the cardinal water, her grip strong around the sharp rim of the basin as she hurried out of the room, leaving Hai to rot in her own anxiety, the presence of the gauze around her left thigh no longer easy to ignore.

The woman had left the solid timber door ajar, and Hai could hear people conversing from outside. She strained, trying to understand even just one word, as her heart leapt from her chest and the pieces finally fit. Her questions, finally answered.

Hai longed, in that moment, for her own foolishness to materialise in front of her eyes so that she could bark at it, the way neglected dogs snarled their protective distrust to passersby. She wanted to beat her recklessness with ineffectual fists, to spit her spite in its face. She should have known the second she opened her eyes and saw the strange woman—who else in this colony had a fleet of French servants at their mercy? She should have known that her delirious courtship with Monsieur Minh was hopeless, that she was insane to have expected otherwise. It was laughable, really, her naivety. Even now, Hai could barely refer to her lover by name, without his title; why would they have their happy ending when she never believed in it herself? After all, Hai would always view Monsieur Minh as her master, one she was destined to serve. They would never be equal. And instantly, like stone and gravel tumbling down uncontrollably from a collapsing mountain, a cruel but honest thought grazed her mind. Guilt threw itself against the walls of Hai's chest, but she didn't resist because Monsieur Minh wasn't here—even if he were, Hai knew there was little he could do.

She should never have loved him.

She should have accepted her fate, spending the rest of her life as the nameless, worthless servant she was always meant to be.

This was her last thought before Leon Moutet opened the door and greeted her with a sinful, crooked grin. Hai felt nauseous as she imagined a snake, its tongue hissing through the gap between Leon's purple lips.

Hai's wound throbbed as Leon came towards her; she glanced at her injury one last time, her expression hardening into something dark.

A retribution.

Of all the things she had seen, all the secrets she had kept, there was one thing Hai could use to hurt Leon back.

"Stunning. Simply stunning."

Oblivious to the determination across Hai's face, Leon clapped his hands together in delight. Bitter bile rose inside her throat, but she swallowed it down. His handywork, his masterpiece—the way he acknowledged her wound, her cap-tivity; she would not give him the satisfaction of looking afraid.

Theatrically, Leon spun around, his stride long and slow—a deliberate mockery of Hai's inability to move. He pulled a crystal decanter off the sleek brown shelf in the corner, then bent and grabbed a small, intricate wooden box from the bottom. He took out a thick roll of a cigar, holding it between his lips, lighting the tip. After one deep inhale, he ran his fingers along the line of fine glasses beneath the row of alcohol bottles.

"I don't suppose you want one?" he asked, but Hai didn't answer.

She needed to wait for the right moment.

"Ah."

Leon let out a soft grunt; he wasn't offended by her silence. He poured himself a full glass—the liquid a silky amber—and tilted his head, swallowing the drink. Using the heel of his hand, Leon wiped the residual liquid from the corner of his mouth. Methodically, he then rolled the sleeves of his white dress shirt to his elbows.

"Your name is Adeline," Leon stated matter-of-factly.

Hai didn't respond, her flaming defiance unfaltering at the sight of Leon's predatorial gaze. The faintest shade of surprise brushed his cheeks, prompting him to square his shoulders, standing a little taller, commanding more authority.

"Say it."

Hai did not.

"You know," he lowered his voice, trying a different tactic. "It wasn't my idea. The Khảis sold you to me."

This, of course, Hai had already realised. Still, the sheer mention of them, their precious last name and what it represented—the wealth and power they deemed Hai not worthy of possessing—enraged her. She averted her eyes, shielding her indignation.

"It's storming today," she said instead. The sky outside Leon's window was gloomy, bloated with grey clouds.

From her peripheral vision, Hai saw Leon's unpleasant surprise—his smirk, frozen with confusion. He heard her words loud and clear, but they weren't what he was expecting. He didn't want Hai's calm and collected composure. He wanted tears, fear,

191

desperate pleas. But Hai would not yield: Leon could take her life, but he would not render her helpless. Let this be the moment, Hai decided. Between where Leon was standing and where she was lying, the space was not unlike the gap between life and death, empty and bright with blinding white light, ready to welcome Hai's secrets.

"I've never been able to speak my mind," she began, louder than necessary. "Silence has always been expected of us servants. We aren't considered human. I suspect you think the same—it's natural to act as though we are devoid of emotions, or rational thinking. It's easier that way, I suppose. How else would you send out your ruthless orders? I wouldn't be able to do it. I wouldn't be able to treat someone like an animal. But I guess that's why I'm the servant, and you are the master. Don't you agree?"

Leon sighed; his face had clouded over with boredom. Like so many others, he didn't care what Hai had to say.

A fool, he tried again.

"Your betrothed didn't betray you. Madame Như sent you to my door."

Hai couldn't help herself—she let out a throaty laugh.

"You think I care what those fools did to me?" She shook her head. "You people and your superiority. You are not that special, I assure you. I simply don't want to die without speaking my mind."

Immediately, Leon's cheeks flushed crimson, the tips of his ears pink with rage—no one had ever defied the great Leon Moutet. He lunged at her.

"You bitch." He slapped her left cheek. "I ought to kill you."

The pain wasn't as overwhelming as Hai had expected, but her mouth was bleeding. She used Leon's white blanket to wipe her face clean, tainting the fabric's immaculate appearance with a thin crimson stroke.

"Go ahead. Kill me," Hai challenged. "But know this: you cannot hurt me. Not the way I'm about to hurt you."

She didn't allow Leon a second to interrupt, pointing her finger directly at his puffy face.

"If you weren't such a monster, I would pity you. Skin so white, eyes so blue, yet your precious son loves a lowly yellow rat."

A veil of realisation draped over Leon's expression, and Hai cackled louder with pleasure, as though she were trying to capture the attention of the vast world outside. *Come marvel at this*, she wanted to say but couldn't because no one would listen to her weightless words, because Leon had already wrapped his bare hands around her slender neck.

"You shut your mouth," he was screaming. The glint of horror in his eyes betrayed Leon: he must have heard the rumours, must have already suspected Edmond's indiscretion.

At once, Leon's brawny fingers tensed, draining the last gulp of air out of Hai's lungs. She didn't resist, staring at the space behind Leon's head: a dreamy world where prejudice didn't exist, where she was alive and well, happy and content next to the man she adored, their courtship no longer something shameful, wretched.

Love was never meant to end this way, Hai thought as the light deserted her eyes. No better universe materialised, only an immense blackness.

Minh

The cigarette was damp between his lips.

Minh inhaled deeply, pretending the smoke carried the relief of opium. How he needed the high right now. His valet had just delivered another telegram, and Minh groaned as he plucked the envelope from the old man's trembling hand.

A plan to burn the forest to ash. Minh grimaced now as he recited the words from the letter, which he had already fed to the orange flames. The managers at the plantation had raided the workers' accommodations and found a stack of crumpled paper, hidden under dry ground. *Creative*, Minh scoffed as he read through the brief report. The men had been nudging one another, telling stories of the abuse they experienced at Minh's family's plantation—working close to twenty hours a day, eating spoiled rice that had gone green, kneeling under the scorching heat because they couldn't harvest enough latex. They had made leaders of the few workers who knew how to write, as though the ability to detail these mistreatments on paper would change anything.

Minh tried to picture their faces: the fools who would attempt something like this. Licking the tip of his pen, Minh wrote back, answering the managers' desperate plea. It seemed the matter could no longer be postponed. He would need to make the trip to Biên Ho.

After giving the valet his order in writing, Minh felt exasperated. He thought of his discussion with Duy when they first heard about the uprising. He wanted to call his friend to complain.

The first cigarette had already dwindled, and Minh's anger temporarily evaporated as he leaned closer towards the candle, its red wax dripping down the top of the nightstand. He angled the tip of the second cigarette so it could catch the flame. Minh inhaled once more, filling his nostrils with a combination of cigarette smoke and body odour. The room was dingy and enclosed.

He was at a brothel. A new one, which he had never visited before. He needed a change of scenery. There wasn't much to the place—creaking wooden floors, a double bed in the middle with two nightstands. Distasteful, plain beige walls. The bedsheet where Minh currently sat was a faded shade of red, and on top of it was a blanket embroidered with golden dragons and phoenixes. It reminded Minh of the scene he had previously imagined for his wedding night, with Hai as his blushing bride. He blew the candle out and lay down, letting darkness arise to consume him. The mattress felt damp under Minh's back, but he refused to move.

He stared unblinkingly at the plain ceiling, hoping for guidance. What he ought to do next, where he should go from here—Minh needed some answers.

He hadn't reached for wine or opium.

Not that he didn't want to. But Minh was resisting the urge. Hai was gone; she had left him, discarding him like a trash bag. He had lost her, his one true love. He had lost control of his own life. It was only appropriate to ignore the urge to drink or smoke—a small, almost ineffectual thing Minh could still control.

But it wasn't enough. Nothing was enough anymore, not even the thought of the dead rodents Minh once killed. When he pictured their broken backs, their organs dangling from their mangled stomachs, he felt no relief. The only thing Minh felt now was loneliness, the same loneliness that he had known before meeting Hai.

He tried to conjure his friends, the memories they made together over the decades, hoping they might help warm his heart. He remembered the year after they graduated. There was a beautiful French girl, whose family had recently moved to Annam to accommodate her father's business. Her appearance stirred the otherwise bland, quiet society—she had long and silky blonde hair and a slender frame, fragile and delicate. People called her The Swan. Other details of her—the colour of her eyes, her name— had grown hazy in Minh's memory, and he knew why. Back then, both he and Edmond remained passive, appreciating her beauty, yet remaining disinterested. And Phong—well, Phong had been Phong, with no regard for anyone aside from his three friends.

Duy, however, was spellbound, his every waking moment spent chasing the beautiful young woman. He competed with hundreds of potential suitors, who showered her with extravagant gifts—expensive jewellery, handbags, and clothes. In the end, The Swan couldn't choose; the mountains of presents were more allur- ing than the prospect of commitment to any one man.

The suitors were restless, and so together, they agreed—the richest of them should be the one to have The Swan.

With Minh, Edmond, and Phong out of the way, the title for the wealthiest heir in Annam fell in the gap between Duy and George Li, the only son of John Li, an American Chinese businessman who had recently arrived with the hope of conquer- ing Annam's textile industry. It was rather difficult to decide who was wealthier, until George—the profligate nouveau riche that he was—suggested a contest. The two young men would use the cash they had with them in that precise moment to feed two separate makeshift firewood stoves; whoever managed to boil the water in the rusty iron pot first would win.

You are crazy. Duy shook his head, condescending, as though he were talking to a child.

What? Are you scared?

George had whistled teasingly, his face oblivious. He hadn't the faintest clue who he was dealing with, his small and boyish face belying a particularly young shade of arrogance.

To the absurd mockery, Duy simply laughed, deciding to humour George; he knew he could easily humiliate this pompous boy. After the countdown, a whistle was blown, and the stacks of money next to the young men quickly grew thinner. Neither cared—both Duy and George could only see the hunger in each other's eyes. They were equally stubborn. Around them, a circle of curious passersby had formed, the men and the women of the local working class. Their faces were hot, not from the flame, but from their own desire, wishing to be the fire that consumed the piles of cash.

It didn't take long. The entire event lasted less than ten minutes because Duy was liberal with his cash, calling over his shoulder for his valet to carry heavy bags filled with notes from the trunk of his car. He dumped them over the fire—a falling rain of wealth. Another second passed, and Duy blinked, a subtle veil of worry brushing over his face. Phong must have noticed because he nudged Minh's ribs, with a hefty pile of money in his left palm, discreetly signalling for Minh to assist.

Out of all of us, Phong whispered in Minh's ear, *Duy is the only one who deserves happiness.*

What about me, or Edmond, Minh wanted to ask. But in the end, he let Phong's comment go. Phong had always been a walking grey cloud, filled to the edge with droplets of rain. Together, they sent the cash in Duy's direction, and for a brief second all four of them locked eyes in appreciation and assurance. Loyalty.

Minh, Phong, and Edmond remained in the background, observing from afar, away from the curious gazes of the poor.

They all leaned against a massive banyan tree trunk with their arms crossed in front of their chests, spectating like they had been watching a horse race. Pride beamed across their faces—Duy looked so tall and proud next to George, the sleeves of his crisp white shirt rolled to his elbows, the top three buttons left open, dissolute. When his forehead was covered in sweat, Duy wiped it dry with yet another money note before sacrificing it to the fire god below.

At last, his water boiled. George was initially breathless with the realisation, then raging with anger afterwards. His tiny hands balled into fists, and his short legs attempted to charge towards Duy. But Edmond intervened, his grip firm and tense around George's wrist. *That's enough fun for one day, don't you agree?*

George didn't respond, his small face twisting with discomfort, struggling to loosen his arm from Edmond's clench. He left quickly after, avoiding the smug expression written across Duy's face. Minh had suspected, and Phong had concurred, that perhaps Duy wasn't that desperate for a date with The Swan; the contest was about something else entirely.

At the end of that memorable summer day, as they giggled over wine and cheese, none of them had mentioned Edmond's timely involvement. But they all thought the same thing.

The power of a Frenchman.

Now, Minh shook his head violently; his heart was heated alright, but not from the warmth of loving recollections. Instead, he felt resentment. George Li retreated because of Edmond, his last name, his skin. A colour so pale, so bland, yet it somehow had the ability to cut deeper than a silver blade.

Edmond Moutet. Leon Moutet. *The whole lot of you, one terrible creature,* Minh thought bitterly as he lay on the brothel bed. *You fled*

from your country to invade ours, begging to live on our land, and somehow
you still believe you are better.

Minh knew he was being unfair; Edmond would never hurt
anyone, least of all his close friends. But the memory returned.
The time Edmond unknowingly stole Phương Liên from Minh.

Like father, like son indeed.

There was a knock at the door.

"Come in. Don't touch the light," he barked, still lying with
his head resting on his left forearm. Minh didn't want to see the
faces of the escort. He would use darkness to imagine Hai instead.

The young woman smelled of fresh, summery flowers, her
shadow a petite silhouette. She stumbled towards the bed, her breath
sultry on Minh's naked skin. He lay still, not touching her. She wasn't
offended; she knew what to do.

Minh heard the sound of the escort's clothes landing on
the wooden floor. She pressed her body against his, running her
fingers along the length of his legs. Minh closed his eyes, ashamed,
like he was betraying Hai. But he had to remember: she made
the decision to leave him behind. He wanted so badly to prove
that Hai made a mistake, that he wasn't an abandoned dog, foolishly longing for the return of a neglectful owner. Yet, his limbs
remained soft, impotent.

"Am I doing something wrong?"

The escort's voice came from the space between Minh's
legs, and all of a sudden, without even a glint of forewarning,
Minh no longer felt loneliness or resentment. Clouding his mind
was a billow of humiliation and spite. His veins throbbed with
vengeance.

"Yes, you are," Minh roared as he pinned the escort under
his arms, panting. Under his grip, the young woman wilted, though

Minh couldn't see her. In darkness, Minh only saw the injustice Hai had subjected him to.

"Please," the escort cried out, begging. "I have a family."

Her voice was foreign, not soft and gentle like Hai's, but raspier. A weak, trembling sound, but it was enough to wake Minh from his wrath. He released her neck, turning on the light.

Minh squinted his eyes, trying to ease the illusion. The escort was not Hai; he repeated this fact in his head. She looked older than the woman he loved, her hair shorter. Her face was now engulfed in terror, and she was sobbing hysterically; around her neck was a nasty bruise. She'd almost choked, but Minh felt nothing. How could he express any remorse when his own heart was aching?

"Scram," Minh said quickly, avoiding the escort's eyes.

Still naked, she sprinted out of the room. The door clicked loudly behind her back, and there Minh was again, all by himself. He sighed, throwing his body against the damp mattress.

He didn't regret his actions, his violence. If anything, it made him feel better. There was something alive inside his chest as he'd wrapped his fingers around the escort's neck. Something primal. Something exhilarating.

He couldn't touch Leon Moutet, Minh knew that. But there were other rats—filthy and rotten just like Leon Moutet. They lurked and hid in the corners of this society, thinking no one saw them at all. Perhaps this was the reason the images of the dead rodents no longer brought Minh relief; his true purpose was to find and eliminate the animals who pretended to be men.

There was one thing Minh could not figure out: Edmond. Leon's only son, sharing his last name. What kind of animal was he?

THAT NIGHT

Phong and Duy came to a stop at the threshold of the dark wooden door. Above their heads was a sandy-yellow arch that served as the junction between the dining and the living areas. A few years back, Duy's parents instructed a decorator to mount a deer head in the middle of the arch, and the deer's eyes had always terrified him. Today was no different. With his back facing the deer as he hovered outside the living room—where the body of his childhood friend now lay—Duy felt those dark brown eyes on his neck, the hair on his arms standing straight.

They couldn't look at each other—both had so much, yet so little to say. Just like Phong, Duy fixed his gaze on the ground; the ordinary entrance in front of them was too imposing. They were about to enter an unfathomable universe—where their friend was no longer breathing. The things they'd seen before the tirailleur's arrival were about to be presented again, confirming this evening was not just a nightmare. One step forwards, and the world Duy knew would simply vanish.

Everything has changed already, Duy told himself.

He turned the brass knob, entering.

The chandelier was still shining obliviously above, its light illuminating the cruel scene below. The flowers in their vases, the furniture, and the other extravagant pieces of decor remained in their respective positions. Duy couldn't help a rueful smile—how did everything, and also absolutely nothing, manage to stay the same?

"Show—"

Duy couldn't finish his sentence. The barrel of a shotgun was grazing his lips.

He stared at the weapon, then back at his friend. It happened all too fast—the return of Duy's suspicion, the sheer surprise upon tasting the metal, and the overwhelming fear that he might have been right. Everything came in the form of a boiling-hot rage, bubbling inside Duy's chest like a volcano. He couldn't breathe. He wanted to shout, but his question came out like a croak.

"What the *fuck* did you do?"

"I could ask the same for the both of you."

Minh's aim was steady. He seemed neither drunk nor high anymore.

"Why did you leave so suddenly? And you." He moved the gun to point at Phong's chest. "What were you conspiring about?"

He held the weapon there, pressing it against Phong's skin, provoking Duy. *It's Phong*, Duy wanted to yell. The instinct to protect Phong surged, and with it, blinding anger. For a second, Duy saw nothing but red, and immediately after, Minh was lying on the ground, his hand holding his left cheek, instead of the gun. Duy's fist ached: he had just punched Minh.

He did not know if Minh was still his friend at all.

"Did you?" Duy pointed to the corpse on the ground. To Edmond. His voice was hoarse. "Did you kill him?"

Minh was still panting, unable to answer. It didn't seem to matter what he might say next—the air in the living room was heavy with distrust. Once, Duy and Minh would not have thought twice before enlisting in the army to fight side by side. But now . . .

"What are you talking about?" Minh barked at Duy, getting to his feet. He looked defeated—his hair was dishevelled, and his striking black moustache was now splotchy with thick droplets of saliva. Minh's shirt was ripped open, revealing his hairless chest underneath. He had been itching, it seemed; there were marks left by Minh's nails, tearing his tan skin.

Had Duy been a religious man, he would have thought Minh was possessed. With almost twenty years of friendship—now with a dead body separating them—Duy didn't know how else to view the person he once called a brother.

Duy glanced at Phong. Phong was still high—he had smoked the most opium out of the four of them. His appearance, though, didn't seem to betray him. Unlike Minh, Phong's clothes remained impeccable on his body. His white shirt was more wrinkly than usual, but that seemed the only discrepancy. He stood with his hands in his navy trouser pockets, apparently thinking.

Duy watched as Phong made his move, walking closer towards Edmond.

Slowly, Phong kneeled on the ground, resting his forehead on the cold tile floor. Duy couldn't watch anymore, averting his eyes again. This time, he settled them on the empty space behind Minh's head. Any other sight would be better than the crimson violence on Minh's face, or the harrowing yellow grief on Phong's, or the pearly white death on Edmond's.

How the hell did they get here?

*   *

We have arrived, Monsieur.

Earlier that day when it was still bright outside, the driver—a chubby man with puffy cheeks and a big belly—stopped the car, announcing their arrival loudly from the front seat.

Let's go then. Duy nodded, his left elbow nudging Minh's rib-cage, waking him. Together, they stepped from the vehicle, walking up the steps of the white stone staircase. Phong and Edmond were early, waiting outside the dark timber door to the Caos' mansion. Edmond was significantly taller than all of them, but his legs seemed unstable, his face buried in the crook of Phong's neck instead.

Sorry, we're a little late. Duy smiled apologetically when they faced each other, already preparing himself for Edmond's complaint.

He didn't respond, didn't even stir; Edmond was already drunk.

The rest of the night unfolded, a familiar routine.

Duy uncorked three bottles of wine for himself, Minh, and Phong. Edmond sat in the tan leather armchair, his favourite, drinking his own bottles from the trunks he had brought back from France. He always refused to drink liquor if he hadn't purchased it himself, and Minh, Duy, and Phong had long gotten used to such pedantry.

After drinking, the young men started smoking.

Boxes from India today, Duy declared gingerly, presenting his friends with shiny golden rectangles of opium from his factory.

Phong reached for the smoking pipe almost instantly.

Duy followed suit, filling his lungs with the alluring smoke. Slowly, his shoulders relaxed, his chest light. It no longer mattered—the dreams he couldn't chase, the opportunities he couldn't take. In that moment, Duy felt invincible.

But of course, he was wrong. It was a wake-up call, what happened next.

Amidst blurry darkness, someone grabbed Duy's thigh, frantic and desperate. Behind the hazy mist, a slender outline materialised, hair curly and blonde.

Edmond.

Edmond was falling to the ground, blood spilling from his mouth. His eyes were haunted, as they stared directly at Duy, condemning him, as though he had been the person blocking Edmond's lungs, denying him his breath.

Edmond was dying, his muscles spasming uncontrollably whilst his friends stood over him.

Don't . . . want . . . die . . . he panted.

And then, cruelly, he did. Those were the last three words Edmond would ever say.

The whole world fell into a tormentingly silent void.

Duy was stunned; it had all happened so quickly. He looked to Phong once more, and his heart ached. On his friend's face was an expression he had never seen before. Something bordered between grief and disbelief. In the corner, Minh was sleeping, oblivious to the tragedy unfolding. The thought to wake him had never crossed Duy's mind; he was still high as a kite. He stepped forward, kneeling next to Edmond, ignoring the gooey mess of red blood, yellow stomach fluid, and lumpy bile under his shoes. He pressed two of his fingers against Edmond's neck, giggling. He was convinced that this was a cruel joke, and soon enough Edmond would open his eyes, teasing their dramatic reactions.

That's enough, Edmond. I'm not falling for it. Duy laughed again, slapping Edmond's unnaturally stiff leg. Of course, Edmond didn't stir.

Duy continued to laugh, despite the ache in his stomach and the blur in his eyes. He couldn't stop, until he felt a hand on his left shoulder.

Phong.

He's gone, Phong said, and Duy repeated it.

Duy then turned to look at Phong and back to Edmond, whose chest was flat. Lifeless. He watched in a daze as Phong crumbled to the ground, wailing. The scene was shocking and heartbreaking enough to propel Duy out of the room, and whilst he was nowhere near sober, he had called the governor.

The worst mistake he had ever made.

Duy blinked, and the recollection halted, his family's living room coming back into focus. His gaze returned to where Phong now sat, pointing at Edmond's body.

Duy and Minh's argument was on pause, their eyes cautious and afraid as they took in the scene in front of them.

Without missing a beat, both Duy and Minh asked in unison, "What happened to Edmond's hands?"

TWO DAYS PRIOR

Marianne

A hundred years from now, a very unlucky archaeologist would come across the Moutets' backyard—they would be horrified to find the graveyard of human skeletons buried beneath. Marianne had this grim thought, standing with her arms crossed in front of her chest. She supposed a proper lady ought not imagine a future so bleak, but this was her only choice. She had nothing but the hope that, eventually, someone would uncover the tragic truth of this house.

Marianne was standing too close to the roaring fire. The red-and-orange flame was devouring the last evidence of that nameless girl's existence, but because the wind was strong, it did not flicker upwards, flaring out to the sides instead. The flames were coming for the hem of Marianne's dress. She noticed but decided to not move—she wondered if her complicity could be burned, too.

The very first night Leon asked for Marianne's help, she was relieved. In some deranged, cruel way, she was glad for the young woman on Leon's bed, bleeding to death. *Better those girls' lives than Edmond's*, Marianne often told herself.

She had been telling herself the same thing ever since.

Now, the fire ahead of Marianne was bigger than ever, swallowing everything it touched. Her eyes were teary, but she held her gaze on the flame. Marianne would do it all over again, to keep Edmond alive.

"Madame, we are done."

The two valets bowed their heads, announcing their accomplishment. The older one had spoken, his voice hushed; Marianne had ordered them to be discreet. She stepped away from the fire, pulling a thick envelope from the front pocket of her cream dress. Marianne placed it in the man's brawny palm and quickly considered them both.

They had arrived in the backyard at precisely midnight, shovels in their grips. Their foreheads were now glistening with sweat, and their clothes seemed even dirtier. They hadn't asked, nor had Marianne explained, and they buried the heavy wooden trunk without any hesitation. Whether a body was nestled inside, they didn't care. *How similar we all are*, Marianne remarked silently. These men would do anything for cash—Marianne would do anything for love.

"Go," she instructed. "Put the shovels back in the shed and clean yourselves up. Tonight never happened."

"Of course, Madame."

They were on their way before Marianne could blink. She was all alone with the greedy fire and the freshly dug grave. Filling a large bucket with cold water, Marianne stopped the burning. She stared at the remnants of the inferno—the young woman's life: her old clothes, the gauze wraps drenched in her blood—and tried to stand taller.

"I did what I had to," she told the wafting smoke.

She wouldn't apologise for trying to protect the child she had long considered her own.

* *

Inside the mansion, the grandfather clock struck one hour past midnight.

Marianne felt her head throbbing, her muscles pleading for rest. She counted the tips of her fingers—Edmond had been locked inside his room, bandaged and miserable, for almost six hours now. If Marianne knew him at all, she would have only half an hour before he kicked the door down. His self-inflicted wound wouldn't help much with slowing him. She needed to move, and quickly. Her plan was based on the assumption that Edmond was still the child she had raised: a boy who hid his most precious possessions in the inner pocket of his suit jacket. A slim chance, Marianne admitted, but it was better than nothing.

She headed for the laundry room.

The space was shrouded in darkness. There were no windows in there. She stood still for a second, considering whether she should turn on the light; Marianne didn't want to attract any unwanted attention.

She lit a candle instead. For a second, Marianne hovered above it, waiting for her eyes to adjust—the flimsy flame hugged the outline of her face, flickering orange along haggard lines on her forehead.

Turning her head, Marianne spotted the wicker basket of dirty clothes left in the corner of the room. Earlier that day, she had instructed the housemaids to leave Edmond's basket aside for her to handle. They were too happy to obey her request; they were all scared of the young master and his rage when he was drunk.

Like a mouse hunting the kitchen for dinner scraps, Marianne made her way over to Edmond's clothes; she knew what she was looking for. Quickly, she sorted through the undergarments and shirts. One by one, she dropped them to the ground, ignoring the mess growing larger by her feet.

Before she could get to the jackets, lying in a crumpled heap at the bottom, Marianne scrunched her nose—the stench of body odour lingered on the dirty clothes. Breathing through her mouth, Marianne pulled the pinstripe suit jacket out of the basket—here was the object she had been searching for. She couldn't contain her anxiety. She was one step closer to discovering the thing that had changed Edmond, the thing that led him to all the drinking. The mansion was very quiet; all the servants had already gone to sleep, and Marianne heard nothing but her own fear, thumping in her ears.

Marianne opened her palm and stared down at the locket.

The memory came back to her, from so long ago.

They had walked together from the Moutets' mansion to the annual autumn fair. Marianne and Edmond. The weather was chilly, and Marianne had summoned all her words to convince Edmond to leave the estate with a grey woollen cap on his head. He hadn't been happy about it, pouting the entire journey. He didn't mind catching a cold; he was afraid for his carefully styled hair.

When they reached the entrance to the fair, though, Edmond stopped sulking. He threw his arms around Marianne's neck, beaming with gratitude. The scene was bustling with visitors, vendors with delicious treats and sellers of exotic animals, making Edmond giddy. He ran ahead of Marianne, stopping in front of random stalls, waiting for her to catch up.

Marianne, please! We don't have all day.

Slow down, Marianne panted. Edmond's small legs always outran hers when he was excited.

Here. In the end, Edmond slowed down, willing to compromise. He outstretched his left arm in Marianne's direction. *I'll hold your hand, and you will hold mine. We will not lose one another in this crowd.*

His small palm was cold and clammy, but Marianne wrapped hers around it anyway. She was relieved, not wanting to chase after him in her thick, heavy coat anymore.

The sun had almost begun to set by the time Edmond got tired. The sky turned a pale shade of purple, and the temperature dropped a few degrees. Marianne and Edmond shivered together, visible breath escaping their mouths. It was time to go home. On their walk towards the exit, a jewellery stall caught Edmond's attention.

Marianne! Look! he called, pink excitement flushing his cheeks.

With pure innocence and childish curiosity, Edmond fawned over the dazzling gold and silver bands. Marianne remained behind, observing Edmond, a loving smile across her lips. How she loved and cherished it, this boy's happiness.

Marianne! Edmond called again, this time not waiting for her response. He was already holding the item—a simple golden locket, threaded onto a delicate chain. The outside had an intricate carving of tree branches, growing vigorously, and inside there was a plain frame, to store a small photo.

Marianne decided to humour the boy—she stared at the piece of jewellery with intensive focus. She didn't get it, Edmond's fascination. It looked as ordinary as anything she'd seen, but Edmond looked as though he had discovered an important artefact. Marianne didn't think much on it; she bought the locket for Edmond on the spot. How could she ever deny him such easy gaiety?

As they returned home that day, hand in hand, stomachs full with hot bread, the corners of their mouths white with powdered sugar from the treats at Edmond's favourite crepe stand, Marianne asked *Why do you love that locket so much?*

Edmond shrugged, admitting *I'm not sure, to tell you the truth.* He'd always sounded much older than his age. *I just saw it and thought, wouldn't it be nice to store the photo of the love of my life inside one day?*

A hopeless romantic, from the beginning.

Marianne realised she was crying; she could no longer see the pendant through her tears, its shape a blur.

Please, God, I'm begging you. Send my boy back to me.

Marianne didn't know which God she prayed to, but she whispered the words anyway.

Rubbing her eyes with the back of her hand, Marianne inhaled deeply. She knew her suspicion would be correct; she always knew who Edmond really was. There could only be one explanation for why he had been drinking so much. Edmond loved someone forbidden, and this had been tearing him in half.

Without any further hesitation, Marianne undid the clasp on the side of the locket.

The small oval portrait inside caught Marianne by surprise, for only a brief second.

Phong with his signature black-rimmed glasses and his half smile, a perpetual reluctance to be happy.

But of course. This made so much sense.

Over the years, deep down, Marianne had already guessed so much, drawing her conclusions from the way they talked, how they touched one another. The genuine crinkle in Edmond's eyes when he looked at Phong, Phong's relaxed shoulders in Edmond's presence. A subtle, almost muted tenderness that helped shield them from the outside world's arrogance.

She'd never said a thing. She'd wanted to give Edmond the chance to confide in her first. *How foolish and cruel,* Marianne thought. She could have come to him, could have explained that it was all good and right, that he did not need to punish himself. That he was allowed to love who he loved, that this affection was no shameful crime. Had she said something before, perhaps Edmond would never have needed the alcohol. Perhaps he never would have hurt that poor servant, or slashed his own arm. Her reluctance, her silence, Marianne realised, had been almost as damaging as Adeline's venomous whispers in her son's ears.

She clutched the locket tighter, her fingernails sinking deep into the flesh of her palm. She had failed the one person she had promised to protect and love.

"Marianne."

A familiar voice. She turned around.

She couldn't see him clearly, her eyes filled with hot tears. Edmond was standing next to the laundry room door. He leaned against the frame, his slender arms wrapped around his chest; he was so thin.

"I see you found it," Edmond said, pointing to the locket. He broke into the smile Marianne always loved, and the ache intensified. She didn't deserve his kindness, not after her failures.

"Oh, come on. Marianne. Say something."

"I . . ."

Her words turned into a hysterical sob, and Marianne ran to Edmond, burying her face in his bony chest. He hugged her, his arms gaunt against her flesh. *How did he get so skinny?* A question Marianne dared not ask aloud.

"Why . . ." Marianne began. "Why must you do this to yourself? Why didn't you come to me? Why didn't you let me help?"

"Because, Marianne, I am too far gone." Edmond was still holding her tight, his reply instant, as though he had anticipated her question. She didn't understand, but she was terrified of this answer.

"You left the locket there for me to find," she said instead.

"Yes." Edmond nodded. "I wanted you to know. I wanted a witness."

"Are you happy, Edmond? With him, I mean."

"I've never loved anyone the way I love him."

"That's not what I asked."

"I know," Edmond said and reached for the pendant, taking the portrait out of the frame. "I want you to have the necklace."

"What do you mean?" Marianne blinked at him.

"I have a safer place to store the photo now." Edmond pointed at the leather gloves that he was wearing, sliding the photograph inside.

Marianne winced at the sight of the bandages around his arm, but she nodded.

"Are you sure about this? I know how much this locket means to you."

"I'm sure. Hold onto it for me, will you, Marianne?"

"I will," she promised. "Now, tell me the story."

The hours passed, deeper into the night, but Marianne did not feel sleepy. Edmond guided her to the very start of the story. Their legacy must be decent and pure, he explained.

"Remember us this way," he told her, and Marianne promised that she would.

214

Edmond

"Come on."

Edmond was sitting with his back against a mighty banyan tree when a familiar voice reached his ears. He looked up, squinting.

That soft, gentle smile. Bright and warm enough to rival sunlight.

Phong was standing in front of him. His hand was outstretched, waiting for Edmond's.

Oh, how he admired such kindness. The pain Phong must feel when time and time again Edmond failed to hold him during daylight. Yet here he stood, willing to wait however long Edmond needed. Without hesitation, Edmond took Phong's hand, hoisting himself up. It was right, this feeling. Safe. Peaceful. Home.

They started walking—around them was an infinite whiteness, blinding. No people, nothing in sight. A world for just the two of them.

Suddenly, the sky above their heads turned black, a strike of silver lightning tearing the ether in half. No sound followed. Everything was completely still. An illusive calm.

It was Edmond who spotted the masked man first—he was charging at them, a black sword swinging on his hip. Edmond was petrified, and he pulled Phong along faster.

"You go."

Phong's smile again, though this time sunlight didn't appear. The world turned a shade bluer. Sadness. Acceptance.

Edmond didn't understand, not at first. His expression turned frantic as the masked man came closer. He didn't want to abandon Phong, didn't want to remain a coward—so he did

215

not run. He let the man approach: one blink, and Edmond was stabbed. He stared at his wound before registering Phong, already dead, in a slump by his feet. Edmond didn't feel any pain, only a hollowness as Phong's chest went still. They were two halves of one vessel; one could not exist without the other.

Blood was dripping from his injury, yet Edmond saw no thick red liquid, only a sluggish black stream. Toxin. Purge. The sins he had committed.

Edmond looked, then, at the assassin, who held Edmond's gaze as he bled out. When Edmond leaned forward, the knife sunk further into his body. He let it, tearing the black mask down.

Familiar blue eyes. That aquiline nose, a wide, smirking mouth.

His father.

Leon Moutet grinned, flashing a set of black teeth.

Edmond opened his eyes, sitting up in bed, panting with realisation. He knew exactly what this nightmare meant. His forehead glistened with sweat, curly blonde locks greasy on his neck. Edmond pressed his back further into the headboard, seeking some futile protection from his memories.

After Edmond told Marianne the whole story last night, he noticed a dirty white bedsheet in the corner of the dingy laundry room. He was surprised, knowing that Marianne would never tolerate such nastiness. Curious, he moved towards the item, and when he realised it was blood, Edmond's surprise turned into fear.

Is it yours? Are you hurt? A layer of panic blanketed Edmond's question.

Don't be silly. I'm alright. Marianne shook her head, a deflection Edmond knew too well.

He wondered if she was terminally ill. Her hair looked suddenly whiter.

Marianne, please. Stop lying to me. I can't lose you, too.

He didn't cry, but he must have looked beyond upset because Edmond had never seen Marianne so startled. She said nothing, only stroking his hair the way she had since he was a child. Under her gentle touch, Edmond felt so little, so fragile, like a toddler.

It's better you stay out of this, she mumbled at last, her voice small. An attempt to convince Edmond to let it go.

Marianne. He whispered her name, pleading.

In the end, like always, Marianne relented. She pointed at the bedsheet, sighing.

That belongs to your father.

She avoided Edmond's widening eyes as she told him the story that would forever change his life. At first, her words were slow; perhaps she was giving Edmond the chance to interrupt, to stop the unravelling of his worst nightmare. He didn't take the chance, letting her go on. By the end, Marianne spoke all too quickly, not wanting to relive her crime for a second longer than necessary. How similar, Edmond thought, to the bedtime stories that Marianne used to lure him to sleep as a child. She rushed the endings exactly this way.

When Marianne finally stopped, Edmond's face was pale, his ears buzzing, unable to take in any sound. He couldn't hear Marianne's guilty sobs, couldn't even hear his own breath, growing shorter and shorter. He couldn't look at Marianne. The wrinkles across her forehead, the way her skin sagged, all the result of protecting his father's filthy secrets.

Later, he followed Marianne to the ground where she destroyed the evidence, night after night, after his father had finished his *business*. They stood with their shoulders touching, staring at the roaring fire, dipping their heads in tandem until the last of the bloody bedsheet was fully consumed.

Go on, get some rest. It's been a long night.

Edmond somehow found his way back to his bedroom, drowning his mangled mind with a few more bottles of wine before lying down, flat on his back. He fell asleep, hoping to forget as soon as he next woke. But it seemed the memory was there to stay.

Now, Edmond stared at the infinite space. He couldn't bear to blink, afraid he would be confronted with the spirits of the women his father had killed—their distorted faces, and their rage, hot and seething. Their feet, raw with injustice, stomped on Edmond's chest until he could no longer breathe.

Groaning, Edmond pushed himself off the bed, ignoring the throb in his left arm. The slashes would take a while to fully heal.

He headed towards the liquor cabinet, reaching inside for a crystal decanter, filled with a strange, translucent liquid. He had hesitated as he gave Marianne the locket last night, with the photograph of Phong inside, worrying that he had chosen poorly. Now, after all he had discovered, Edmond knew something needed to change. It was his fault, really. He shouldn't have been drinking that much, blinding his eyes and blurring his ears to the tragedy inside his own home. Had he not been such a drunk, he could have prevented it. Those innocent lives.

His fingers turned white around the bottle's neck; Edmond reached his final decision. Atonement, for his family's sins.

Madame Như

Madame Như sat in the living room for far longer than she had originally planned; she must have been in this chair over an hour already.

It was almost noon, but the space remained dark; the curtains were drawn. Madame Như felt tired and slightly sick. When she looked at herself in the mirror earlier in the morning, she was startled, her face haggard, her eyes empty. Such a ghastly sight; she couldn't let anyone see her now.

There had been a viciously cold wind last night—a violent storm would arrive soon—and today Madame Như's muscles were paying the price of her forgetfulness. She had gone to bed without closing the south window of her bedroom. Madame Như curled her fingers into fists, lightly beating them against her aching limbs. She cleared her throat, grimacing. A flu was coming, Madame Như could feel it. No amount of herbal tea could help her now.

She sunk deeper into her armchair, straining to listen for any sign of life on the other side of the tall oak door. She couldn't hear anything other than the timid footsteps of her servants. After the violent beating Minh carried out the other night, the Khải' mansion had turned into a graveless cemetery. The valets and the housemaids tried their best to remain invisible. Even Tattler had disappeared, leaving Madame Như utterly alone.

"Water! Water!" the orange-bellied parrot chirped from his wire cage.

Maybe she wasn't completely alone.

Smiling, Madame Như got to her feet; she was suddenly grateful for the companionship of her pet. She traced the black metal bars with her index finger, pretending the bird chose to stay with her, that she didn't need an enclosure to keep it from flying away.

Madame Nhu unhooked the door to the parrot's cage, peering inside for the parched stone bowl. She couldn't remember when she last gave the animal fresh water.

"My dearest!" Madame Nhu exclaimed before calling for a housemaid. "How could you forget his water?"

"I beg your pardon, Madame. I will see to it right this second." The maid dipped her head.

"Take the cage and go."

"Madame."

Madame Nhu walked back to her favourite chair, trying to stifle a cough.

Another rasp on the door.

"Come in."

"Hai's mother has arrived, following your orders, Madame. She is currently waiting in the yard."

The butler avoided Madame Nhu's gaze. He was a tall man, much taller than Madame Nhu, yet from the way he now stood, with his back hunched and his head lowered, he seemed just as small as the young valet Minh had beaten the day before.

"About time," Madame Nhu breathed out. "Take her to the kitchen and give her an early lunch. Let her eat whatever she wants, then bring her here."

"Of course, Madame." Despite the peculiarity of her request, the butler asked nothing more. "Is there anything else, Madame?"

"No, you may leave."

Hai's mother was here. Madame Nhu shifted inside her chair, crossing and then uncrossing her legs, annoyed with her own limbs. She knew this visit was vital, yet she dreaded it. Perhaps, as a mother herself, Madame Nhu was reluctant to announce the death of someone else's child.

She felt inside her trouser pocket for the letter that had been delivered by Leon Moutet's valet a few hours prior. There was only one sentence written in black ink, but Madame Nhu had read it more times than she could possibly count.

"A fine gift you offered me. Unfortunately it was quite short-lived, though I appreciate your family's loyalty."

She sighed, feeling uneasy.

Hai was a life-sized doll, which Madame Nhu had directed to Leon Moutet's lap—now he was free to implicate her in his despicable crime. The Khais' loyalty—their ability to keep their mouths shut, to satisfy all the Moutets' future demands—was the price Leon Moutet ordered Madame Nhu to pay in exchange for his assistance in solving her little problem.

It was a pity, the way it unfolded—not at all what Madame Nhu intended. It was not her fault Hai had decided to climb this mountain, a place she did not belong. Oh, it was a long list, the things Madame Nhu told herself, so she could fall asleep.

Leaning forward, she reached for the box of matches in the middle of her tea table, planning to burn Leon Moutet's letter to a crisp, along with her sin. What she did was wrong, Madame Nhu knew, but she would do it again if she had to. The family Madame Nhu was trying to protect—the reputation she was struggling to maintain—was much more important than a worthless maid. She angled the paper on top of the flickering orange flame, refusing to let go, even as the fire licked the tip of her finger. Shame and humiliation were only feelings, after all. Insignificant. Meaningless. Her family's name was worth everything—worth creating an inferno for. She would do it, without hesitation, without regret; it wouldn't matter if the blaze swallowed Madame Nhu whole.

Duy

"Monsieur, are you certain you would like to close the shop today?" the club's forewoman asked cautiously.

Duy looked up from the chessboard, narrowing his eyes in her direction. Her question was laced with insinuation—Duy's mother would soon discover his impulsive decision—but this didn't offend him. His mind was busy with curiosity; he could not seem to remember the forewoman's name.

About a month ago, Mother had appointed the woman to oversee the bar girls' health and well-being. She entered the club a small and timid person, wearing a plain, simple black tunic with brown linen trousers. Today, she stood in front of Duy in a fine turquoise silk top and a dark pair of navy pants. Her hair was gathered in a sleek low bun, and she wore a dainty gold chain around her neck. She fashioned herself the way Madame Mai would, her real identity now disappeared. This realisation unnerved Duy.

"My mother won't know, if you won't tell."

"Of course, Monsieur." A sheen of discomfort spread across the woman's face, but she regained her composure quickly. "What would you like the girls to do today, then?"

Duy looked to the corner of the club where a group of young women waited. They appeared almost identical—petite figures, long black hair, bewitching red lips. The women avoided Duy's gaze, and for a brief moment he wanted to apologise, assuring them that he wasn't one of their usual clients. But why would that matter? After all, Duy allowed those men inside.

"They can rest," he said at last. "Order the other workers to start cleaning and polishing the equipment. And counting the

223

stock on hand," he added, "we are due for some maintenance. Don't you agree?"

"Monsieur." The woman replied curtly, dipping her head before walking behind the bar, pretending not to notice the hole in Duy's lie. Madame Mai would never permit such a thing; she needed to see the money, constantly and physically. At times, her greed seemed to know no boundaries.

Duy had to disobey Mother today, he supposed. He was tired and restless; he could hear Master Cần's words, echoing in his head. He could see her ancient face, her gleaming black eyes. Death would soon appear, and he couldn't stop it. Duy needed the escape, however temporary. The raunchy men and the addicts be damned.

Tilting his head back, Duy drained his black coffee. He set the white ceramic cup on the glass table in front of him, quietly observing the manager, who had been watching him through the thin curtain of her eyelashes. Duy had discovered a while back that Mother also hired the woman to spy on him; she wasn't exactly subtle. Still, Duy had to admit, she was somewhat efficient—just then, her fingers were swift as she rinsed and dried the dirty glasses, wiping away smudges of lipstick and hand prints, all whilst carefully eyeing him. Mother always feared that Duy would abandon his inheritance, and in truth, he couldn't really blame her.

They were close, once, Duy and Mother. When Duy was a child, he spent most of his days following Mother around their grand garden, laughing and playing under the warm golden sun. In the afternoon, Duy sat behind her back, parting her striking black hair in search of strands of white.

One, two, three, he counted afterwards, exclaiming in utter delight when Mother dropped a few spare coins in his chubby palm.

Why, thank you darling. Her smile was always tender. *You have been so incredibly helpful!*

As Duy grew older, those moments came to an inevitable stop. These days, Mother wanted to discuss nothing more than the family's business, her silvery locks neglected, left to multiply freely.

The memory caused a sweeping pain in Duy's stomach, forcing him to stand up, seeking distraction elsewhere. The liquor cabinet, he decided. He could do a stock count there.

Before he started, Duy poured himself a full glass of imported whiskey, letting his fingers roam free on the smooth surface of the bar counter. He usually only spent time inside the club to entertain his business partners, to ensure that the workers were serving his guests with utmost diligence; he'd never had the chance to properly admire the club's interior. The club maintained a fine combination of both Western and Asian aesthetics—plush leather sofas, armchairs and daybeds on peacock chinoiserie rugs, fine porcelain smoking pipes with delicate drawings of tigers and horses on their stems, served on luxurious black velvet trays. Around the room, the walls were covered in hanging scrolls with hanzi characters written in cursive calligraphy. They were there to seal the space shut, protecting the Frenchmen's exquisite opium high.

Raising the glass, Duy finished his drink in two big gulps, pretending to focus on the sweet and slightly spicy notes. The urge to seek his life purpose returned, dominating his psyche; he didn't know why he kept doing this—running a business he didn't much care for.

You have such a comfortable life. Could you ever really leave?

The sound of Minh's question echoed in Duy's ears. He had everything, Duy knew—but at the same time, his life was lacking *something*. A meaning. Without it, Duy was no different from the scrolls Mother hung on the club's walls, existing only to serve the elite. The French. At times, that vague ambiguity made Duy believe he had it harder than most, even when he compared himself to the

225

pitiful servants. He was not ignorant; after all, no human suffered a pain greater than their own.

"Monsieur." A cleaner approached Duy from his left. "I was cleaning the Red Room and found this locket. One of the guests must have forgotten it there."

"Here," Duy said, dropping a 100 piastre bill in the man's calloused hand. "For your honesty."

"Thank you for your generosity, Monsieur." The cleaner lowered his head, accepting the cash with a heavy gratitude hanging over him.

"You may leave." Duy waved the worker away. He was tired, hearing the gratitude. He was no gracious saviour—he was just a spoiled heir with too much time and money.

The golden pendant glinted in Duy's palm, a much needed diversion from his exhausting reflection. He narrowed his black eyes at the object, raking his memories; he had seen this before, this intricate design. Immediately, Duy's face brightened with a flash of recognition.

"Edmond." He mumbled his friend's name, shaking his head slightly. How did it end up in the Red Room anyway? Edmond loved this piece of jewellery; he had never misplaced it before.

Clumsily, Duy's thick fingers undid the pendant clasp, his eyes peering inside to see whose photo Edmond had been keeping close. He was instantly disappointed. Inside was . . . a black-and-white portrait of Edmond. He wasn't smiling, but the corner of his lips lifted. Teasing.

Was he serious? Duy laughed. He couldn't afford to love anyone more than himself?

Of course, the necklace didn't belong to Edmond, but Duy had not realised this yet. The letter *P* had been carved rather loosely along the back, like an afterthought. No one would notice, unless they knew exactly where to look.

Madame Nhu

"Here."

Pointing to the black bone bench next to her favourite arm-chair, Madame Nhu ordered the old woman to sit. She averted her eyes almost instantly, pretending not to see the anxious expression on Hai's mother's face. In Madame Nhu's presence, Hai's mother looked even smaller; she kept her head low, curling into herself. She couldn't have been much older than Madame Nhu, yet her skin appeared saggier, her hair whiter. Across her wilting face was a splatter of brown spots, a constellation of hardships and poverty. Before today, Madame Nhu knew, Hai's mother had never been full. The woman fidgeted in her seat, a white grain of rice still stuck to the corner of her dry lips, her breath pungent with the smell of fish sauce. Discreetly, Madame Nhu glanced down at the woman's scrubby grey tunic and her bare, dirty feet.

Hai's mother's eyes roamed the room. She took in the lustrous black bamboo stool, its intricately carved and sculpted legs mimicking the curves of a dragon's tail. On the stool rested a tall ceramic vase. The painting on its body depicted five cranes flying towards blue sky, their wings outstretched majestically. Behind the vase was an imposing liquor cabinet, filled with glimmering crystal decanters.

Madame Nhu kept her silence, sitting with her legs crossed, giving the old woman a moment to take in her beloved living room. Before the meeting, Madame Nhu had changed into a five-piece aodai in emerald green, ignoring the similarity between this dress and the one she had picked for Hai that fateful day. She wore her hair high on her head, keeping it away from her carefully powdered face. On her neck was a long strand of white pearls, on her feet a pair of black clogs with colourful, hand-painted peacocks on the innersoles. Madame Nhu smelled of her favourite fresh floral perfume, chosen from the expansive collection in her wardrobe, and she was thankful that the scent helped mask the remnants of Hai's mother's lunch.

They sat side by side, two mothers from two different worlds.

Leaning forward, Madame Nhu reached for the teapot; she was still considering what she ought to say. Earlier, she had planned to quickly present the old woman with a distorted version of the truth, then send her back to the rural area she came from, but now she thought she should be more delicate with her approach; her story must carry no holes. There was no need to tell Hai's mother what *really* happened. That poor family would never come searching for a daughter they had sold anyway. Still, Madame Nhu couldn't afford the possibility that she might miscalculate. She was no longer just protecting her family but also Leon Moutet's powerful world. The reminder of her new responsibility sent a wave of nausea through her stomach, and briefly, she closed her eyes, hoping to conceal her fear. In her ears, she could still hear the parrot's mocking chirps.

Like the animal, she too had been caged.

"Here."

Madame Nhu repeated the first and only word she said to Hai's mother as her willowy fingers wrapped around the curvy handle of the teapot. Her teaware was made of fine bone china with elegant white colouring, their rims glinting with golden paint as delicate as thread. She pushed the warm, relaxing jasmine tea across the table, leaving it within the woman's reach.

"Your journey must have been tiring. Have a drink."

"Thank you, Madame. But I'm not thirsty. There is only one cup here. Please don't waste it on me," Hai's mother responded dutifully, not daring to look at Madame Nhu. Her voice was husky, worried.

"I insist."

Smiling now, Madame Nhu held the cup to the woman's face, pleased. She ordered the maid to bring only one cup, wanting to see if Hai's mother understood her place within the Khải' mansion, and she did. She had passed the test. So far, the meeting had been just as easy as Madame Nhu had hoped.

"Madame, you are too kind."

She lowered her head once more, accepting the tea with both hands. When she finally looked up, though, Hai's mother's submissive smile slowly faded, replaced by a concerned expression.

"Do you know why I requested you come here today?"

"No, Madame. I do not," the woman replied promptly, the sheen in her eyes dense with caution.

"I wish I didn't have to be the person to tell you this." Madame Nhu staged a sigh. "I want you to understand that we have exhausted our resources and that we did all we could."

The woman shifted in her seat; her spirit grew visibly tangled with dread.

"Hai has passed away."

Four simple words, but they left Madame Nhu breathless. For the first time in her life, she nervously awaited a servant's response. It wasn't because Madame Nhu felt guilty or remorseful; she reserved those emotions strictly for the altar room, kneeling in front of Buddha, begging for the deity's forgiveness. She was anxious because she could not predict what Hai's mother would say next, and this scared her.

"How did it happen?" The woman struggled to speak, dropping all formality. The pain was obvious, raw and fresh.

"She caught an infectious disease." The lie rolled so easily off Madame Nhu's tongue, her posture stoic, her face calm. "The physicians did all they could."

"Can I see her, Madame?" Hai's mother asked, looking directly at Madame Nhu. Her eyes were two black wells of regret; she had sent her own daughter to this family, this society, this fate.

"She has been cremated."

Madame Nhu shook her head, explaining almost too quickly. She previously anticipated this question from Hai's mother, and she was relieved to follow the script again. Still, Madame Nhu's heart skipped a beat, thinking she might have sounded rather feigned, rather practised. She blinked innocently and reached for the woman's calloused hands, an impulsive act that made Madame Nhu's spine shiver. "The physicians have advised doing so in order to prevent any potential spread. I have arranged for her ashes to be sent to the pagoda myself."

There weren't any ashes. Madame Nhu couldn't possibly guess what Leon had done with Hai's body. But there was at least a pagoda—Madame Nhu knew a monk who accepted the Khải' generous donations, agreeing to spare a wooden plate for Hai's name atop the altar. An absurd compensation for the tombstone Hai was denied at the Moutets' mansion but a compensation nonetheless.

Madame Nhu leaned forward, signalling the end of their meeting.

"Perhaps one of these days, we could go see her together."

Of course, she didn't mean it, but this seemed like the right sentiment. Madame Nhu needed to prove that she had nothing to hide, that she was utterly innocent. She lifted her hands from the woman's and replaced them with a sealed brown envelope. Her muscles were still tense, her jaw still clenched, but Madame Nhu assured herself she had done everything she possibly could.

"For your travels," Madame Như said softly.

"Thank you, Madame," the woman mumbled. Her fingers wrapped tightly around the envelope, the prize of her silence about her daughter's death. It must have been humiliating because abruptly Hai's mother rose to her feet, struggling to excuse herself.

Madame Như was surprised.

"There isn't . . ." she hesitated; Hai's mother's meltdown had been far less intense than Madame Như had expected. "There isn't anything else you want to know?"

"No, Madame."

Hai's mother shook her head; her irises glimmered with sorrow, her scrawny face contorted in a nameless pain, a pain so harrowing, so vast, Madame Như could not bestow it a name.

"Maybe this was easier on her," Hai's mother said. "I only pray that wherever my child arrives next, it won't be like this life."

With that, Hai's mother bowed; her heavy steps led her away from the room. Her shoulders hunched, her tears dampened the brown envelope she clutched in her palm, each note soiled with her daughter's blood.

Madame Như said nothing. She silently positioned herself behind the balcony of her living room, which oversaw the front yard. She crossed her arms in front of her chest, hugging herself whilst she watched the butler escort the woman away from the Khải' mansion. Madame Như watched as Hai's mother shrank into a blurry smear, her house—a place Madame Như couldn't see where the woman would now return to grieve her child—remaining somewhere far on the orange horizon. The sun, a crimson dot, slowly left the sky. Madame Như welcomed the darkness.

She would keep watching, for the rest of her life, she was sure of it. She would keep watching for ways to protect her family, for ways to survive this world, no matter the cost.

231

THAT NIGHT

A rich note of music from a piano cradled Duy's ears, calming his mind.

Surprised, he blinked to discover that he was no longer standing in his mansion's living room. On his left was Minh, and on his right was Phong, their faces younger, more innocent, more hopeful.

In front of them was Edmond, alive and well. He was sitting on a leather stool, pouring his heart into the melody. His fingers glided seamlessly across the black-and-white keys, and Duy, Minh, and Phong were all in awe. Under the warm light of the Moutets' grand chandelier, Edmond's pale skin glimmered, his appearance ethereal, as though he had been carved from holy stone.

Afterwards, the four of them drunkenly lay together on a random hill after strolling the streets around the French Quarter, a high-profile residential community reserved strictly for the elites. It was almost midnight, but they didn't care, talking and laughing loudly with youthful obnoxiousness. The air around them was hot and damp, sweet with plans and ambitions.

I don't want much, you know, Minh began, rubbing his bare chin thoughtfully. *I want a small family, with enough money to survive. More resources, more responsibility. More problems. Who needs that?*

I want freedom, Duy said, shaking his head; he knew such a thing would never exist within their world. He left the sentence at that. He hadn't the heart to speak aloud the things that would never come true.

Phong, as they all expected, remained quiet. In response to the things he couldn't say, the boys simply squeezed his shoulders. A declaration that they would love Phong the way he deserved to be loved. An assurance: they were his family.

After a second or so, Edmond chimed in, breaking the woeful silence. *Piano. I want to perform, to dedicate my life to the art.* He pointed at the shining stars in the navy sky, smiling coyly. *Who knows? Maybe they really do listen to our wishes.*

Maybe, they all agreed, savouring the taste of fleeting happiness on the tips of their tongues.

Suddenly, a whimpering sound came from somewhere far away. Duy was startled, stiffening in his spot, turning to his friends. *Did you hear that?*

No one answered.

No one could answer because those boys existed only in Duy's memories. They were real no longer.

The spell lifted. The hill, the glimmering stars, and the midnight sky faded, and in their places, the Caos' living room materialized. The noise Duy heard was coming from Phong. He was unable to answer Duy and Minh's question from earlier, tears choking his words.

"His hands," Duy repeated helplessly. He couldn't believe his eyes. They didn't resemble Edmond's hands, so graceful in his vision, flying across the keys of the piano.

Now, they were covered in skin lesions and discoloured patches.

"Go on." Looking back at Minh, Duy grunted, challenging. "Explain yourself, Minh."

"Are you mad?" Minh's voice was raspy.

Rushing him, Duy pinned Minh to the wall.

"Didn't Edmond's father just take your toy away? You're the only one with a motive. You just pulled a gun on me and Phong. If you aren't guilty, why the *fuck* are you blaming us?"

Duy didn't give Minh the chance to reply, his grip tightening around Minh's white collar, his face red with rage and betrayal.

"You've never liked Edmond," Duy spat. "I always thought it was because you were childish and spoiled. I never thought you would actually kill him. You monster!"

As soon as the words left his mouth, Duy released Minh from his grip, panting. He realised he had misspoken.

"I didn't mean—"

"That's fine." Minh raised one hand in defeat. "I guess now I know what you really think of me."

"I—"

Duy didn't know what to say next, the corner of his lips tightening with self-contempt. He lowered his head instead. A peace offering.

He couldn't bear looking directly at Minh—he was the only person Minh had ever come to with his fear of isolation. The extra emotion overwhelmed Duy, and suddenly he was furious. He was angry with himself for betraying Minh's trust, with Edmond for dying—which in itself was such a selfish anger—and, most of all, with the damnable mystery that took Edmond's life, ruining theirs in the aftermath.

Like a guilty puppy, Duy glanced at his friend, who now closed his eyes in utter exhaustion. He no longer believed Minh was the murderer; the expression on his face when Duy threw the accusation across the room was too raw, too painful. Minh, of all people, never knew how to pretend.

234

That left only one person.

No. Duy suppressed the thought before it could arise. It couldn't have been Phong. Not in a million years. Not Phong, who longed only for affection. Not Phong, who couldn't even hate his own father.

Then, what the hell happened?

"What, um," from behind Duy, Minh's voice came out as a muffle. "What was Edmond holding there?"

Duy followed Minh's finger, looking at the flat object in the palm of Edmond's left hand. Hearing this, Phong finally stifled his sob, peeling his forehead off the ground, sliding the picture towards Duy.

In that instant, nobody moved. Nobody made a sound. The living room was as quiet as the inside of a coffin.

A young man's face in black and white, black-rimmed glasses resting on his upturned nose. His forehead was tall, his cheeks chiselled, his half smile warm, intimate.

"Why was Edmond hiding a photograph of you, Phong?" Duy asked, his brows furrowed in confusion. There was something familiar about this shape.

"Oh," Duy exclaimed, feeling for the heavy locket in his trouser pocket. He undid the clasp of the pendant in a haste, placing the portrait inside. A perfect match.

A stream of understanding flowed through Duy's veins: the close-knit bond, the protectiveness, the teasing glance that he some-times saw. Turning the locket over, Duy squinted his eyes, noticing the faint *P* at last.

"This necklace is yours."

"Yeah," Phong replied weakly, standing up. "Edmond had it made for me in France. A replica of his original."

"I see." Duy nodded weakly, not knowing what else to say.

For a while, the three young men stood, wordless as the minutes passed. It was difficult to speak, confronting the two decades' worth of secrets they kept from one another.

In the end, it was Phong who broke the stillness, answering the question Minh and Duy couldn't ask.

"I love him, okay? Edmond. I have loved him all my life. I have loved him more than I've ever thought was possible. I have loved him in the dark, and I have shielded our love from the sun. And now he is dead. I love him still, but he chose to leave me."

"Why . . . What are you saying?" Still holding the locket inside his palm, Duy sounded confused.

"I'm saying . . ." Phong stammered, his tears falling again. "I'm saying that Edmond killed himself because of me."

"How do you know?" Duy mumbled inside his throat. There wasn't a trace of accusation or doubt in his question; he always knew Phong wasn't a liar.

"The slashes on his arm. It must have started then." Phong struggled to speak, choking on his words. "He must have done it to numb his mind. And it didn't work, I suppose, because . . . his hands . . . skin lesions are caused by excessive consumption of arsenic. My guess is he attempted to enhance his wine with it, day after day, trying to poison himself. The cuts, and then the wine, they weren't enough to silence his thoughts."

Duy gazed at the six empty bottles lying near Edmond's feet.

"You think he meant to do it? That he was suicidal?"

"Yes, I suppose he was."

But of course, they would never know for sure.

"When did you—" Duy began, hesitating.

"When did I know that I loved him?" Phong smirked ruefully. "When he asked if I could tutor him. When we were kids."

"From the start, then."

"Yes, I guess. I have loved him from the start."

"Why did you never mention anything?"

"Edmond," Phong shook his head, "Edmond couldn't even admit it to himself."

"My love could only love me there." Duy repeated the words that Phong had spoken all those years ago when he booked the Red Room at Lavie for an entire month.

"You remember."

"I do. I'm sorry. I wish I could have helped."

"I wish you could have, too."

"I think I should give this back to you." Duy opened his palm in Phong's direction, revealing the locket inside.

Phong stared at the object, shaking his head. "I don't want it anymore. They were meant to be a pair. I don't even know where Edmond's is now."

Duy nodded, placing the locket inside Edmond's cold, mottled hand. The three of them sat with their backs against the wall, their eyes bearing down on Edmond's body, their shoulders touching—Duy in the middle, with Phong and Minh by his sides. Even in death, Edmond was still their sun.

They tried to breathe calmly, all wondering what would happen when the governor arrived. If he would believe that Edmond had simply killed himself. They allowed the silence to rise, to swallow the unspoken thought: someone would have to pay for Edmond's life.

The worth of a Frenchman.

But it wasn't the governor who knocked on Duy's front door, just minutes later. When the young men looked up at the door, standing in front of them wasn't the portly old man with the big, round belly, but Leon Moutet. Like a hungry shark, Leon had arrived, following the scent of blood.

ONE DAY PRIOR

Minh

After hearing the news of the commotion at the rubber plantation, Minh was fuming; he went straight to his private estate to consider his plan. The rebels were braver than he had anticipated, making their move the previous night. The leader was smart enough to keep his identity a secret until the very last minute: when he was arrested, nine other men had decided to surrender and follow him. Foolish loyalty.

As for the rest, Minh had yet to know; he intended to question the factory manager that afternoon.

Now, he turned the knob to his bedroom, frowning when the door hinge screeched. The noise echoed within the vacant space, a tantalising reminder. His house, no longer a home. He headed towards the writing desk in the corner and grabbed an apple from the fruit basket, peeling its red skin with a paring knife. He sliced the flesh into smaller pieces, then left them on a white ceramic plate.

"Fuck," Minh cursed as the simple wooden chair groaned under his weight. He leaned against its flimsy panel, his eyes darting from the empty room to the breakfast he had just prepared. An undying habit, he realised. In a fit of rage, Minh threw the plate against the wall. He didn't want to remember, but memories had a mind of their own—the morning routines he had taken for granted.

I know how much you love apples. Minh often woke Hai with the delicacy in hand. He hated them—the taste overly sweet, the texture a hybrid of soft and crunchy—but he never denied her anything.

You shouldn't have. Hai would smile when she accepted the gift, her eyes glistening with sleep, twinkling with affection, never leaving his.

Minh adored it—the direct, tender, innocent way Hai looked at him. She held his gaze without flinching, even when he was upset. She wasn't afraid of him. She didn't see the monster the other servants saw in Minh, and for that, he was grateful. Hai knew that behind his hardened façade, Minh had only ever wanted love and acceptance.

Together they would move to sit, quietly, at the writing desk, Minh opposite Hai. It was enough to be in each other's company, peacefully enjoying each sunrise. Minh would lean across the table to hold Hai's hand, and she would blush an adoring pink. Eventually when Minh prepared to leave for work, Hai would excuse herself to the kitchen, working alongside the maids Minh had hired to serve her. He would beckon her over first, holding her chin between his thumb and index finger, placing a soft kiss on her lips. Quick, without thinking. A reflex, a natural moment he'd never thought he could lose.

"No." Minh shook his head, slapping his thigh violently.

He did not cry. Not ever.

"Bring me the grey suit. The one with the black buttons," he yelled towards the hall. He was better than this—he refused to shed a tear for a woman who had wronged him.

He stared blankly at his reflection in the tall mirror as he waited for his clothes, conjuring the face of the rebel leader gaping back.

The maid helped Minh get ready in a haste; he was becoming restless. He didn't wait for the valet to open his car door, climbing in with a frightening determination.

"Let's go."

Behind the driver's seat, Minh's head throbbed with an irritating hum. Even the monotonous sound of the engine made him furious. The bags under his eyes felt puffier than ever, their colour a shade of purple insomnia. He was exhausted—Hai haunted him whilst he was awake and asleep.

He had to stop thinking about her; he needed something positive. His newfound purpose, perhaps. The mission he had recently discovered, his true destiny. The reminder alone helped elevate Minh's mood; he tapped his fingers erratically against his knees. He had successfully harvested an agenda, and he couldn't wait to see it through.

After an hour, the vehicle came to a stop.

"We're here, Monsieur."

The weather was hot, the air damp. Minh let out a scoff of disgust as he got out of the car. He looked down at his feet, noticing a faint smudge on his otherwise pristine leather shoes, failing to register the driver's bare feet on the searing concrete ground.

In front of the red iron gate stood Liêm, his father's close friend, the factory manager. Liêm stepped forward, his head slightly bowed.

"You've grown."

A clumsy comment to start a painful conversation.

Minh bobbed his acknowledgement in a dismissive manner. Liêm had gotten older; his black hair was spattered with silver strands, and his hooded eyes sunk deeper into his skull. His frame was rather slender, leaning against the gate, his left hand waving a military-green hat, attempting to cool the air by generating a soft whiff of wind. Liêm's skin was red from the heat, his dark navy shirt drenched in gigantic patches of sweat, and around him came a buzzing sound from the hungry flies.

Minh never liked visiting the plantation. He felt more like a conqueror, enjoying the expansion of his rubber forest without the annoyance of daily decisions. Like his father had before him, Minh left those decisions in Liêm's hands—and Liêm was a well of knowledge when it came to the factory politics.

"Can you brief me on what happened?" Minh asked. His mouth quickly opened, then closed. He was afraid to breathe in the putrid scent of rubber tires.

"It started late last night," Liêm began, his face drooping with exhaustion. "The rebels snuck out of their accommodations and travelled towards the forest, torches in their hands. I was up late. Old age, you know. We got lucky, really, that I caught them in time. They would have burned the forest down otherwise."

Minh saw a flush of pride warming Liêm's face.

"Where are they now?" he asked sharply.

"They're waiting in the forest, according to your order," Liêm replied promptly.

"Take me there."

* *

241

The walk was long, starting from the factory gate and winding through the factory itself, past the measly accommodations for the workers, and towards the forest entrance. Liêm remained a sensible twenty steps ahead with his men, leaving generous space between themselves and Minh. He was trying to avoid conversation, Minh realised. As for the rest, they knew better than being friendly with the boss. Just as well. Minh wasn't in the mood to entertain anyone.

It was lunchtime, and aside from the tenacious shrill of the cicadas, the village was strangely still. Minh caught a glimpse of a few scrawny kids, running away at the sight of him, perhaps to the safe embrace of their parents. He assumed he was a bogeyman around here.

Minh passed two families, cooking a meal together in one rusty pot. Thin grey smoke twirled through the air of the small courtyard where they cooked. The fire barely heated the thick, rusty cookware; Minh grimaced as the water struggled to boil. Inside, the leaves of the cabbage remained a crisp, pale green. The smell made Minh nauseous, and he picked up his pace with his nose scrunched. He couldn't comprehend why these people would voluntarily consume such an abomination, forgetting that food—however rotten and revolting—was still food.

The men came to a stop for a quick rest in front of another small stone house with a wooden sign, marking Lot C. Its residents lingered in the yard, their eyes dark with fear. For a while, no one spoke. Minh, Liêm, and his men were all tired from the long walk, and the workers fell silent under Minh's heated gaze. Afraid. He paid their discomfort no mind, studying their appearances, their strangeness like they were another species entirely. The women were dressed in brown linen shirts, the splits and patches on their outfits nearly identical. The men wore black from head to toe—their shirts were unbuttoned and their shorts were rolled high to combat the heat, exposing dirt-smeared skin underneath. Their knees were the colour of ash from hours spent kneeling in the mud; their arms and chests were branded with open wounds in the shape of thin, slender whips. The workers seemed both ravenous and scared, their faces like those of tigers, imprisoned, hungry in their cages. But like house pets, they surrendered to their captors.

"Well don't just stand there," Minh urged Liêm after his heartbeat returned to its regular rhythm. "I don't have all day."

Reluctantly, Liêm nodded. He led Minh further, leaving the dark grey roof of the stone house behind.

When they finally reached the rubber forest, Minh could tell there had been a storm the night before. The grass was a gooey green mass under his feet. The sun was hot and high in the cloudless sky, its searing golden light cutting through branches of rubber trees, heating the last of the rain to a sticky, humid mist. *Idiots*, Minh laughed to himself. The rebels wanted to burn the forest in the rain.

Minh walked with deliberate steps. Around him, the air was very still. Other than the crunching of brown, crisp leaves beneath his shoes, the forest appeared to be sleeping.

It wasn't until Liêm stopped at an isolated piece of land—where the rebels were being kept—that they finally heard the voices. The leader's persistent words, his voice exhausted as he murmured to his loyal comrades.

Minh stopped in his tracks, his hands resting in the pockets of his charcoal trousers, his left eyebrow an unpleasant arch as he turned to Liêm.

"Is that . . . ?"

He needn't finish the question. The skinny manager had already nodded, confirming his suspicion.

"The leader is indeed Monsieur Phong's step-brother."

*   *

Minh had decided to come with a group of fifteen men. His shot-gun probably would have been enough—the ten malnourished workers had already been beaten half to death, their necks chained to the young rubber trees. Together, Minh's men assembled a bar-ricade, their faces austere; the congregation was a show of power more than a necessity.

Minh signalled for them to stand down; he didn't need their assistance anyway. He wanted to listen to everything Phong's step-brother had to say.

He trained his eyes on the young man. His arms were crossed in front of his chest, his true expression concealed under a pair of round sunglasses. Minh squinted, struggling to identify any resem-blance between this nameless man and his close friend. Phong's step-brother wore a torn grey tunic with a worn round collar, a group appointed crown for the group appointed leader, his thin body lost beneath the excess fabric. His hair was cut short, identical to that of every other man at the plantation. Across his tan face was a long, fresh wound in the shape of the leather whip that was limping at Liêm's side. His eyes were bruised black and purple. He looked nothing like Phong, Minh decided coldly.

He recalled the day he was informed of this man's existence at the plantation. *The bastard*, they called him. No name, no title, no golden bloodline. Even his own father denied him any relation. The man might as well have been born the son of a beggar.

"His name is Tư," Liêm whispered.

Minh didn't respond, glancing at the silver hour hand of his watch, noting that the time had moved past midday. The workers had been kept there less than twenty-four hours, chained to the very trees they'd spent all their time nurturing and protecting.

244

Tư ignored the group of tyrants standing around him, his attention focused solely on his shackled comrades.

"When was the last time you were given the chance to admire the infinite, vast blue above your heads?" Tư's voice was raspy and hoarse as he called to his beaten friends. "From sunup to sundown, your eyes are glued to the ground, clearing the forest of plants and bushes."

Tư stopped for a second to swallow his saliva, as though that would ease the scorching thirst clearly burning through his throat.

"Look at yourselves!" Tư continued. "Your clothes are hanging off your bones, your flesh torn, your skin injured. You must strike to demand better working environments. You must strike for change!"

Minh let out a taunting laugh. His hands clapped, mocking, forcing Tư to turn his head in Minh's direction. It was only a fleeting second, but Minh was sure he had just seen Tư's red, passionate face dim a shade paler. Minh smirked as he walked to where Tư was sitting. Slowly, he lowered his shotgun to Tư's forehead. Its chilling barrel must have brought some comfort to Tư's feverish skin, but his expression remained impassive.

"What a beautiful speech," Minh commented sarcastically. "Though I must say, it doesn't look like you'll succeed."

Tư averted his eyes, refusing to give Minh a chance to relish in his failure. He couldn't utter any objection; Minh was right.

"Do you understand the meaning of your name, Tư?" Minh asked.

Tư glared back at Minh now, but still said nothing, his gaze the embodiment of words he couldn't speak aloud.

"Very well," Minh sighed theatrically. "Since you are so stupid and I'm feeling charitable, I shall explain it to you."

He circled the ground Tư was kneeling on, the same way a cat circled a mouse. The forest was now a stage for his performance, the dying men his reluctant audience.

"You see, Tư means four. So, naturally, you might immediately associate this number to the meaning of your name. But here is where it gets interesting."

Minh raised his index finger, keeping his posture straight.

"Phonetically, Tư also sounds similar to a particular word, which also originates from the Chinese language. Want to guess what that word is?"

Minh couldn't coax a retaliation from Tư, but this did not deter him. He continued. "The word is tử—death. You hear me? You were born to die."

Minh waited, allowing the words to seep under Tư's wounds. Somehow, the forest grew even more quiet as the two men stared at one another, two lions readying themselves for an inevitable fight. It wasn't a fair fight, by any means, with one man chained to a tree. But it was a fight nonetheless.

"You are nothing but a pretty boy with a weapon," Tư finally spoke, stabbing at the tension with the sharpness of his words. He spat them out of his mouth along with his phlegm, right on the patch of grass where Minh was standing. "You really think I'm scared of someone who hasn't the bravery to come here without a gun?"

To Tư's surprise, Minh only laughed. Tư's insult was more pitiful than offensive, the words a weak beating against Minh's sturdy ego; this sort of ego was only fragile in front of men like Leon Moutet.

Minh crouched to his heels. His right hand patronised Tư's swollen cheek with a soft pat, his smirk condescending.

"You might be correct. Maybe in another life I would humble myself, offer you a chance to fight. But in this life, I can hold a

246

gun anytime I please. You won't even get to decide how your life will end."

Minh didn't care what else Tư had to say. He had made his decision. He did hesitate, of course. After all, Minh did sense that flickering desperation on Phong's face from time to time, whenever he mentioned the plantation. Minh had always known that Phong was curious about his stepsiblings, relegated to the fields—though because his friend had never actually asked, Minh went on dismissing this as a vague, meaningless concern. In the end, the indecision solidified into a determination. Minh would not offend anyone.

He was right to pull the trigger.

The blast sent a ripple jutting through the forest, and Tư's friends let out a collective, muffled whimper. They rubbed their bony hands together, begging for Minh's clemency.

It was then that the impossible happened—the relentless whine of cicadas somehow receded in Minh's ears. He couldn't hear much else, not the scrawny men's pleading voices, certainly not Liêm's screams, begging him to stop. The power he felt when he executed Tư was exceptionally overwhelming, fuelling the fury of his newfound bloodlust, devouring all of his senses. His index finger felt magnetised to the trigger.

His surroundings blurred: even after blinking frantically, Minh could still only see the face of the woman who betrayed him, the woman who held his heart in her hand and had cruelly grounded it to shards, the woman who brought out the compassionate and humane side of him, only to abandon him to his true, animalistic nature. Hai.

The woodland and the people melted, their presence now as black as Minh's resentment. Hai seemed to smile at him, satisfied with all she had just consumed, so satisfied she didn't notice spiders crawling out of her mouth. She was no longer the light at the end of his tunnel, no longer the person who could save him. She was now the demon who gobbled his happiness, who ignited his lonely rage.

The realisation burned through Minh. He raised the pistol, firing until the gun was deprived of bullets.

When Minh finally woke from his rampage, he panted, the bloody aftermath of the massacre dyeing his vision red. The nine men from Tư's group had all been killed; they couldn't outrun Minh's wrath, not when heavy silver shackles were restraining them. Their corpses collapsed onto one another, forming a distasteful hill. The men who rebelled against him were now dead, their blood feeding the soil one last time. They would be left here in the wilderness, Minh decided, their decomposing flesh serving as fertiliser for the greedy trees; even death failed to save them from the fate of slavery.

Minh looked at the scene unblinkingly before turning his back and walking away. Along with the corpses, he left behind the last shred of his humanity. On and on he marched, out of the forest, failing to notice the horror that filled Liêm's face. The fifteen men that Minh had brought as a show of power now recoiled at the sight of him, terrified for their own lives. He didn't care. His mind was blank, free from guilt and baggage; he felt no remorse, nothing but boundless relief.

Phong

"Monsieur Lê asks for your presence at four o'clock sharp, Monsieur. He will be in the study then."

The maid was knocking on Phong's door, announcing his father's peculiar request. Phong felt immediately uneasy at her words: his father never needed him, and the last time they met in the study room was when his father revealed the truth about Phong's stepsiblings. He couldn't imagine today was different—his father would not be bearing good news.

Phong ran his fingers through his wet hair; he had just taken a bath. He was still naked, standing with a white cotton towel around his waist. Phong lazily eyed the black outfit that he laid out on the bed, reluctant to put it on. His father's rule, of course: everyone, masters and servants alike, must wear pure black in his presence. The traditional colour of mourning. After twenty-four years, Phong's father still mourned his wife's death. Day after day, the man fought time to preserve what he still had left of the past, his unyielding fingers closing tightly around the broken shards of his delusion. Phong resented it, being the source of his father's loss, yet at the same time, he understood it. He could only imagine the life he would lead, if Edmond left his side for all eternity.

From the corner of Phong's room, the grandfather clock struck four. He couldn't delay the matter any longer. Like a spoiled child, Phong was suddenly angry at his friends. His successful, busy friends who had duties to tend to, lives to lead, more important tasks to perform than his dreaded walk down the hall.

Just as well, Phong breathed out.

In a few more hours, when tomorrow arrived, he would be in Edmond's car, heading towards Duy's mansion in Đà Lạt. They

249

would arrive before Minh and Duy, would avail themselves of those few stolen moments of privacy. Phong would bury his face in the nape of Edmond's neck, breathing in his scent, saying aloud the phrase he often whispered. *My beloved.* The feeling of their fingers, laced together. Edmond—half-drunk, half-sober—would cry, overwhelmed with feelings he didn't want to confront. Phong would run his fingers through Edmond's fine hair, kissing the tears dry, as if to say: *Let me always bear your pain.*

Such prospect should have dampened Phong's spirit, but he was smiling. The constant heartache seemed much too small a price to pay, so long as Edmond was by his side.

Phong unclenched his fists and started dressing himself.

He tossed the towel in the wicker basket by the door. His fingers followed the line of buttons on his black shirt, considering whether he should leave the top two open, before closing them altogether. He didn't want to prolong the conversation with his father, and he certainly wouldn't give the old man a chance to lecture him on inappropriate attire. Next came the vest and the jacket; Phong had already started sweating. The socks on his feet felt uncomfortably clammy, but he put his shoes over them anyway. He wouldn't be in the study for long, Phong reasoned. His cheeks hollowed on his face as he let out another puff of air, then headed out the door.

That day, the corridor was unusually dark, reminding Phong of Minh's mansion and his mother's insistence on natural light. Phong couldn't see much other than the faint outlines of some flower vases, so he lowered his head, staring intently at his footsteps to ensure that he wouldn't trip. He didn't understand why his father had ordered all the lights off.

When Phong reached the study room's door, his father called out.

"Come in."

His father was sitting in the dark, though Phong could make out the shape of a wine bottle in his hand.

"You asked to see me, Father."

Without moving from his chair or looking directly at Phong's face, his father nodded. "You're late."

Phong dipped his head, bored. They'd had this conversation at least a hundred times before. For as long as Phong could remember, this had been their lives—a series of repetitive, formal courtesies.

For a while, neither man spoke, and Phong was forced to stand awkwardly in place. He watched his old man's grip tighten around the neck of the bottle while his chest ached with longing. His father's gesture was angry, violent, and still Phong resented the innocent object. All his life, he had never known a touch so gentle, affectionate from his father. He shifted his gaze to the corner of the room where a timber cabinet stood, a vase of white chrysanthemums resting atop its surface. One by one, the petals fell from their buds, gathering around the base of the vase, a white-and-blue ceramic bowl of burning incense sitting next to them. The work of one of the women that his father remarried, surely. Each morning each of the women woke, got dressed, and moved from one room to the next, mourning the death of a woman they unfortunately resembled.

Next to the cabinet, neatly arranged in a line, was Phong's father's herbal wine collection. Inside each glass jar was the corpse of some reptile or insect—a scorpion, a brown snake, a king cobra. When he was a child, Phong was afraid to look at the creatures, but now he felt only pity for them. More than twenty years had passed since he first laid eyes on them, yet their bodies were still refused the natural process of decaying, imprisoned for all eternity in a cramped space, with only alcohol as a companion.

251

"Well don't just stand there. Sit down." His father pointed at the hardwood chair on the other side of his writing desk, pulling Phong out of his thoughts.

Reluctantly, Phong obeyed. He settled uneasily onto the seat, avoiding his father's eyes.

His father reached for the switch on the wall behind his back, turning on the copper chandelier above their heads. It cast a ghastly yellow light on his father's face, and for a quick second, Phong felt a pang of sadness inside his chest. His father seemed even older now, his eyes glassier. It was cruel, the way time gradually slithered through them all, sparing no one.

"I received a telegram just now." Phong's father gestured towards a torn envelope in the middle of the table. "A boy I once knew was killed as punishment for rebellion. The Khải' young master delivered the sentence himself."

Phong opened his mouth, the question balancing at the tip of his tongue. Why was his father involved in Minh's business? But quickly, he caught on, and Phong sealed his lips into a deafening silence.

His stepsibling, one of the children his father created, then rejected.

His only chance at having a family. A chance Phong never quite knew how to grab. A chance now taken away by one of his oldest friends.

In that instant, Phong felt a raging anger towards Minh, something he had never felt before, even during moments when their friendship seemed most strained. Phong was certain that somehow Minh had always known of his desire for family—and Minh had killed his step-brother anyway. Phong and his stepsibling had never met because of Phong's fear and reservations, and now they never would because of Minh's shotgun.

Abruptly, Phong stood, the legs of his chair scraping against the floor. He could no longer sit in front of his father, who reminded him so much of Minh; how easy it was for both of them to reject a person's life.

Phong stormed out of the study without excusing himself, leaving his father behind, alone in the dim space. He reached his room in no time, his fingers clumsy, slippery around the opium pipe. The equipment rattled atop the metal tray, but the sound was drowned in the volume of Phong's sorrow. He needed an escape.

But when he closed his eyes, allowing the soft grey smoke a grip around his throat, once again Phong thought of his step-siblings. His severed relationship with his own father, and his precious last name—he got to keep it, but his stepsiblings did not. He thought of another universe where his step-brother wasn't his step-brother but himself, Minh's gun aimed at his head. Would Minh still have pulled the trigger?

On and on, Phong's mind circled until his grip on reality loosened and he lost himself in the chasm of uncertainty, the abyss a cheerless shade of black with nothing but a pair of yellow king cobra eyes, leering back at him.

Marianne

One. Two. Three.

Marianne counted the droplets of water that trickled down her jawline, bursting as they landed atop the copper basin. She was still nauseous, but she forced her head up, scrutinising her reflection in the humble oval mirror. In the span of a few short hours, she seemed to have aged ten years. Her hair was icier, her wrinkles deeper. Her eyes were a paler shade of blue, lifeless. Her dress was no longer pristine, and her shoes were no longer impeccable. She hadn't the energy to care about her appearance.

She feared for Edmond's life.

Last night, after the conversation with Edmond, Marianne sat at the small desk by her bed, turning the golden locket over in her palm. She couldn't understand it, why Edmond suddenly became adamant that she know about his secret relationship, his insistence that she keep the piece of jewellery. *Was he sick*, she wondered. He did look much skinnier than before. *Was he in danger? Was he planning to run away? Would he hurt himself again?* One after the other, different theories presented themselves in Marianne's mind, luring her into a lucid dream. At six in the morning, as her green alarm clock went off, she hadn't managed a single second of rest. Frantically, she'd leapt out of bed, making her way to Edmond's room, intending to question him further, but he wasn't there.

None of the servants had had any clue where he went.

He would return, she tried to convince herself, suppressing the uneasy feeling constricting her throat. He must have been at Duy's opium club. The secrets she had revealed about his father were heavy, she knew that. Edmond must have needed some time to process the horror.

She simply needed to get on with her day. He would come back to her. He always did.

Morning dragged into noon before yawning into early evening, pinching Marianne's flesh with restlessness. She moved around the mansion the same away a lost soul would, bumping left and right into furniture she did not see. As the sun started setting, Marianne made her way towards the servants' quarter. In a dark corner, muffling a sob, she saw Anne, one of the housemaids recently arrived from Paris.

I really don't have the time for this, Marianne sighed. But in the end, she had asked. *What's going on?*

Madame, forgive me. Startled, Anne turned around, wiping her tears with the heels of her hands, standing up straight. *I didn't mean to be a nuisance.*

There was a cut on the girl's forehead, and she was bleeding. Around her bare feet was a small puddle of blood. Marianne blinked, trying to keep her voice level.

Who did this to you?

Truly, it's nothing. I shall clean the floor in a minute, Madame, Anne replied, avoiding Marianne's gaze. She seemed utterly afraid.

It's not, um— Marianne struggled to finish her question. *It's not Monsieur Edmond, is it?*

Oh, no! Anne shook her head, eyes widened with surprise by the mention of her young master. *Monsieur Edmond has been nothing but kind to me.*

Well, go on, then, Marianne urged. *I can't help if you don't tell me.*

It's . . . Anne bit her lips, perhaps trying to decide whether a confession would be worth it. *It's Monsieur Moutet, Madame.*

He did this to you?

It's nothing, really, Madame. I don't think he meant it. You see, I was cleaning his bedroom when he walked in, and forgive me, I'm not smart enough

255

to see that he was in a rather unpleasant mood. It was my fault, truly. I resumed my task despite his presence, and when he realised I was still in the room, he threw a crystal glass at my head.

Anne was crying again. Blood trickled down her temple, diluted by the tears that rushed down her swollen cheek. The sight unnerved Marianne, and she had to look away.

Go ask for the valet. He'll know what to do about your wound. Tell him I sent you, and he won't ask any unnecessary questions.

Marianne could always trust the valet; he was one of her oldest friends.

Madame . . . Anne nodded, but her eyes were wary.

Your secret is safe with me. Now, go on.

Thank you, Madame.

Once Anne was completely out of sight, Marianne knelt on the ground and began cleaning the blood with the towel on her belt loop. Twice now this fabric had tasted blood from two different people. What would come next? Her hands trembled with fear; Anne's words lingered. Something wasn't right with Leon. He used to make a point of remaining delightful with the servants in his household, always trying to win their support and loyalty. Why the sudden and drastic change? Was it that young Annamite maid? Did she offend him somehow, even after her death? Or was killing her no longer enough to satisfy Leon's bloodlust?

Was he done with the practice?

Marianne's body went cold at the thought. No. Leon could never touch Adeline, the *real* Adeline who remained a continent away.

But there was someone else within Leon's reach.

Marianne couldn't explain it, the trepidation in her stomach. Immediately, she set off in terror, sprinting towards Leon's bedroom. What she would do when she stood in front of that cruel man, Marianne didn't know. She couldn't physically stop him, but did it really matter? She would become a human shield if she had to, separating Leon from Edmond.

Marianne was so distracted, she did not watch her feet—a few seconds later, she collided with the valet in the brightly lit corridor. An entire day had passed, nighttime had arrived, and Edmond still hadn't returned.

Are you okay? The old valet offered Marianne his hand, helping her up. *What's the rush?*

I need to see Monsieur Moutet.

Oh, you missed him. He just took the car and left. He said he had an urgent meeting in Đà Lạt.

Dinner time? Driving by himself? Marianne's eyebrows furrowed, her voice doubtful. The Leon she knew never missed a meal, always preaching about the importance of consuming the right nutrients. Food first, business second—such was Leon's life motto. An attempt to soothe his body into forgetting the aching hunger during the early years he spent living in poverty. *Did he say anything else?*

It was strange. The old valet stroked his chin thoughtfully. *When I came to inform him that the car was ready, I overheard a funny thing.*

What? Marianne asked impatiently.

He was on the phone, I assume. He was murmuring something over and over—"That fool is in love with a yellow rat." Who was he talking about, do you think?

I have to go.

Hey— the valet called, but Marianne heard only her thumping heart. She ran and ran, locking herself inside her bathroom, washing her face again and again as though the liquid could somehow wake her from the nightmare.

Four.

Five.

Six.

Marianne continued counting the droplets of water again as her surroundings—a small bathtub, a copper basin, a white toilet bowl with a brown lid—slowly came back into focus. So did the woman in the oval mirror, staring back at Marianne. The woman looked beaten, defeated.

The valet's words returned to her ears.

In love with a yellow rat.

The never-ending rumours. The portrait she found. The battle that Edmond himself was fighting.

Who else could Leon be referring to?

Somehow, Leon had managed to uncover Edmond's secret: his love for Phong. Marianne had never once believed that Leon was capable of killing his own son. But this might just be the final straw—loving an Annamite. An unforgivable sin, in Leon's world.

Closing her eyes, Marianne tried to slow her breath. She was far too late. She couldn't find Edmond anywhere, could do nothing to shelter him from what Leon might be planning. She could only get on her knees and pray that a god truly existed, that Edmond would be protected against his father's uncontrollable violence.

Such helplessness broke Marianne, and she started to cry. Unlike the droplets of water that trickled down her face earlier, Marianne couldn't seem to count her tears. She could only feel their heat against her skin, could only watch as the tears fell to the ground, shattering on impact, like broken pearls.

THAT NIGHT

Leon entered the living room with two hands behind his back, his face calm, free of emotion. He did not glance at his son, dead on the floor. His gaze was trained fiercely on Duy instead, where he stood with Minh and Phong. He scrutinised their expressions and demeanours, like a judge observing criminals. Over Leon's shoulder, the governor and his small army of ten men stood waiting obediently, like a pack of hounds.

Duy's face turned a shade grimmer at the sight; it was clear that Leon wasn't interested in finding the truth. He wanted to save his pride.

He wanted to make them pay.

"The governor and I were having a friendly dinner, you see, when his phone started to ring," Leon began, his voice booming. "He informed me of some sketchy business within the Caos' residence that might involve my heir. We left our meal in a hurry, only to show up here and discover that my only son is dead."

Fixing his gaze on Phong, Leon continued.

"I'll give you one chance. One. To confess. What happened here?"

"Edmond killed himself. There was nothing we could—"
Duy replied, but quickly he was interrupted by the governor.

"Monsieur Moutet wasn't asking you."

Surprised, Duy stared at the Frenchman in annoyance. He
didn't understand it at first, but when the governor squared his
shoulders and clenched his jaw, the purpose of his presence at the
Caos' residence became crystal clear: to restrain Duy. The governor wasn't here because of Duy's insistence. He was here because
Leon had requested it. The shelter the governor had been offering
the Caos was now an anchor, holding Duy down, preventing him
from challenging Leon's authority.

"He consumed a mixture of arsenic and wine," Minh continued, picking up the rest of Duy's sentence.

Raising his right hand, Leon's gaze was as cold as steel. "I
didn't ask you, either."

No one would have believed the ease with which Minh lowered his head and closed his mouth at a Frenchman's request.

Duy's heart sank. From the instant he first heard the news
about his friend's senseless massacre at the rubber plantation, he
had expected this outcome. No one, not even a man as powerful
as Minh, could get away with killing so openly, so ruthlessly. Duy
could imagine them, the grim lines of Madame Nhu's lips as she
came to the same realisation that she must rely on the ever influ-
ential Leon Moutet to protect her only child, to save him from
prison. Perhaps that was the price for Minh's freedom, becoming
Leon's newest puppet.

Duy was furious, with himself, with his friend. How did
they get here, crouching like ants under the powerful thumb of
the French?

"You, go on. Speak." Like an emperor, Leon pointed an
index finger at Phong. "Why are your clothes drenched in blood?"

Amongst the three of them, Minh was the most dishevelled, his hair tangled, his moustache unkempt, and his shirt ripped open. Duy was certainly the dirtiest, with Edmond's blood painted on his sleeves, as he was the first to attend to Edmond's body. But Leon ignored both of them, focusing on Phong instead.

"Go on," Leon urged, when Phong refused to speak. "Have you anything to say for yourself?"

A vicious glint of satisfaction brushed Leon's smug face, and Duy's chest tightened with dread. Leon could have listened to either Minh or Duy, but he chose not to. He could have pointed his finger at any of them. But Leon was only interested in Phong.

Duy's heart exploded. Like a lightning bolt, the realisation struck his clouded mind. There could be only one explanation.

Leon knew.

Somehow, Leon knew of Edmond and Phong. He didn't care what Edmond did, or what Phong didn't do. He didn't care that Phong's shirt was white and clean; Leon would look at any stain and claim it was his son's blood.

He wanted Phong to pay. Not for Edmond's death but for Phong's audacity: he had dared to love a Frenchman.

"Uncle—" The word Duy used to call Leon when he was a child now sounded foreign at the tip of his tongue. It was useless, he knew that, but Duy couldn't stop himself; he never stood by, leaving Phong unprotected.

"I'm not your uncle," Leon spat, offended. "Governor, get your minions under control, would you?"

"Monsieur." The governor nodded, gesturing for two men to march forward: Pierre, the first tirailleur to respond to the scene earlier this evening, and another officer Duy had never seen before. He stared in utter dismay as Pierre came closer, his light brown eyes mocking. The tirailleur's footsteps were slow but confident, as though he already knew how this would end. Perhaps he did. Duy and his friends were trapped.

How long had Leon been planning this? That *friendly dinner* he referred to—had he orchestrated everything? Had he been betting on Edmond's suicide? No, that couldn't be right. None of them, Edmond's closest friends, not even Phong, had seen this coming; how could Leon? Yet, Leon's motive was as obvious as ever. He might not have expected Edmond's death—but he had intended to punish Phong from the start. Had Leon killed Edmond himself?

Quickly, Duy glanced at Phong, who held Leon's gaze with defiance. He wanted to say something, anything, to defend Phong, to save Phong from Leon's rage, but Pierre already stood in front of him, blocking the way. A rifle was hanging across his thick chest, the strap frayed. The baton he'd dropped earlier in a laughable show of power dangled on one side, mocking Duy. *Look how the table has turned.*

"This might be a tad uncomfortable," Pierre smirked, gripping Duy's arm. The fearfulness he wore when they first met vanished.

Together, Pierre and the other tirailleur led Duy and Minh out of the Caos' residence.

With one heavy foot after another, Duy followed, no longer resisting. There was no point. They were outnumbered and out-powered. Like dispensable prawns, both he and Minh were taken off the chessboard. It was comical, pathetic, really—the almighty Annamite heirs reduced to marionettes under French control.

"It's better I follow him. Edmond," Phong whispered in Duy's ear as he walked past.

You've decided, Duy thought, an acute pain pounding in his heart. He looked at Phong and lowered his head. Their final goodbye.

"How could you do it, Phong?" Duy heard the last of Leon's performance behind his back. "How could you kill Edmond?"

The door to the Caos' residence was locked before Duy could hear Phong's answer—but he supposed it no longer mattered. There wasn't a thing to be done, not with Leon's involvement. The admission made Duy feel small, incapacitated, his illusive power destroyed. He was drained, exhausted. He no longer knew how to move forward—they were like his arms and legs, his friends. Limbs he needed to survive, united, inseparable. Yet somehow, in one short night, Duy had lost two of them, his body now forever paralysed.

ONE DAY AFTER

It took Phong longer than usual to observe his surroundings; his glasses were broken, his eyes swollen, his head throbbed. Everything was blurry, and everything hurt.

The guards didn't try to be gentle, discarding him with violent force into the corner of this dirty holding cell. The nauseating scent of urine attacked Phong's nostrils, and his wounded face crumpled as he scrunched his nose.

He was to remain there a few more hours, awaiting immediate execution.

The ground was damp and filthy, the ceiling above dominated by black mould. There were no windows; not even a speckle of light could enter. Phong smiled, imagining this was one of Duy's cheap opium dens. A rather exotic experience.

An undying habit, the thought of opium made Phong's fingers twitch restlessly, begging for a bit of dough to roll between the tips. One thing kept him grounded—the locket Duy had found. Phong wanted to pull it out, to touch its surface; perhaps, the sight of Edmond's portrait could ease the pain Edmond himself had created. Phong summoned the last of his strength to reach inside the left pocket of his now soiled trousers.

He felt nothing, his fingers frantic inside the empty space. Phong closed his eyes, trying not to remember: his foolish determination to reject the locket, to leave it with Edmond's body.

I don't want it anymore.

Bile rose from the back of Phong's throat; who had it now, he didn't know. The last piece of evidence, the only proof of his love.

Drowsy with a newfound pain, Phong recalled the night before. A twisted decision to push his limit.

Bright yellow light from the grand chandelier.

Phong was back in the Caos' living room, kneeling next to Edmond, the sound of Duy and Minh's argument dwindling to a faint murmur in the background. Phong couldn't tell what possessed him in that moment when he took Edmond's gloves off. One look at his own portrait was enough; guilt was a hungry and greedy monster, devouring him whole.

How could you do this, Edmond? Why? Phong croaked, kneeling next to Edmond's cold body, but of course he knew why.

Perhaps this was the reason for his unprompted confession in front of Duy and Minh. Phong had been blaming himself—their secret love pushed Edmond to his death. Phong had always known of Edmond's dark thoughts, yet he persisted with their affair anyway. How hard, how brutal it must have been, the battle between Edmond's feelings and the world he'd always known.

No wonder Edmond insisted on coming here, to the Caos' residence, where they shared countless memories. One last souvenir to give his friends.

He couldn't have anticipated the blame his death would evoke.

When Duy accused Minh of killing Edmond, Phong had looked up, catching Minh's eyes, which darted immediately away from him. Minh was embarrassed by what he'd done at the rubber plantation, Phong assumed. Once, Phong would have cared, crying for the missed chance to have a family. But Edmond was dead, and nothing mattered anymore.

It hit Phong, the realisation—he was meant to follow Edmond. The fortune teller's prophecy all those years ago. Words Phong had long forgotten.

One will pay.

All along, it was destined to be him. Phong, who would sacrifice to atone for Edmond's death, saving Duy and Minh from Leon's rage. It seemed almost too good to be true, how Leon had arrived, armed with the same determination: Phong's downfall.

After Duy and Minh were led away, Leon had nodded in the governor's direction, and the eight remaining men from the governor's pack emerged, a flock of vultures. They didn't speak much, carrying out the order previously arranged between Leon and the governor. One by one, their feet stomped on Phong's chest, their fists hard against his flesh. Soon enough, their faces became a blur in Phong's swollen eyes. Before he fainted entirely, they dragged him by his collar, leaving a trail of blood on Duy's glossy white marble floor. His body was thrown in the back of a patrol car, the same way he had seen his servants throwing out bags of trash.

Not long after, the vehicle came to a stop at a nameless prison, one with a well-worn, battered gate. The French never bothered naming these institutions—the places they utilised to hold the Annamites captive.

A bullnecked tirailleur had dragged Phong across a crude cement ground, the sky a gloomy grey above their heads. The sun

266

had yet to rise. Phong had let his limbs go limp, ignoring the excruciating pain as his flesh scraped over the rough cement surface. The heart did that sometimes: numbing other nerves to contract its muscles in a different kind of suffering.

Ever since then, as Phong withered away in this holding cell, alone with his thoughts, the unanswered questions refused to leave his mind.

Why now, Edmond?

Did it really matter? Phong had seen the look on Edmond's face, the ache that Edmond had been carrying everywhere he went. Phong always knew that Edmond might hurt himself, but, with a naive stubborness, he never expected anything beyond the self-inflicted wounds across Edmond's arm.

What happened to your locket, Edmond?

Edmond had thrown the precious locket somewhere Phong would never discover, discarding their love like dust, like filth. Perhaps it really was. If it hadn't been for those feelings, maybe Edmond would still be alive. Maybe his thoughts wouldn't have torn him in half. The portrait that Edmond carried of Phong felt no longer like a testament of affection but a condemnation: Phong would hurt everyone he ever cared for.

Was I not worth staying alive for?

Edmond had decided to leave, abandoning Phong to navigate a life he never knew how to lead. Like the locket, Edmond had thrown himself into the gap between life and death, a space Phong could not touch unless he followed.

A clatter of noise came from outside his prison cell. Phong sighed—at the very best, it was time for his execution, which he had grimly resigned himself to. At the very worst, it was yet another beating orchestrated by Edmond's father. Regardless, Phong didn't care.

"You look horrendous."

A feathery voice rose from the entrance. Phong was agitated—he had planned on wallowing in his despair all by himself. He wanted no interruption.

"You don't know who I am," the voice pressed again, ignoring his silence, refusing him the solitude he had hopelessly been yearning for.

"I do," he corrected her, the two words like tired breath.

"Phong, I know everything."

The statement swayed Phong, and he glanced her way, unblinking. She was crouching to look at him more closely; a strand of light blonde hair escaped her otherwise sleek low bun, brushing the side of her broad forehead. Her eyes were a pleading shade of blue, wishing for a chance.

* *

Monsieur Moutet's order. Phong heard Marianne's vague, faint explanation to the guards as they prepared to escort her and Phong to another room. Like the mention of a god, Leon Moutet's name.

This new cell was just as small, its four corners just as dingy as the last. The foul smell, though, no longer seemed as nauseating. Phong could only assume that the room had been cleaned to accommodate Marianne's unexpected appearance; he doubted they had a special holding place for the more important criminals, those who came from noble and powerful families, rooms like Duy's clubs had for their richer clients. After all, this wasn't an opium den, and Phong's estranged father would rather lose yet another son than offer Phong a helping hand. Phong's status, his bloodline, the vanity of his last name: these things hardly mattered anymore. Still, though he did not need his father's rescue, Phong's heart ached, registering the empty ground his father should have been standing on.

A brawny hand violently pushed Phong forward, forcing his ankles to drag forwards the rusty, heavy iron cuffs. Their rims raked atop the dark cement ground, a screeching sound like the cry of a starving hyena.

Phong paid little attention to his discomfort, his eyes scanning the new surroundings; in the middle of the room sat a set of bamboo tables and two three-legged stools. Their designs bore a world of difference from those he had seen in Madame Nhu's extensive collection—tall, proud treasures. This prison furniture was made from rustic pieces of bamboo, carrying thick layers of dust and gunk on their ridges, black paint peeling.

"Five minutes," the stocky guard with dark brown hair declared curtly, leaving Phong and Marianne locked inside the cell.

Marianne moved first, perching on the stool's edge, careful not to dirty her blindingly white dress. She looked directly at Phong without saying a word. Reluctantly, he followed, taking the seat on the opposite side. He lowered his head, face hot from Marianne's knowing gaze. Phong felt exposed and vulnerable; the things he and Edmond had kept as secrets, now one sentence away from breaking free.

"It's on the front page now. Everyone is talking about it. Everyone thinks you're guilty."

"Well, I suppose I am." Phong shrugged, his voice rough and harsh. He hadn't had anything to drink since the previous night, and his mouth tasted awful, like his own blood.

Marianne sat with her hands knit together in front of her belly, preparing her speech. Grief loomed over her otherwise expressionless face; she was trying to pretend at stoicism.

"Phong, we don't have time for this. You can be honest with me."

"I'm not following."

"It wasn't you, was it?" Marianne said impatiently, the calmness on her face already evaporated. "It was Leon who killed Edmond."

"No. What are you talking about?" Phong cleared his throat, his thick brows bunching together.

"I think he found out about you and Edmond." Marianne lowered her voice. "I haven't seen him since yesterday. And now Edmond is dead, and Leon sentenced you to die as the final punishment. It's far too much for a coincidence, don't you think?"

"Marianne . . ." Phong started, then faltered.

"I knew it. I knew it couldn't have been you." She continued, oblivious to the guilt on Phong's face. "When I first heard it, I could tell there was more to the story. I snuck out, you see, and I asked the valet to take me here. We ought to do something about this, you and I. We can't let Leon get away with this."

"Marianne," Phong repeated himself, exhausted. Momentarily, he hated Edmond for leaving, putting him in this position.

"Phong, listen to me."

"Marianne," Phong raised his voice, trying to capture Marianne's attention. "Listen to *me*. Leon didn't kill Edmond. Edmond . . . he killed himself, okay? He diluted his wine with arsenic, poisoning himself. Because of me. And his hands! They were covered in skin lesions. All because of me, our love. So I guess Leon isn't entirely wrong, punishing me. I am guilty. I am responsible for Edmond's death."

Silence erupted in the small space. Marianne stared at Phong with glassy eyes.

"I'm sorry," Phong said, breathless.

"The locket." Marianne gasped, reaching inside the front pocket of her dress. "He gave me his locket the night he told me about you."

She revealed the piece of jewellery, tucked inside her palm.

Phong couldn't reply, blinking emptily at Edmond's locket. Edmond had entrusted Marianne with it, but Phong foolishly rejected his, leaving it cold and unloved with Edmond's body. Had Leon found it? Had the governor? Would they burn it? Discard it?

"It's possible he decided it then, when he handed me the locket," Marianne mumbled to herself. "Maybe it wasn't a gift. Maybe it was his goodbye . . ."

Tears swallowed the rest of her words, and Phong winced. He forced himself to look away from the pendant—to tell Marianne to leave—but she stifled her sob, speaking over him.

"I can't let this happen to you. We have to get you out of here."

Funny, Phong wanted to say. Marianne used the word *we*, as though there were someone else out there who cared about Phong's survival. Duy and Minh might have, sure, but they were in no position to disobey Leon Moutet's orders.

Phong shook his head, holding her gaze. He didn't deserve this love, didn't deserve Marianne's pity. She seemed utterly broken, the better part of her world ripped apart—a mother now without a child.

"Marianne . . ." he repeated her name.

"No." She raised her hand. "I know what you're going to say. You are going to tell me that you want to follow Edmond, that there isn't any point trying to fight Leon Moutet. This isn't what Edmond would have wanted."

"We can never know that for sure, can we?"

Phong didn't say those words to be cruel, but Marianne looked as though Phong had just slapped her.

"He told me the story," Marianne said, another attempt to change Phong's mind. "He was crazy about you, do you know? He loved you so much. A man who loved you that much would never want this ending for you."

"He abandoned me," Phong said coldly, not because he resented Edmond, but because that was the truth. Their love wasn't heavy enough of an anchor to keep Edmond alive. Marianne didn't respond, staring as Phong bit his fingernails. He was trying to choose his words, deciding if he should be honest with her.

Perhaps he should.

"Don't be sorry for me, Marianne. The truth is I plan to follow him whether or not Leon Moutet is involved. We promised we'd be together forever. Did he tell you that?"

Phong smiled bitterly.

"Edmond's gotten his forever, and now I intend to have mine."

Outside the cell, the guards were growing restless, and they barged in as the last word left Phong's mouth. They ignored Marianne's protest, her declaration that they were making a huge mistake. Her words, futile and pointless, like wind against a mountain.

In one swift motion, the burly guard picked Phong's slender body off the stool, grinning sadistically. His cigarette-stained teeth flashed under his thin lips, his muscles eager to help rid the world of yet another filthy Annamite.

"Phong," Marianne croaked from behind, her voice imploring.

Hearing his name, Phong glanced back, his eyes an empty void.

* *

The air was parched, and the sky was cloudless.

The guards walked ahead, trailing Phong slowly behind on a tight leash. Phong's last name had evaporated the moment he entered this prison, and the French could treat him accordingly. Like a stray dog, an abandoned animal.

The ground was hot under Phong's bare feet; the sun was now high and bright. A taunt, mocking his sinful love. The kind of love that could only exist under subdued moonlight. Under righteous golden sun, Phong was alone.

"Hands." A guard turned and wiggled his index finger, signalling for Phong to follow. He obeyed. They had reached the execution ground.

This guard was taller than the guard back at his cell: his lips were tight as he uncuffed Phong, as he tied Phong's back to a tall, fractured wooden pole, with dark spots trailing its length. The blood of the people who had died before him.

Phong squinted as the firing squad came into focus. Five men in total, each carrying a Winchester rifle. Their faces were covered by thin black masks—a weak attempt to make the execution less personal. After all, the men and Phong, they were one and the same—the needle and the thread Leon Moutet had used to sew over his broken pride.

A flag was waved, not the flag of his country, but the flag of the group of tirailleurs—French flag canton on a bright yellow field. On cue, the men raised their weapons. Phong held their gaze for a second longer before closing his eyes, a strange calmness flowing through his veins.

They fired.

Somewhere close by, the birds startled, their yelps tearing the ether in half as silver bullets exploded from five guns. In the blink of an eye, Phong's body folded to a slump, lying in a crimson pool, his lips bearing the slightest hint of a smile. He died picturing Edmond at his happiest—eyes lazy, lashes fluttering like fragile petals under gentle wind. And so Phong died happy, too.

Later, when the time came, Phong's body would succumb to the elements, turning into the dust and sand that floated in the air, searching for the last of Edmond's essence on this earth.

TWO DAYS LATER

Sen panted as she ran along the quiet streets, the brick houses and the small, unopened shops a blur. The usual smell—a mixture of urine, sewage, and rotten food, all scattered over the grey pavement—made no appearance today. Or perhaps her senses had gone adrift, muddled by speed.

Her mind was empty. She did not know where she was running; the thin scarf she had tied loosely around her head suddenly felt heavy. The road was devoid of people—the men and women who woke before dawn to ready themselves for work on the street were nowhere in sight.

It was far too early.

Sen spotted a small alleyway on the left side of the road ahead and picked up her pace. Her heart pounded when she stopped, her back pressed against the peeling white wall, her hands instinctively reaching for the pockets of her trousers, ensuring the money was still in place. The bulging pile of notes she had been accumulating over the years.

She could go home.

That had been her first thought, until she dismissed it completely. It would be dangerous and unfair to her poor mother.

Where else then? Sen didn't know. Her whole life, servitude and subservience were all she had known. Her whole life, she answered to a name that wasn't hers.

Tattler.

She would stop now. She belonged to no master. She was no handmaid; she served no one.

She was Sen.

Sen looked at her fingers, which had known only mud and dirt before. They trembled. Sen closed her eyes and tilted her head back, allowing her tired limbs a moment to rest as she relived the pivot when she decided she would really, *really* risk it all.

It happened when she'd followed Marianne to the servants' quarter during that silent, endless walk from Edmond's bedroom. In front of Sen, Marianne was lost in thought, leaving Sen to herself, processing the horror she'd just experienced. Her mouth had still been sour from her vomit, the same vomit that Edmond later ordered her to swallow. The taste refused to disappear, clogging the tip of her throat.

For so long Sen had built everything around the dream of becoming a madame, her every action a steppingstone, delivering her closer to the life she had always burned for. She listened to others' well-kept secrets, sneaking from one corner to the next in search of the right moment to rise. But when she finally got her chance, Edmond had ripped it away with a mere pair of scissors, a bottle of wine, and his calculating words. When he held her face above the puddle of her own vomit, Sen saw clearly for the first time how Edmond viewed her—a lowly inferior, fated to burrow in her own filth. The power he'd exerted diminished her sense of self—she was helpless, reduced to begging for mercy. The image she had treasured of her future, smart and capable, smeared to a humiliating smudge.

When they had reached the main floor, one level above their final destination, Sen noticed two imposing ceramic vases. Their creator had painted a drawing of waterfalls amidst a bamboo forest on their chalky white bodies—Sen knew that these soulless objects were more valuable than a servant's life. *Her* life. Such thoughts swayed her fright, and by the time Marianne told her to use the washroom, her stomach was torched with something else. Something intense, fiery. She splashed cold water on her face, staring at her reflection in the small, tainted mirror, trying to understand the new sensation in her organs. The images of what she saw—the shiny marble steps, the striking bannisters, the sturdy handrails that formed a mesmerising spiral, the vain items these wealthy men collected—helped ignite a violence she did not recognise.

Wrath.

Fury.

Why don't you do us all a favour and disappear?

Edmond's words echoed, their edges sharp, piercing.

Why should Sen be the one to disappear? Sen, who suffered more losses than Edmond could possibly imagine—her father to alcohol, her brother to famine, her mother and her entire life to poverty. Why shouldn't it be Edmond who disappeared?

She couldn't lose, not to people who already abhorred her. She knew from the core of her existence she deserved something better: she deserved to live. People like Edmond, they needed a lesson—to learn their actions, their cruelty, had consequences.

She would fix this broken scale, restoring it to balance.

Sen had pushed the washroom door open to the other side, where Marianne awaited with a prepared speech, her eyes big and innocent, pleading. She saw a flicker of pity when the old woman nodded yes to her begging, and she was pleased. Her entire life, she had been trampled by her masters. She knew it was a weapon, how her superiors let their guard down when people thought her harmless.

She spent that night in a new room, unable to sleep, her ears straining to familiarise herself with the sounds of this strange house. When she was certain everyone had fallen asleep, Sen snuck out, the sky outside her new window smaller than the sky back at the Khải'. Carefully, she made her way to Edmond's bedroom, the place of her worst torments. She positioned herself next to the door frame, and she studied Edmond's sleeping face. It appeared Marianne always left the door open. The next part of her plan began to form.

Quietly, Sen walked across the yard, and this time, she admitted, she was lucky. The gate was unlocked: a slight push and the blinding white mansion was behind her. The temporary freedom was liberating, and for a second, Sen considered abandoning her mission. Her pocket was thick with the few notes Marianne insisted she take for her troubles. She could leave with her head held high, with no nagging worry trailing her steps. It was tempting, but in the end she shook her head. No. After an eternity of tyranny, Sen owed herself the chance to be in charge.

Once she made it outside, the rest was easy. The countless days and nights she spent running errands for Madame Như had finally turned helpful—the map of Sài Gòn had never been clearer. She turned left and right with deliberation, the directions long ingrained in her mind, the way a horse knew the route back to its barn. Humans and animals, she concluded, were merely creatures of habit.

Sài Gòn's streets were more tangled than they were big, and after a few more turns, she reached a herbal pharmacy. There was no sign, the brick house standing as ordinary as any, solemn at the end of the alleyway.

She knew of this place from the other servants' gossips back at the Khåis'. They discussed the pharmacy often—a secretive institution that sold a discreet herb that helped with early pregnancy termination. The vulgar affairs between the housemaids and the valets were carefully swept under the rug, quietly discarded.

The ether was a mixture between dark navy and grey; the sun had yet to make its appearance, its seat still dominated by the crescent moon. It was too early for the door to open, for the bags of ginseng roots and rhino horns to hang outside, welcoming. Sen rasped her knuckles against the dark brown panel anyway; she hadn't much time.

The man who greeted her with his eyes half-closed wasn't someone she had seen before, and she was confident he would not remember her forgettable face. She was cautious enough, wearing a palm-leaf conical hat to conceal her ugly, shorn hair. She kept her voice low, shielding her excitement.

I'm here to pick up Madame Nhu's order.

As she said it, Sen startled, a leftover reflex; the name of her old master felt risky, but it had to be used. A crucial part of her revenge. Should a detective manage to discover this pharmacy, the suspicion would fall immediately on the Khåis.

What?

The man asked, confusion clouding his question. She almost rolled her eyes.

The order for Madame Nhu? From the Khåis' residence? she repeated, louder this time. *The one she came to ask for just yesterday.*

We didn't receive any order from Madame Nhu, the man replied curtly, his face half-doubtful, half-worried.

That's unfortunate, she shrugged. *What was your name again? Just so I can clarify with Madame when I inform her that the pharmacy has failed to fulfil her order.*

The subtle threat worked; the sleepiness immediately evaporated from the man's face, his skin flushing pink with concern. He stammered. *Could you, you know . . . Well, do you know what Madame asked for? I can weigh it out for her right now. It will only take a moment.*

Right, Sen pretended, a finger tapping the corner of her lips. *Madame came yesterday to ask for strychnos wine, the kind that kills rodents and insects. We have such a big mouse problem, you know.*

Of course. I will just be a moment. Please, don't go anywhere.

With that, he turned his back, promptly disappearing to measure the order.

Sen stood with her eyes watchful, scanning the pharmacy whilst she waited. The space was smaller than her old bedroom, crowded with multiple woven panniers; the air smelled dry and stale with bitter herbs and leaves. She failed to spot any labels, only fine specks of dust floating and landing graciously on cluttered surfaces.

The man returned with a seemingly innocent bottle, the collar of his tunic darkening with sweat. His breath was heavy.

There we go. Please tell Madame to be careful. One drop is enough to kill an animal, and remember not to breathe it in. The toxin is fatal, you see. Any direct contact is poisonous.

I see. Sen nodded. *How much for this?*

It's on us. The man made a gesture with his hand. *After all, we almost forgot about Madame's order.*

Well then. She dipped her head in pretentious appreciation, wrapping her scrawny fingers around the bottle's neck. *I'll be sure to tell Madame of your generosity.*

The walk from the pharmacy back to the Moutets' mansion was much quicker than she had anticipated, and Sen was back within the walls of her new bedroom before sunrise. The whole journey, if she were to time it, took only half an hour. Efficiency. Sen loved this most about herself.

With meticulous care that almost bordered on paranoia, she sat the bottle on her bed, admiring its deadly yellow liquid. She grinned; it would not alter the colour of Edmond's favourite liquor.

The stories from her childhood came flooding back then: how fatal the strychnos seed was, how no one without extensive knowledge of oriental medicine should ever attempt to turn it into something useful. She closed her eyes, dreaming of the plant's deceptive leaves and stems, its innocent, benign appearance, inky toxins running discreetly within its roots. Sen was like strychnine, too, she thought: a nameless servant with a forgettable face, and a burning, fatal vengeance. She could see her small body, all those years ago, leaning against the trunk of the tree, like she was writing this moment into her future.

She drew a heavy breath in, her head poking beyond the doorframe to see if anyone had woken. The hall was a murky grey; brooms and shovels were blurry outlines in the dark, shadows engulfing most of them. She made her way upstairs, each step a graze over icy marble.

Finally, she reached Edmond's floor, where there was a gypsum ceiling with intricate, lifelike reliefs of birds and butterflies, sculpted in flashy golden brass. She squinted her eyes in disdain; the colour was far too extravagant, too arrogant. Much like the man who lived there.

For a second, Sen hesitated outside his door. Her mouth had

gone sour, and she swallowed her saliva, along with the knot at the back of her throat, stepping inside.

Edmond was exactly where she'd expected—flat on his back, the same way her father used to lie, his mind surrendered completely to the alcohol. It was, again, almost too easy: his bottles of wine lined the trunks by the foot of his bed, their corks already undone, thanks to a dedicated servant. Edmond never liked to waste his precious energy.

As Sen squatted on her heels, she couldn't help tasting the bitterness that rose to the roof of her mouth, replacing the smell of vomit in her memory. For the first time in her life, when she finally decided to stop trying, to stop pleasing her masters, things had suddenly run smoothly, like a touch of silk against supple skin.

How effortless, how simple, succumbing to darker intents.

One by one, she poured the strychnos wine down the neck of each bottle, imagining Edmond's throat. It didn't take her long to empty the glass decanter; the liquid inside remained a pulsing red.

After that, she only had to wait.

The news arrived late, so late Sen thought she had failed. She was angry and disappointed, her perfect chance wasted. But then she caught Marianne hiding in a corner of the servants' quarter, crying the same way her mother had cried, all those years ago, for her dead brother. A triumphant smile appeared on her lips; she couldn't contain it, knowing she had succeeded. She felt like a warrior, blooming with power.

Edmond had actually died.

She had been waiting ever since, shielding herself from the Moutets' other servants, readying to run. She needn't have worried. In these foreigners' blue eyes, she was as invisible as a strange ghost, her disappearance forever unnoticed.

Now, Sen stared unblinkingly at the grey cement beneath her feet. She doubted anyone would be looking for her. She didn't know why she had fled; her plan was meticulous, smooth-sailing from start to finish. Perhaps, deep down, she knew she was trying to outrun herself, for even now she carried no guilt; this life was rightfully hers. Yet, somehow, that same thought scared her.

Finally, Sen decided to move. A walk this time, no longer a run. She didn't want to bother herself with what tomorrow might bring. She only knew for certain that Edmond's slender frame, his peculiarly green eyes, his curly locks—all that made the powerful man himself—were now forever a part of her.

MANY, MANY
YEARS AFTER

It was the first day of winter. The trees had finished shedding their old leaves, and the birds had started migrating somewhere warmer. He estimated the time to be around five in the morning—the sun had yet to rise, but the rooster they kept as a pet had already started crowing. He dragged his stiff body off the wooden plank bed and slowly dressed himself. He winced as he put on the long-sleeved tunic; his shoulders were strained from a rigid sleep. He rubbed his eyes, feeling the wrinkles on his thin skin. His feet were cold, so he decided to put on a pair of black socks. The weather outside seemed bitter, prompting him to cover his bald head with a torn skullcap in dark brown.

Duy stood, breathing out in the pagoda yard with his fingers curled into fists, tensing. The wind was far too violent, and he was trembling. He had gotten much older, weaker. After all, more than three decades had passed from that night. The night Edmond died.

Slowly, he made his way to the old frangipani tree, something he had been doing every morning before sunrise. He lowered himself to the cold dirt, leaning his back against the tree trunk, closing his eyes, reminiscing. He had never been a deeply religious person, yet more than thirty years ago, like the birds that flew south, he found himself at the door of this pagoda, seeking warm solace from the piercing cold of his family fortune, his past, his sins. The master teachers had graciously offered him a hand, taking him in, teaching him their ways of life. In turn, Duy learned how to cook, how to garden, and how to grow and to harvest the most basic leafy greens. He learned the proper way to clean the shrines, without disrupting the bowls of incense and fruit offerings, and he also learned to appreciate their humble shade of brass—even though they weren't the shiny, flashy gold that he had treasured in his mother's altar room.

Shortly after he'd arrived, Marianne came to see him, bidding him a final goodbye. Duy invited her in, and he sat with her in the common area, where all the monks greeted their guests. It had been a quiet, peaceful day, and they were the only two there. Duy settled on the stool opposite Marianne, placing a freshly brewed cup of jasmine tea in front of her, but she declined, claiming her insomnia was getting worse. They both knew the real reason she had trouble sleeping, but Duy nodded in agreement and commented casually on the hot weather. An easier topic, to get the conversation going. They couldn't look up from their hands, unable to face one another, each representing something the other had lost.

Marianne didn't say much as she dropped a golden locket inside his palm. Duy held onto it, staring unblinkingly at the faint *P*. Somehow, Marianne managed to convince the governor to release this piece of jewellery from the evidence vault after Phong's death. The benefit of living a life under Leon Moutet's wings.

Holding the pendant tight, Duy asked why she was giving it to him instead of Minh, though in truth, this was his discreet way of requesting an update on his old friend.

285

His mother sent him to an asylum. She declared him medically insane, with Leon's help, of course.

Marianne's tone was flat, detached, as though she had just recited a random story found in the local newspaper, the story about a stranger whose fate did not concern her.

Duy felt a drop in his stomach, a sadness for his oldest friend. His short-tempered but loyal friend. His friend who wanted nothing other than companionship and profound understanding from others. Duy wanted to defend Minh, to prove that Minh didn't deserve such an ending, that Minh's mind had simply betrayed him. But in the end, Duy kept his silence, shifting in his seat, letting the old timber stool groan under his weight. His words would change nothing.

They had sat together as such for a little while longer, Duy and Marianne, not speaking. The hollowness of what could have been swallowed the rest of their conversation.

Later, as Duy uttered his goodbye, he learned that Marianne was leaving for France the next day. Her business was finished, she smiled ruefully, allowing a sliver of sorrow to show. Without Edmond, Marianne assumed a new task—she would return to Madame Moutet, to help take care of her old, broken friend. They didn't mention Edmond's father. There was no point. Leon would forever remain the charming, powerful French diplomat.

Duy bowed his head as Marianne turned away—the way his people expressed respect. He had always considered her the mother Edmond had never had, and he hoped Marianne knew that. She waved without looking back, her steps turning frantic, eager to escape the memories Duy called back. She followed the grey stone stairs down an equally grey road, her shoes disappearing over the growing moss. Duy remained behind, watching.

Just like that, they parted. They both knew they would never see each other again.

When Marianne faded into a dot on the horizon, Duy had closed the bright red door, his pace quickening. He walked to the middle of the courtyard where the frangipani tree stood and dug a shallow hole, burying Phong's locket beneath the damp dirt. He hoped that the soothing fragrance from the flowers would bring his old friend's soul some comfort, because that was what the people who were left behind did—they claimed solace in the name of those who had passed. Duy did not believe in the spirit realm, but he mumbled a prayer. An apology. A goodbye. He needed to believe that his friend was still out there somewhere.

From then on, like a ritual, he sat in this same spot every morning, his back leaning against the tree trunk, his eyes closed, imagining the now wrinkly, weathered faces of his friends. A tragedy, he often admitted, that they would never grow old together.

The wind rose, forcing Duy out of the memory. Shivering, he made his way towards the kitchen. The space was always shrouded in darkness when he first came in, but Duy knew his way around the room. Day after day, time unfolded this exact way—he woke before everyone else, tearing up as he dreamed of the brothers he had lost. He cooked a simple breakfast for the other monks, then swept the pagoda yard in silence before visiting the rooster they kept as pet. He had never felt more unremarkable. But somehow, this brought him peace.

The menu Duy'd chosen that morning was steamed vegetables. After waiting half an hour or so, he opened the lid of the pot, checking to see if the sweet potatoes were cooked, picking a small one for himself as he exited the kitchen. Above his head, the sun slowly appeared, the sky turning white. Duy didn't want to be around when the monks emerged; he didn't want to converse with anyone other than the chicken. He was no longer the young heir, with servants polishing the ground he walked on—and he certainly didn't believe he was better than them. No, Duy avoided them because he was constantly afraid of being disappointed.

With the fowl, it was simple. It hadn't another companion, left to navigate the rest of its life in loneliness, just like him. He told it random stories from the life he used to lead; and because more than thirty years had passed, he sometimes repeated himself. The chicken didn't seem to mind, its black eyes blinking intently every time he spoke. Duy planned on telling and retelling his past, repeating the stories until they lost their meaning, until they became merely history, nothing more, and nothing less. He would stretch himself thin, the same way a person would an elastic band, ensuring the memories could no longer haunt him, that the poison in his veins from his time in that elite world would be finally cleansed.

Those opulent days, Duy would begin, as the rooster circled his spot on the cold ground, ready to listen.

ACKNOWLEDGMENTS

For an author, I must admit that in this very moment, typing my acknowledgments, I'm lost for words. Not because I don't know who to thank or what to say, but because a few sentences don't seem to be enough to convey my gratitude.

I'll try.

To Danya Kukafka, who I am lucky enough to call my agent, I owe so much of *Those Opulent Days* to your brilliance—the final plot twist wouldn't exist without you. Thank you for believing in the manuscript since the early days. Thank you for your encouragement, not just with this book, but also other drafts I have been working on. Thank you for understanding the stories I wish to tell, at times better than I understand them myself. Thank you.

To everyone at Trellis Literary Management, thank you for the kind feedback you have given me and *Those Opulent Days*, back when the manuscript was under a different name entirely.

To Joe Brosnan, the sharp editor who sees my characters for who they are the same way I do, thank you for all your generous suggestions to push the book to the best version it can be.

To everyone at Grove Atlantic, thank you for taking a chance on my debut novel.

To all the booksellers, future readers, and reviewers who take the time to read the story I have created, thank you for allowing my work to be a part of your life.

To the 2024 Publishing Children discord, thank you for your companionship. You make writing a much less lonely process.

To Arlia Bowness, I know you never take the credit, but thank you for sending me that fateful message that one time we were talking about dreams and goals—"Write that book!" Thank you for always lending me an ear, listening to all my complaints, and answering my self-doubts with the right amount of bullying and affirmation.

To A Bob, whom this book is dedicated to, thank you for your unwavering support. Thank you for everything.